SWINGING THROUGH DIXIE

Swinging Through Dixie

LEON ROOKE

A JOHN METCALF BOOK

BIBLIOASIS
WINDSOR, ONTARIO

SWINGING THROUGH DIXIE

OLD MAN HUBBARD has made his appearance. He break-fasts daily on a stool at the Dinette, always one cheese biscuit, one sausage biscuit, grits, a slab of country ham, two runny fried eggs—if his stomach is con-sidered reliable—jelly. He hovers at the café through morning, padding in knee-high boots from one stool to the other in the receipt and giving of news—which family had fights the previous night, who has come down with broken bones, who got laid off, which mill super is the flaming bastard to work for, which one of those on hand suffers worse rheumatism, how long will this dry spell continue, what is intended with all those confounded nearby acres some fanatic has cleared and has now set a'fire.

What fire? Where is it? What are you talking about?

Fire is today's hot topic at the Dinette. A barn at the town's edge has come down, trees have been felled, and now stumps blaze day and night. No one knows why. Is a maniac meaning to burn up the town? All except Hubbard agree the burning makes no sense. Hubbard says, "Everything makes sense if a sensible person chooses to bring sense to it." The others say to him, "You don't make no sense either. Hubbard, you've gone and *got old!* Your marbles have disappeared downstream."

Today a news item heard at eight a.m. at 1220 on your radio dial, has aroused strong speculation about the other fire: *"Before daylight this a.m., an early-vintage Ford automobile was discovered in fiery blaze on the road shoulder this side of State Line. Occupants alive or dead, if any, unknown at this hour. Slick Jess Helms, on the fiery spot, reporting. Tune in next news hour."*

"That bastard won't on no spot. I seen him in the studio flirting with—"

"Guy thinks he's Gabriel Heatter on the Mutual Radio Network. Thinks he's the Eyes and Ears of the World."

"Gabriel Heatter ain't on Mutual."

"Is."

"'Adolph come right down Main Street paddling his U-boat. Enemy subs spotted off Kill Devil Hills.' That's Mutual and Slick for you. Trying to keep us on our toes."

"The war's done over."

"Gabriel Heatter done good on that Lindbergh kidnap mess, didn't he, Hubbard?"

"When was that?"

"Sixteen years ago come June. You wrote more editorials opposing that baby-killer's execution than you did arguing the cotton mills ought not to come here."

Shhhhh. Hubbard's asleep.

The burning car: several Dinette patrons have exercised their God-given right, as well as satisfied their curiosity, by driving out to State Line to view the vehicle. "It was still blazing when I come upon it," all reported. "Tires, you know, will take a man's lifetime to burn. What Slick said about occupants living or dead, I'd be bound to agree with. What looked to be a skull turned out to be the gear shift shot into the roof, if that crate had any roof left. I got right singed, looking. But if that buggy wasn't Grey's, you can boil me in your onion soup like you would a housefly."

"Naw. Can't be Grey's."

"Why in tarnation not?"

"He ain't never coming back here. His wife would kill 'm."

"I might myself."

"You and me both."

"All I am saying is was it looked like his car. I seen what looked like burnt cue sticks. That damn fool would save his pool sticks before he saved his own self."

"You're saying Grey's kicked the bucket?"

"He's kicked the bucket and all hell loose if he was in that inferno."

"Grey and Essie couldn't drive that Ford to the corner store without something befalling it."

"Well that's a Ford for you."

"Now hold on. He was a good man to work for."

"Who?"

"Henry."

'My pappy says Henry Ford was good to women and black people and Chinamen but couldn't abide Jews. It was his paper—"

"Everybody gots to hate someone."

"—published them…"

"Pappy'd go hysterics he saw anybody driving anything except—"

"—them *Protocols* made your hair stand up."

"Jesus Christ and save matches, what are you talking

about? We got only one Jew in town and that's Sam at the shoe store. Sam don't drive a Ford."

"Five. Sam's wife, Vitria, and three offshoots."

"Vitria is First Baptist."

"Henry and Adoph were good buddies. They had snapshots of each other on their desks. Ask Hubbard. He'll tell you."

"Hubbard?"

"How would I know? I've not seen my own desk in twenty years. And I sure as fire never saw theirs. Sorrel is right about those *Protocols*, though. And it may or may not have been Grey's scorched auto. If so, he would have got his butt flying. He's too dad-blamed ornery to git hisself burnt."

"I won't come near a Ford my own self."

"Not mine you won't."

"Damn. I can't open my trap around here without one of you jaspers putting your foot in it."

Amarantha came through with more coffee for Hubbard, should he want it. The others she was inclined to treat with total disregard. They were too garrulous. They were stupid. They were sex fiends. They didn't tip. Hubbard always left a dime. A few pennies more, if his pockets rattled with too many. "Here you loungers sit," she said to them. "Bunch of useless buzzards."

Now Mandy, they said. Buzzards ain't useless. Buzzards are the salt of the earth.

Mandy—Hubbard called her Sunshine when not employing her actual name—held that all men were sex fiends. She had no interest in the business her-self—most were stupid, and so cheap they wouldn't hold out a bone to a starving dog, which in this town many were. She had been at the eatery through all its rebirths. The original building, a barn midst scrappy farmland before the town became one, finally surrendered to rot. For decades, the rot remained as it had fallen, in the town centre, threaded through with crab grass, dandelion, and finally overtaken by kudzu. Hubbard, through that period publisher, editor, and owner of the *Weekly Herald*, had written countless editorials bemoaning the eyesore. When the new building went up, a board-and-batten structure imprecisely plumbed, Mandy came with it. She was by then a hundred pounds heavier and looked a good deal shorter. She's put on the weight herself, she said, but marriage to Finn had done the rest. *You married Finn? No, he got me drunk and married me.* That was on a Thursday. By Saturday noon the marriage was over. In and out like a coo-coo bird, as she told it. Finn was told she never wanted to see him again, but she'd seen him every day since, Finn being a Dinette regular. It was Finn opting for Grey's death by fire out by State Line.

Amarantha was going through the place now, thumb-tacking Today's Menu on various uneven walls. Everyone, including Hubbard, was interested in that.

"What's your special today?" he asked.

"Okra in slime," she said. "Everything today comes ladled in slime."

Hubbard laughed. It was sometimes difficult getting the truth out of Amarantha. She liked having fights with the kitchen. She thought the kitchen received entirely too much praise. Praise made her uncomfortable.

"The onliest way to git slime off okra," Finn said, "is to take a blow torch to it." This statement, containing a whiff of truth, elicited strong opinion.

"The hog jowls with collard greens is good if you got your teeth in and have a hankering for grease," Amarantha said. Her mood was foul.

All ears were tuned to 1220 on the radio dial when the next news flash came, Slick Jess Helms reporting. *"Fire by burning automobile, now said to be a 1942 Ford coupe, still rages out by a notorious State Line Nitespot, there apparently being no fire brigade servicing the area. A local resident of some repute is rumoured to be the vehicle owner. Body or bodies have not yet been discovered. Nitespot resident, entrepreneur, and entertainer Debora Doon refused comment. Next report on the Farm Digest, high noon. Stay tuned."*

"'Ill repute,' he meant saying. Ain't that so, Hubbard?"

"That puerile loudmouth Slick don't consult with me," Hubbard said.

The regulars knew the lecture they would be in for if they asked what puerile meant.

The Dinette cat, Douglas MacArthur, nicknamed the General, had hopped onto Hubbard's lap. It was trying to dislodge the hearing aid from the old man's ear. It satisfied the Dinette regulars to watch that.

At noon when the Dinette begins to swell, Hubbard will parlay the cane chair known as his personal property, either by dint of his own hand or another's, to the sunny spot outside the café, where it and he will lean against the charred wall between two stumpy barrels in which half-rooted evergreens vainly seek longevity. The bushes are less nourished than is Hubbard, more threadbare and decrepit, while seeming to reflect Hubbard's calm outlook on a world into which he has been unwillingly cast and against which he stubbornly persists. Dogs familiar to him will nose his crotch and prod his hands for food and settle into sleep around his legs if they are so disposed. On hotter days, if his old bones allow a pittance of relief, he will nod off himself, deaf to those passing who murmur, "How are y'all today, Grandpa?" or some such inane civility. He's a likeable old man, kind to dogs and children and polite to those who demonstrate the same to him. For sixty years he ran, honourably, it may be supposed, the local "weekly rag." On his seventieth year he had sold the paper to a consortium of citizens for fifty cents, a fifth of Gentleman Jack, a free subscription for the remainder of his years, a country ham cured for one full year, and the promise of a crippling defamation suit if ever they editorialized favourably for the Republican Party. Then he had walked the Gentleman Jack home in a paper sack. His wife of 47 years, Ruth by name, reminded him to remove, please, his shoes at the front door, and to take off his hat. It was an invitation to bad luck for a man to wear a hat indoors. What hat? He had forgotten the hat was on his head, having already sipped plentifully at Gentleman Jack. He wanted to know why bad luck haunted only mens' hats. She said only imbeciles asked such naïve, if not plain foolish, questions. She wanted to know, had he put the promise of a suit in iron-clad lawyerly writing? He had. She wanted assurance that the free subscription continued if he chanced to predecease her. It did. Where is the ham? she asked. Still hanging, he said. I hope it's a genuine Smithfield, she said. Our own are every bit equal to a Smithfield, he said. Possibly, she said. She wanted to see the fifty cents. He put the five dimes into her hand. "All right," she said. "Now let's sit on the back porch with a bowl of these roasted peanuts I pulled fresh from the ground this morning, and have a go at that bottle."

They did.

She said, "A sane man would have demanded two bottles."

He said, "I didn't want to sound greedy."

She said, "I feel I must personally acknowledge that while Gentleman Jack is delicious beyond all human reckoning it has never been a personal favourite. It hails from Tennessee, a backwards state."

"You prefer the Kentucky offerings?"

"Never mind. Jack will do nicely. Now that you are an unemployed journalist, what do you intend doing with yourself? Are you just going to sit there and age gracefully?"

Ruth now was, unhappily, gone. Few disputed that she'd been a better wife than Hubbard deserved. He'd been a wilful, opinionated young man, and had no doubt these absurdities still clung to him. He'd often been stubbornly cranky, too quick to take offense, and still was. When he'd proposed, Ruth said, "Why on earth would I want to marry a man who keeps shooting himself in the foot?" But she smiled, kissed his lips, and did.

In the fall of 1936, Hubbard drove his DeSoto over the rough roads to the adjoining county, Northampton, for a meeting with his friend and former advertiser, Owen Myles, who owned the Riteweigh Cotton Gin. Owen told him he had enough cash to keep the gin going another week, maybe two, if he skimped on salary payment to his single employee, a steady bastard with a wife and nine children.

"Yes," said Hubbard, "he certainly sounds steady."

Owen said, "If I had another hundred, with good luck and if hell don't freeze over I can keep the gin going a whole 'nother month, by which time the wagonloads will be rattling in heaped with cotton. Then it will be Easy Street till this same time next year."

"By which time your steady will have ten children," Hubbard said."

At this point Owen walked down to the spring behind his gin, returning with two bottles of home-brew. Uncapped, the foam caught both of them.

Owen said, "I don't suppose you're in cahoots with any big-time bankers, are you?" Hubbard said his understanding was that the bankers in this neck of the woods were jumping out of high windows. Owen said he hoped to hold off on that solution just yet. "For that one hundred smackers," he said, "I'll give you ten per cent interest in the business, and make you comptroller with a desk bigger than mine."

"You don't have a desk," Hubbard said.

"So you're saying for one hundred I can get ten per cent of a business set to kick the bucket next week."

"That's the size of it," Owen said.

Hubbard pulled out his wallet. He had twenty-eight dollars inside it. He said he could maybe raid Ruth's purse for another ten. He could cash in his insurance policy, which had cost him fifty cents a week through the past three decades, and pull in another dollar or two that way.

"You're still short that hundred," Owen said. "Let's make the gin twenty per cent yours for whatever you can come up with."

They shook hands and had another cold home brew down by the spring where the water trickled free, travelled a few few yards, then disappeared back into whence it came. Owen had set out two logs there, and the hired hand came out of the rusting gin to join them. The building set up high off the plain on which it stood, the aluminum siding boldly reflecting the afternoon sun, all three regarding it mournfully.

"How are you?" Hubbard said to the new man.

"Fair to middling," the man said. "I be better come payday."

"What do those children of yours do?" Hubbard asked.

"The best they can," the man said.

Hubbard and Owen agreed such was the best you could ask of them.

Lawyer Allsbrook would draw up the papers, each further agreed. Assuming he hadn't jumped town with everyone's life's savings.

Sometimes when Hubbard is feeling talkative, or wants to brag about how he came to be co-owner of a cotton gin, or merely hopes to keep his memory in training, he tells this story. What he always leaves out, and has no need to tell because nearly everyone he is telling the story to knows that part, is what he found when he drove the DeSoto back home. The ironing board was up in the kitchen. The print dress she'd been ironing, one of their favourites, had been drying on the clothesline when he left. She'd been heating the iron on the stove. The iron had burned through the dress, through the ironing board, and lay on its side close by her body.

Hubbard was blessed to have received from her loins three that lived: one lost in one war, a second in another, the third presently enduring her private combat in a foreign nation Hubbard can neither spell nor with ease pronounce any more than he can decipher the strange syntax employed in letters irregularly received, those letters bearing passages inked away in black oblong stripes, the envelopes a sea of obliterated stamps. The war was over but the War Department remained vigilant. Apparently, Nip Ears Still Listened, Loose Lips Still Sunk Ships, your home grease was still to be saved to make explosives. *Hello dear father…I am well and hope to God you are, I am now*xxxxxxxxxxxxxxxxxxxxxxxxxxxxxx *xxxxxxxxxxxxxxxxxxxxxxxxxxxxxxxxxxxxxxxxxxxxxxxxxx xxxxxxxxxxxxxxxxxxxxxxxxxxxxxxxxxxxxxxxxxxxxxxxxxx xxxxxxxxxxxxxxxxxxxxxxxxxxxxxxxxxxxxxxxxx*my *boyfriend who is* xxxxxxxxxxxxxxxxxxxxxxxxxxxxxxxxxxxxxx *I commemorated my beloved brothers' passing with shots of* xxx *xxxxxxxxxxxxxxxxxxxxxxxxxxxxxxxxxxxxxxxxxxxxxxxxxxx xxxxxxxxxxxxxxxxxxxxxxxxxxxxxxxxxxxxxxxxxxxxxxxxxx miss you, your cronies, miss Mom, miss that oaf pool shark Grey, stalwart Essie, funny Grey Jr. etc*xxxxxxxx xxxxxxxx *tell me who it is who writes that. Soc(i.e.)ty col. in your old weekly smut sheet?*xxxxxxxxxxxxxxxxxxxx xxxxxxxxxxxxxxxx*Your loving* xxxx *next time when*xxxxxxxxxxxxxxxxxxxxxxxxxxx

Hubbard has not seen this errant, supernut child—for to his mind child she remains—since she appeared of a sudden three years ago for his 84th birthday, and, as suddenly, disappeared, removed, Grey and others claim, by a helicopter landing in the dead of night on the high-school baseball field.

"What does that gal of yours do, Hubbard?"

"Nigh as I can determine she's a spy."

"Ours or theirs?"

"Ours. Damn you."

While his own body falls apart daily, those of his sons' decompose in whatever field it was the pleasure of foreign wars to leave them. Today he has hobbled in for breakfast on feet dead to all except a numb, useless tingling, to be directed into the hot, not-that-busy kitchen, to find slumped on a stool the girl, the woman, he has known a sizeable chunk of her life, little of it he would call praiseworthy.

"*You!*" he says. "What the devil are you up to now?"

It is Essie Valentine Peterson—now, so to speak, Essie Valentine Grey, though she denies it.

Essie is hunched over double, her legs slung over through and around the legs and rungs of the stool, in that peculiar manner he's noticed women have for address of a peculiar situation. And it is peculiar, for Essie is not one usually prone to tears. She is going full steam now, cheeks spotty, eyes as though dipped in red-eye gravy, wringing herself one way and another, gulping for breath, emitting odd snorting sounds, fusillades they might be called, a bleating reminiscent of a lurching locomotive not built to carry the heavy load of cars latched to it. At any rate that is Hubbard's thought as he approaches her in wary resignation. "Been like that since she come in," he hears someone, one of the cooks, the bearded one, say, "I reckon Grey must of be come home."

"Must of be."

"If he don't kill her first I reckon she will kill him."

"Hush," Hubbard said to them. "You don't want to go giving her ideas."

"If Grey was in that conflagration out by State Line she's been saved the trouble."

"Slick says not a soul was in that car. You can count on Slick—"

"Not me."

"—to git his facts straight."

"Slick has got more bullshit in his craw than a dump truck can haul."

"Slick?"

"You must be thinking of that dust-up Slick got into over at the prison farm when the woman come to visit her man got holt of Slick instead. A broom closet, I heard, and the man chasing both Slick and the woman with the same broom he used sweeping the yard."

"Slick?"

"So the tower guard gits off a shot and who is it falls down dead?"

"Who?"

"The guard. He's so full of hisself from firing that gun he falls daredevil outen' the tower kersplat onto a body of mud."

Essie was not listening. She had clearly left home in a hurry: in bare feet, dressed in ugly red-dot pajamas over which she'd thrown a frazzled cotton dress, hair tangled, a sheen over her mottled flesh.

Hubbard clears his throat, he pronounces her name, lifts his arms. Essie looks up, both hands dab at her eyes, she casts upward a skewered half-smile, unhooks her limbs from the stool, and plunges into his old man arms. He isn't overly disturbed. She's a strong woman suffering failing moments. Grey comes home and she shatters like broken glass.

"Grey's home!" she cried. "Yesterday I saw a family of cardinals and I knew they were an omen. My water tap ran rusty and that was another. Then I wake at four a.m. in a hysterical fit: he'd entered the town limits. I knew it. I want to borrow somebody's pistol, put on my boots, and shoot him in both kneecaps."

"Not both. Both would be a dire handicap in his profession."

"Just one, then."

"There's your son."

"I see him."

"What? The two of you are not on speaking terms today?"

Has Grey Jr. been tracking his mother? Does he worry about her? An emaciated string bean boy of ten or eleven, in oversized sneakers and overalls bleached near white, standing half-hidden behind the dusty dwarf tree fronting the pool hall, for some moments had been in mute observation of them. A black rag tied around his head, concealing his brow. Hubbard snorts. He wants to know what name the boy is calling himself this week.

"Tecumseh," Essie tells him.

"*Which* Tecumseh? The lauded Indian warrior or that sojourner through biblical nightmare, William Tecumseh Sherman?"

"How would I know?"

The boy has ventured forth. "Wipe your nose," Essie tells him. He ignores her. He is tugging at Hubbard's sleeve. "What will you give me for this here precious object unearthed from pure rubble?" he asked. He projected a wooden spool into which he'd thrust a popsicle stick, wads of grimy chewing gum anchoring tattered chicken feathers embedded at each end. "Son, try me later," Hubbard said. "We got us a domestic situation to unravel." The boy again poked the object at him.

"How much you give me," the boy asked, "for this one-of-a-kind foreign specimen, probably Navaho."

"Leave us alone," Hubbard said. "Go make something else."

Essie had ceased weaving about. She had her breath back and was wiping her eyes on her dress. "What is it?" she asked. "What do you call that thing?"

The boy was not quick to reply. He avoided looking at her.

"Do you want your britches switched? Answer me."

"You the one liable to git her behind switched."

"Now you two hold on," Hubbard said. He was put out with both of them, and with himself as well.

"It's a domestic bird of antiquated origin," the boy finally said. "Only it don't fly."

"Give him two cents for it," Essie said to Hubbard. "Tell the little hotshot if he comes back with one that flies you'll pay him a whole nickel."

The boy waited with a brightened face while Hubbard rooted about in a pocket. "I don't like this one bit," Hubbard complained. "Hellfire. I'm being taken to the cleaners and it's not yet—"

"Pay up," the boy said. "I got business elsewhere."

A time later Hubbard was outside taking in the sun in his tilted chair; Essie sat beside him on a patch of weeds, her back leaning against the wall, long legs spread wide. "Keep them knees covered," he told her. "I don't want having no wicked thoughts this day." Across the street, under the moving picture marquee, Grey Jr. was seen attempting to sell something to a man in a hat the colour of tobacco juice. The man kept shoving him back, the boy immediately returning. "That urchin go-gitter must somehow got contaminated by your Peterson blood," Hubbard said to Essie. "Before he's fourteen he'll be building cotton mills in Mexico, same as your greedy forefathers would of done."

"I'd be obliged if you don't mention that name," Essie said. "Nor that other one I know is on the tip of your tongue."

"Well, you're the great-granddaughter of one rogue industrial baron and so far as anybody knows still hitched to the other rascal."

"I'm not married as much as you think I am. Before nightfall the day me and Grey married, we were fit to be tied trying to get ourselves annulled, but the office scum in your dumb county refused to open the door."

"I don't want to hear about it," Hubbard quickly said. "This whole town has heard about it 'til tar-and-feathering the lot of you is the recommended action. A dollop of female circumspection on these matters wouldn't kill you."

"You know what you can do with your circumspection. I'm claiming 'til my last breath, the marriage wasn't consummated. Everybody knows an unconsummated marriage ain't a real marriage."

"Don't talk like that, please! Hell's bells, woman, you got a near-teenage son walking through town like he owns it, or would if it was worth owning."

"I can claim Grey had nothing to do with that. The woods are full of fools who could be my son's daddy. That's my story and I'm sticking to it."

"Shootfire, I'll be danged if you. …Yours and Grey's trouble ring in my head like clanging pots sun-up to sunset. Now sit there like a setting hen with a shut mouth and let an old man catch his rest."

"That paregoric bottle in your pocket is what's addled your brain. Me and Grey have nothing to do with the sorry mess you make of yourself."

"That's verbal assault. You take it back."

"I apologize."

"Accepted."

"I can't help hoping Grey got a tiny bit singed in that goddamned wreck of a Ford. I won't ask what was engaging the randy S.O.B. at State Line."

"You know very well they have pool tables at that Nitespot."

"Uh-huh. And Lulabelle and Trixie Foxtrot and Peach Blossom and … Say, what explains all that activity over at the movie palace?"

"Are you ignorant? This town is on the map. We got ourselves a movie star."

"Who?"

"A woman you'd like to hang."

Hubbard could have supplied Essie with the significant updates. He was tempted to, but wasn't sure he dared. She was a poor windswept heifer curdled by love. He thought of her as—*normally!*—a sensible woman of considerable accomplishment, of respectable if unquiet disposition—a caring mother—*normally!* A fine cook, if ever one could guide her into a kitchen. Better educated than he, more humanely decent, more gracious, generous, responsible, dedicated, resourceful, and funny—*normally!* Of her housekeeping virtue, well, he'd reserve judgment on that, not being much of one himself. One thing for certain: she was—*normally!*—without being vain about it, just about the best-looking woman in the county. Her competition in this regard were the certain beauties at Bon Vivant Hair (and foot) Emporium, the ticket seller at the Imperial picture show palace across the street (he was this minute studying Carol Bly's comely features as she set up shop for the matinee), and the Myrna Loy lookalike who worked the pumps in hip-hugging fatigues at the gas station out on the highway. Several he had courted in the long ago—and not to mention those many breathtaking Aphrodites involving haystacks and wet furrowed fields and barn lofts and pea patches upon whom only *in stark, doomed imagination did I once lay*. Or about a hundred others whose faces had become smudged over the years, and certainly not to usher into this privileged interrogation his own dear daughter across the seas or dear dead-departed Ruth, who could have pitched all of them into deep shade with the sheer wave of her elegant hand. But certainly to admit into this fabulous ensemble the woman he had unabashedly claimed that Essie might well, and possibly with good reason, want to hang: Viota Bee, bless her curves, the town's reputed movie star.

Debuting on the silver screen, by God, this very day, not thirty feet from where Hubbard sat sunning himself, as—mindless now—he scratched the head of the mongrel dog which daily, hourly, insisted upon. Thoughts of beautiful women wafted away. "What's your name, dog?" he asked. The dog whimpered; it licked his hand. It vexed Hubbard that few dogs in this rank mill town had names and none wore collars. If you named a dog or put a collar on it you might then have to feed it. Someone at the *Herald* ought to editorialize on that.

Amarantha hung by the Dinette door. "Your scalawag friends are having a nip in the back, if you want to join them. Otherwise, the pork rind marinated in sorghum molasses with mint and string beans is halfway edible, if your stomach is churning."

"It is now," Hubbard said. "Godamighty, Sunshine, you know damn good and well this is the best dining parlour in the state."

"I guess you already had that nip," she said.

*

It was Varner or Varmer—or even Vaneer as they sometimes called him—who first passed word that Grey was in town. Old man Varner had come across Grey passing the time of day with Cindy on Varner's back porch. He'd had to smack little Cindy's face to get it out of her that Grey only wanted, or seemed to want, only to know if her older sister, Viota Bee, was anywhere around. Had Viota skedaddled or was she hiding out from some boyfriend or was she that minute asleep upstairs in her four-poster satin-sheeted bed? "That was three questions too many," Varner said, admitting he'd had to smack the nine-year old three times *"pretty hard"* to get replies satisfactory to him.

Naturally Varner's wife, Dottie, flew out at the first screech, meaning to rescue little Cindy, which got her face slapped in the bargain. It got the porch railing broke and a foot put through the newly-screened back door, the Varners and Grey scrambling one way and another, tugging, kicking, scratching, and punching at each other. Varner claims insults and dire threats were made to his person and to one and all, Grey telling them they were not one of sound mind in the whole family, save little Cindy and Viota Bee, the latter having been his confidante and troubadour since they sat beside each other in first grade. It was agreed by sightseers straggling rapt-eyed into the yard that Grey passed no such remarks, that Grey was a hallmark of gallantry and civility, only doing his best to fend off old Varner's slaps, head-butts and throat holds and to torpedo Varner's hollered intention to knock little Cindy's perfumed head into next week. That madame Varner had scooted in outfitted in no more than a transparent nightie, bosom flaring, folks said, was what catapulted Varner into full-fire rage. It was clear, they said, that the nip or two the old juice-head had enjoyed in the peace and quiet of his rec room had helped promote him into a huffing toe-stomping bull, just as it was likewise clear Grey would have been wise to refrain from any approach, discreet or otherwise, to the Varner property, neither the front door nor especially the back door through which it was generally assumed he'd of dark night trespassed regularly. As evidence, who else but him until that fracas knew of the luxurious finery in which Viota Bee reposed, the four-poster bed, the haunting (red? black?) satin sheets she and who else but Grey were like to dwell within or on top of or beneath, whichever way they liked it, and proclivity or mood, impulse—demon blood—drove them.

That whichever being none of our business, an innocent passerby might think, though that uninformed party would be dead-wrong and is hereby invited to keep his or her mouth shut, since the bitter truth, the raw facts, await the unfolding.

Such is how Hubbard would have told it, and *did* tell it, once affairs taking place on Varner's back porch got sorted out. He was a newspaperman for God sake, a tinkle or two past his prime, for goodness' sake, but it was a newsman's job, come hell or high water, to *report*, to deliver the news as objectively as humanly possible. He was not, however, a machine, and if some little sap of brotherhood was omitted in his report on those lousy Varner parents, or Varmer or even Vaneer as they sometimes said the name, then that was hunky-dory with him because he didn't mind confessing he didn't like the pair, never had liked them, only raving imbeciles did, because they were the two-bit kind that people had in mind when they resorted to the opprobrious, not to say slanderous, term *fry in hell*. Whereas, if you didn't like Grey (and Essie and their little hotshot seedling, Junior) then you were outright stiff-necked windbags with no true claim to humanity.

Ratty-rat-rap. What can be taken as solemn invocation here is that Grey ought to have known that Viota Bee had shed her hide of these parts. Essie knew it, Hubbard knew it, Bon Vivant staff and clients knew. Who didn't? *Goodness gracious me*, hadn't it been reported in the *Weekly Herald*? In the column signed by Anonymous: **Soc(i.e.)ty (that is)**. On the Women's Page, worse luck, alongside a recipe for Pork Belly Raisin Stew, flower arrangement hints, side-by-side columns by gossip queens Louella Parsons and Hedda Hopper, a Katzenjammer Kids cartoon. *Miss Viota Bee Vadier, 29, long-term prized employee at Bon Vivant Hair (& Foot) Emporium and familiar figure about town, has tendered her resignation and is now seeking fame and fortune in Far Portsmouth to our wicked north. Go-Away festivities were held after-hours at the popular salon, which saw presentation to the former pulchritudinous Miss Homecoming Queen (1946), Miss Captivating Personality (1945,) Miss Buy War Bonds (1942), of a gold necklace (courtesy inspired proprietor Sallie Forth), and new pumps (courtesy Sam's Shoes w/financial support from Bon Vivant staff (Joan, Judy, Bertha Bell)). J. Scrubbs performed on the mandolin.*

Legendary midget Alonzo Rapt delighted all with acrobatic feats. Ralph's Barbecue of Weldon Road provided hush puppies and barbecue made, Ralph told **Soc(i.e.)ty** **(that is)**, *from midget pigs. "I'm happy the big priss is going" one sulky blonde was overheard saying. An overjoyed Miss Vadeen (Varner) was escorted to her new domain by Jim Beam Talley, former football star, now VP of Mercantile Dynamics, who predicted a gossamer sale of two bull cows at an agricultural fair en route. Happy sailing to the lustrous chickadee!*

Struck by the glittery, hyperbolic tone of the column, Hubbard had made inquiry to his old friends at the *Herald* consortium. Who is this Anonyous? he asked. We don't know, he was told. It came in freelance. A madhouse of spelling errors, punctuation breeches.

"Typed?"

"More or less. You disliked it?"

"Offered free?"

"If we printed it we were asked to leave a dollar under a rock by the back door."

"Ah!"

Essie and Grey Jr. were having an argument.

"Those Varners or Vaneers or however they like calling themselves can, for once, shut their own traps," is what Essie says. "Fools are born every minute and they are the living proof. Yours Truly is another one, if you are going to sit here and tell me all the time Grey was busy making you he was skulking through that Varner back door to wedge his way under or between or on top of red satin sheets that don't exist in that house in the first place. Weren't me and Viota good friends? Not in recent times, no, but haven't I been a thousand times in that room? Where this four-poster idea comes from is the other side of the moon. If you ask me. Well, you didn't ask me, and you better not, but I am telling you Viota Bee don't tread on angel dust how you and Grey and this town claims."

"Telling me what?" Junior said. "What you tell me changes with each breath. In this house nobody can mention Grey's name while your mouth froths it your every footfall."

"Hush. I can't rinse my mouth without you finding fault. You are not too old to git whupped. I'm washing my face and mopping the floor now. You're itching to go find Grey, then go. Just don't bring the beastly man one hundred feet of my door."

"You've said yourself it is coincidence rules this earth. Grey shows up, it will be not one lick of my doing. I'll remind you also the beast, as you put it, remains my father."

"I might argue there's some doubt on that front. Now git out of my sight. Go to that picture show. I am sure some low-brow hulk, known kin to a snake, will slip you under-age squirts in by the side door."

"No way I'm not seeing Viota in her own picture show."

"Take that band off your head. Trash that feather. Wipe your nose. You look stupid."

"I *am* stupid. It is my one prideful fact."

"Scat."

That show: *Mean! Moody! Mendacious! Magnificent! Bosomy! Bestial!* So the picture Grey Jr. has seen described on the big posters. *The immortal picture that couldn't be stopped! Is this the last breath of Billy the Kid! In that woman's arms!*

In the first place, who is *that woman* is a question a boy might well be led to ask. It's a question that stews a boy's brain. Is Billy to perish on the bosom of Jane Russell or slavering (such a *good* word!) on the famous hills constituting the whole—*so a boy of reduced intelligence might be led to think!*—of the town's own Viota Bee? Whether Daddy Grey has also *slavered* there is the pertinent query. People *of all ages* hint at such. Essie has. Oh, Essie has suspicions, no doubt there. If verified, then a boy's life drops like Tarzan in quicksand. The marriage goes kaput, home and home life, such as it is, goes sailing off into the blue. Essie and plucky little hot shit Junior (*what* were they *thinking,* loading him with that name?) and Grey himself will all be leaping headfirst into bubbling quicksand. So doesn't that make it mandatory that a boy find Daddy? Villainous Daddy. Unloving Daddy. The rake. The rogue. But a boy's hero, whatever louse he is said to be.

He's *burnt!* *To a crisp!* Maybe that's why Grey hasn't checked in. A neat little injunction wouldn't halt Daddy.

A few minutes earlier, so it would seem, judging by a verbatim report rendered by Earl Tillich, the knock-kneed schoolboy not one in Junior's party hardly knew—him being one among an inexhaustible swill of Tillichs living in scratch huts on hillsides just outside the town limits, much to their satisfaction. According to the verbatim report, Junior's Daddy Grey had been seen on the street not fifteen minutes before, giving severe and prolonged study first to them colour titty posters, then to every 10 x 12 shot behind dirty glass. Says he, Tillich we mean, to no one in particular, because who wants Tillich to think anyone in this world cares what rubbish is issued from a Tillich mouth: "Well? Well? Well?"

We say, "Well, what? Damn you, Tillich, has your well gone dry?"

"Well, well, well," says Tillich. "If it isn't standing before me, in company with dopey friends, the half-orphan boy proudly claiming ownership of a split personality. How yawl, Jr.? How yawl holding up this fine day?"

"Cut that mess out, Tillich," we say. "What we want to know is what was Grey doing other than looking at a naked woman in a hayloft, which we already would have guessed without you opening your fat mouth."

And he says, "I was just telling you."

"Telling us what?"

"Your pappy Grey had come and gone from the pool hall and sooner than later meant going back for a high-stakes game. 'If anyone in this town has more than two dollars in his pocket and the guts to take me on.' That's what the better informed among us call a direct quote."

"Quit showing off. We know all that."

"You can know it or not know it but mine was the body standing right here with Grey's hand on my shoulder."

"Your shoulder! My God," we said.

"You'd think I was his own son, how Grey was being so palsy with me. He give me twelve cent for this picture show and a nickel for popcorn. He said if I wore his hat and his jacket I could stride right into the picture show, everybody thinking I was him. I practically popped. A Tillich could be him. Just imagine."

"You're a fabricating cockroach, Tillich. Cut out the hogwash. You're straining our credulity."

So we hit him. We scrubbed his scalp raw and gave him about a hundred Charlie Horses. To our consternation he did not once cry. What the marquee lacked in neon it made up for in mostly-shot light bulbs, and he looked at those. He looked at a man at the booth wanting a ticket, which Carol Bly wouldn't let him have because he was drunk. "Go home," she told him, and he said, "I am home, you slut." Carol said, "I am certain it gives you pleasure to think so," before slamming down the shutter on his fingers, sending a smile our way. We knew Carol Bly's sister right well, and shoplifted at the five and dime, McCrory's, it's called, where her mother worked. The drunk man was not one seen before. He'd slid into town to see *The Picture They Dared Us to Make* but had got side-tracked by the corn liquor still paper-bagged in a back pocket.

We pinched and punched Tillich 'til he went on with his report.

"Grey couldn't take his eyes off that scrumptious Jane Russell picture: sprawled onto a hay bed, aiming first to shoot Billy, pitchfork him, then to cascade into romantic worship and shoot anyone coming for the Kid. Was how he summarized the action. Something about a horse, too. I didn't git that part. Grey says—what he says is, I quote: 'There is surely some strong similarity, as rumoured, between Jane Russell and Viota Bee. You can see the chest works, the leg span, the facial aspect, the brunette hair, the absence of socially approved modesty as applicable to female beauty, is a near duplicate. Ditto brassy voice, sultry movement, pouty lips, the handling of pitchforks. I'd say on the glamour and talent front, both are works of sound composition, soothing as rain-water to the eye. Will you grant me that?' he says. Will you grant me that? His hand still firm on my shoulder. What Grey's saying I can barely think to think about. Truth is, I can't hardly breathe from trying to not think about all that sprawled nakedness of whichever one it is. Like in front of you is all you're seeing is a full pastureland going on miles and miles barren of tree, bush, and brush, because that pastureland only got room for the one body sprawled on it. Hers! Theirs! Viota Bee's or Jane Russell's, either one. 'That's right smart,' Grey says to me. 'That there pristine statement has the many layers of profundity found in Essie's scalloped potatoes cooked in a deep-dish bowl. I reckon such is how all men of good faith would see both them fine, auspicious though un-shepherded female forms. It's like an Article of Confederation drawing us each to each. As opposed to something asomatous, a word, my dear boy, I know will have immediately leapt into your brain, meaning, as you doubtlessly know, without bodily form.' He says. Your daddy says. Giving me that warm smile. I bet you are ignorant of that useful word, asomatous, aren't you, Junior?"

"……………"

"Hit the gas, Tillich. We not got all day."

"'Two matters to consider,'" Grey says to me. "'One, Viota Bee will shake herself silly, ever she holds a gun. She's fidgety and will shoot herself. Two, no matter the chills, the fever, the expiring Billy the Kid, mortal gunshot wounds befolding, Viota Bee would suffer severe mental deprivation before she'd climb naked in bed with the Kid or with me or you or anyone else except a certain party I could name. Therefore, brother Tillich: Therefore: it can't be Viota playing that Rio role, that Russell part, in yon picture show, no matter her talent displayed being Homecoming Queen, Miss Captivating Soul, Miss Buy War Bonds and all that rigmarole. She won Top Tap Dancer in the Coastal Plains when she was seven years, a fact you may not know. Or be aware, coincidentally, that Essie Valentine Grey, the dear wife I hope to see one of these days, captured the New England version of this very same title when she was that very same tender age. I am indeed a lucky man to have these dual visages strutting within my horoscope. But, again, why against all odds and contrary to all desires I argue it is not Viota Bee playing the role of dazzling Rio in this noble United Artists feature presentation is because...because that divine girl flies with virginal wings, dines on angel dust, and will remain pure in heart and spirit the whole of her life unless or until a certain unnamed party begs her hand in marriage. Ask Jim Beam Talley. Rich, handsome, good as gold, but ask Jim how far he got with her on that auto trip. Hardly past the left cheek, I believe he said. Wrung out and never within closing distance of first base. You do know about first base, don't you, Tillich? Never mind. Viota Bee's an Aphrodite clean of thought, the same as I expect Miss Russell is. Over in the Tidewater, at Norfolk's historic Byrd Theatre, I seen that picture six times. It is not Viota Bee in that picture. It is skilful playacting, which is all any picture show is. In other words, a picture show is a reflection of anguished reality or primitive escapism played out by them not our own selves, better or worse.'"

"That don't sound verbatim to us. Grey don't talk nonsense. You're going to git it, Tillich."

"Hit me again—"

"I'm fixin' to."

"—and I'll tell Grey you did and he'll knock your block off."

Hummmmmm...

"What's that burning down there?"

"Down where? I don't see no smoke nowhere."

"Them stumps. Be a damn fool, Junior. You're looking the wrong way."

Four things—paramount issues!—stick in Junior's mind after this report from Tillich. One, that remark about scalloped potatoes, which is the single dish Essie will cook, if you hold a hot poker to her fanny. Two, is her tap-dancing, which he had forgot she could. Three is where Tillich has heard Grey saying, *The dear wife I hope to see one of these days.* What can *one of these days* mean? Does Grey mean *if I can ever git around to it?* Or does he mean *this marriage is reopening for business?* Either one, Essie will have a hissy fit. *I'm not one of those Sabines,* she will say. *That wretch can't walk rough-shod over me.* The fourth thing sticks not in Junior's mind but in his craw—a-so-ma-tous. Greek. Because of Little Turd Tillich he's been forced to look the word up.

Otherwise, it ain't no way it ain't Viota Bee in the picture. Grey's smart but he ain't omnipotent.

*

Hubbard observed more and more people were congregating around the ticket shed and spreading out into the street in patches under the blink and hiss of marquee light bulbs. Two sailor boys were in guarded conversation with a trio of khaki-uniformed soldiers shod in smart combat boots. Not one a face he recognized, but bright faces all. All limbs intact, maybe on furlough and on their way home, maybe en route to Fort Bragg for demobilization. A hard war, possibly the hardest yet, who knew? He felt extraordinarily old, watching them. The activity across

37

the street made his bones ache. But, then, everything did. Perhaps it was time for a surreptitious swig. How many times in the day did he give consent to a secret chug, only to have some pop-eye hop in from nowhere, blurting out, *I saw that! And you a civic leader! Be ashamed of yourself!* Was he? Not yet, damn their eyes.

Carol Bly emerged from her shed, to a blitz of admiring whistles. She was plumb out of tickets, she said, and had to run to the dime store for another roll. "Why, it'll be my pleasure to go git that roll for you," the military boys said.

It tickled Hubbard to see all five shoot off.

Well, she was a cute girl. Feisty as a diamondback snake, Ruth would have said.

"And bring me a little sprig of daisies to brighten my booth," he heard Carol shout.

Flirtatious, too. Just look at her jiggle that skirt!

Hubbard wondered if Carol Bly had what they called further south a steady beau? Here, plain boyfriend and girlfriend appellation was considered elevated enough. To say someone had "airs" was about the worst that could be said of someone. Other than "drunkard," "worthless," "a cotton-mouth pea-brain," "a bucket of shit," and like rudimentary encomiums. Carol Bly had "airs" all right. Good for her, was Hubbard's thought. Hadn't he heard something about Carol being seen cutting the mustard at dances out at State Line with that Talley boy of the Dynamics firm? Or was it that tall carpetbagger bozo at the pool hall, the galoot Grey was so fond of? Certainly he'd seen both giving her the eye. But, then, that Talley boy had been seen his arms around nearly every pretty girl in town; he was a dyed-in-the-wool Romeo, that boy.

Now here came the military roaring back, waving ticket spools, shouting, "Take mine, Miss Bly!"

"Goodness me," Carol said back, "Aren't you handsome boys sweet as cupcakes!"

Late tonight the whole gang would likely be kicking up their heels at the State Line Nitespot. Then, no telling what.

Bless my soul. He was getting catty as old lady Hubbard peeping from her cupboard. But what else did he have to do?

"Talking to yourself again, are you, Hubbard?" someone asked.

Definitely, time for that swig. A few old boys emerged from the Dinette, rubbing their tummies. They stood by, lighting Chesterfields.

"I ask Mandy was the river catfish fresh today and she said it had just swum in the door. She said did I want my catfish with whiskers or without. *With* costs extra, she said. Then when it come, I et it and I says to her, Mandy, how do you make this cat so all-fired good, and she says we rub it down with ass-of-elk. Can you beat that?"

"We don't got no elk around here. Elk is an absent species. And you can't do nothing with that gal. She's got a mouth on her would make a crocodile blush."

"We don't got no crocks around here. You want a good crock burger you got to go all the way to Jacksonville."

Across the street, shouts were going up along the lines of *When do the show start? When do it? Shake a leg in there!*—as though some doubt existed that it would, a practical worry since frequently what the Imperial advertised was not what was to be seen on the screen, commonly on account of the Trailways bus having lost the reels or the distributor fled to Hawaii.

"Do I have it keerect that in this show Viota Bee is seen crawling naked in bed with—"

"If she crawled in with me I wouldn't crawl out for two weeks."

"No, you wouldn't be able to."

"By cracky, ain't she still working at Bon Vivant?"

"No, by God she ain't."

"Durn. And me wanting to git my hair bobbed."

"What hair? You're balder than a doorknob."

"You aim to see that picture show, Hubbard?"

"I'm thinking on it."

"You seen Grey?"

"Naw."

"Well, is he living or dead? I hear Essie done took a pitchfork to him."

They stomped on their cigarette butts and lit up new ones. They looked awhile through the Dinette's screen door and at the cotton ball stuck there to keep out flies. They studied with mute regard the metal strip across the door, which said COME AGAIN, CAMELS, which led them to inspect their own Chesterfields. They watched a group of children out in the street chucking rocks at the light bulb hanging high overhead. Another group was farther down, poking sticks into a pecan tree. They smiled as the tree owner ran out waving a broom at them.

Not for the first time did Hubbard acknowledge that every kid in this town was skinny and underfed. They'd break an arm just throwing a baseball.

The white bookmobile puttered slowly along the street and came to a stop between two cotton-webbed pine trees in the Mercantile lot. A lone boy of six or seven stood waiting for the side door to open. The van worked three counties and usually showed up in this same lot once a month for two or three hours, less if rain was falling and never if snow was coming down.

A Mrs. Sphere drove the van and presided over the several hundred Reader's Digest condensed volumes shelved inside. She did not like talking to people. From the driver's seat, pillow-elevated to enable her to peer short-sightedly through the windshield, she would abruptly inform her clients when they had been browsing long enough. "Make your mind up," she'd say. "It don't matter nohow which you choose, since one is so much like another." She did not like her shelves depleted. She gave close scrutiny to any borrower's card; if any such card was in any manner stained, folded, dog-eared or dog-chewed, she'd declare the bearer ineligible and confiscate the card, no renewal permitted through whatever period she felt the card's state justified. If they didn't like how she conducted her business they could take their business elsewhere. They could git their own condensed library.

But she conferred on the boy waiting at the book-mobile spot an authority denied others. She could be heard clanging open the door, saying hidy to him; she assisted him on the high step, straightened his clothing, slicked down his hair with some spit, gave dispassionate study to any loiterers hanging about, shooed away any others wanting entry, and clanged shut the door.

It might be an hour or so before either again appeared. It was not known what exactly the two did in there. From the beginning she had put pink shades over the front windows. Over the back window as well.

The shades were frayed some. The tassel string pulls had gone missing. From the way the tires wore, treadless to begin with, you knew some while had passed since they'd been aligned. They were tires of another age: a lattice-work of wooden spokes. In the distant past she'd applied pink paint to them, or likely had hired someone. The paint was mostly gone now. Inside, she had a small aisle chair. She called it a chair—her "browsing" chair—though in fact it was no more than a three-legged stool. People grave in weight were not permitted to sit—or put their feet—on it. Not that many wanted to, as they'd have a devil of a time getting up. Maybe the chair existed only for the boy; certainly Mrs. Sphere never sat on it, being weighty herself. And handicapped by "that bad leg." Spindly legs and an overlarge caboose, as people said.

True enough, one leg was foreshortened, which explained the van's extended, all but defeated, clutch. From time to time, she arrived in town accompanied by an invalid. This was presumed to be Mr. Sphere, although he was never introduced or referred to. He sat beside her up front, a pasty-faced, heavy-necked man wearing a bright tie, usually asleep but affable enough when not. The trouble was one could rarely tell what he was saying; he slobbered a lot. Mrs. Sphere might say, "Honey, clean your mouth," but he would go on slobbering, talking gibberish, often throwing in a laugh or two, like he was the jolliest man on earth.

Still, what was the boy and Mrs. Sphere doing in there all that while behind the drawn curtains, the closed door? Rap on that door, you'd be told to beat it. *Scram. We ain't open yit. Come back next month.* Once, to stubborn knocking, she opened the door waving a pistol in the faces of the man and woman standing there. "Go away," she said. "You won't be the first loving couple I've shot." And she did shoot, if only into the air. In astonishment, the man collapsed onto a dusty bed of petunias the Mercantile had put in. The woman unleashed an unknowing smile, clutching all the tighter the straw bag into which she'd hoped to drop the newest condensed best seller. "You've shot…"—shot my husband, she meant to say, but stopped because the victim was grappling at her ankle. She looked down to see him wallowing about—exactly like a rooting hog, was her thought. He stood, finally. He said, "That was a close call. My God. I thought I was back on Iwo Jima."

What went on in there? An old crazy woman and a boy you couldn't git a word out of. So there was talk about that, as well as talk about what went on at the boy's slat house out behind the radio tower where nothing else was. How did the house go up without anyone knowing about it and why out there where the land was swampy and smelt to high heaven and nothing grew except weeds and thistles past your neck. The broadcast tower, up no more than ten years, was already leaning, which maybe was why the WCBT signal didn't carry beyond the county and hardly next door when the weather was bad. Somebody was always trying to shoot out the sparkly red lights atop the tower; somebody was always breaking into the tiny white hut behind which the tower stood. The lights were said to serve as warning to aircraft but aircraft never showed in these parts. Maybe it's for the birds, then? The birds, oh sure. Birds come here by accident and don't stay long. The stench of old man Peterson's paper mill soon gits to them.

43

Some, eavesdropping at the bookmobile door, said they heard a high chirping voice reciting in dramatic monotony such words as you might expect to find, if ever foolishness led you to look, in what Mrs. Sphere called "these everlasting classics." It was believed that Johnny Little—such was the boy's name—was the illegitimate son of an illegitimate daughter of Mrs. Sphere, living in the house behind the WCBT radio tower out on the lane that, one way or another, got one eventually to Highway 301. About four miles, give or take, the boy had to walk to git into town proper; another four back, for Mrs. Sphere had never been known to give him a lift. Gas don't grow on trees, she said. I don't put myself out for anyone. Well, she was gitting on in years. No one could expect her to be a Biltmore. Philanthropy wasn't in the cards. A neurotic the town could stand, so long as the visitation was reasonably spaced. The boy was known to refuse any ride offers. He pretended sightlessness of anyone making such overtures. "Won't look at you. Won't say a word. Just trudges on with that downcast face, in those knickers and tennis shoes his mama makes him wear."

Grey had made his way out there, of course. Somehow he knew the boy, the mother, and even the man Little with whom the pair was living. It could be he knew Little because he was a drinker and Grey took it upon himself to see that he got home and got there without beating up the boy and mother, which was Little's inclination when carousing. What Little did for a living was speculated upon, Grey not assisting with these speculations. He'd spent a while in the farm prison over by New Bern, that much was official. Grey said Little was not as violent as he thought he was, and that the most harm he ever had brought to the mother was to gently fling her aside when she sought to take away his drink. The fact is, Grey said, those three set the good example in this rat-trap town which makes everyone look eighty before they've turned thirty. Grey said Little was "All right," and that he'd be partway decent if only he would stick to his medication and could get past his need to kill people.

The reason this is being told is because here they come. Little and the woman—who is hardly past being a girl and stands less than five feet in the decorated moccasins she's wearing—are coming hand in hand with smiles on their faces. They have come to see the picture show. They have heard of its marvels and depravity on WCBT and seen the editorials in the *Herald* opposing the presentation of *"smut which has appeal only to the base among us."* Everybody voices agreement with this but can't wait to see it.

Several farmers had rattled into town by mule and wagon to stand, sombre as undertakers, watching in stolid deliberation those assembled, by nature monosyllabic in the unfamiliar environment, roughened hands holding onto galluses, the odd one pinching a wedge of Prince Albert beneath the lower lip and spitting, when it came to that, into the palm of the hand and discreetly wiping that hand on the overalled behind, wanting for their own sensibility's satisfaction no violation of supposed town conduct, conduct which they'd personally been witness to through the perverse, obtuse, deliberate, necessary, often forced action of sons and daughters fleeing farm for town, where everything was rush rush rush and dog eat dog—"That," one now was saying, "or setting down day in and day out to doing nothing, unless you call doing nothing keeping busy."

Two of them have spotted old Hubbard sagged against the Dinette wall and have drifted over to pay their respects.

"How you, Mr. Hubbard?"

"I'm right pokey," Hubbard tells them. "You boys' crops chugging along?"

"Corn is."

"Peanuts is."

"Melon is."

"Potatoes is."

"You boys put no cotton in this year?"

"Oh, cotton for dang sure. Boll-weevils paid a visit. Cotton ain't knee-high to a bedbug."

The two men went inside, returning with a Coca-Cola for Hubbard and two Red Rock sodas for themselves. They squatted down alongside Hubbard, all gazing out at the hubbub.

"Mine too. A dead grasshopper stands higher. I'll be hip-deep in snow before that cotton thinks to say hello."

"Yes sir. Farming was God's first nightmare. What if that dang tree produced no apple?"

"Last evening my child Blossomer, just-born baby whimpering from a slapped fanny—says to me—in the cracker voice they talk here, 'You mean to tell me I've got myself all the way up off the sofa to make you yo' dinner and now you is tellin' me you has already et!'"

"Yes sir, you town folks are right backward, no insult intended for your Blossomer."

"It was like hearing scripture, how she said it."

"This here picture show, my boy tells me, is the new scripture. I've got profound regret for what I'm entering into, like Satan is rubbing my backbone. My three gals, mill hands at number two mill, still sleep on a corn shucks mattress so I reckon they still see theirselves as country gals. It's music to the backside, they say."

"All in the one?"

"Not one ever married, and don't mean to. Say, Stonewalls the name. Us Stonewalls got a parcel of acres on the road 'bout seven miles up from you."

"Plunket's mine."

They shook limber hands, wary of touch, eyes scoring the other's shoe leather as if divining themselves elsewhere. "I reckon as how I've seen your wagons at that Owen fella's cotton gin. You still got a hand in with Owen on that cotton gin, Hubbard?"

"I do. But have I seen one red cent yet? How did your mule-riding adventure go, Mr. Plunket?"

"Let's see. The proceeds are tied up here in this pocket rag. Five cent a ride. Nobody fell off, thank God. No matter how hard they tried. Looky here: two dollars and forty-eight cents. Better than I can do with my cotton. I took them young'uns up one alley and down another. You got more alleys than streets in this metropolis, Hubbard."

"Maybe them alleys are streets."

"The gospel's truth. I think the young'uns liked seeing the stump-burning best."

"I might myself."

"A boy with a feather sticking from his head come up to me. He's pulling this Red Ryder wagon. He says he will rent me that wagon. I says, son, what use would I have of that wagon. He says I could hitch the wagon to my mule, haul a pair in it and triple or quadruple my payload. Two or three little squirts are at his heels he's already sold tickets to."

"That'll be the Grey boy."

"The Lord does help those who help themselves. The boy whose daddy got burnt up at State Line?"

"Uh-huh. You done any coon-hunting lately, Stonewall?"

"Wife runs the dogs now."

"By God, she don't!"

"The big question in marriage is would you do it over again, to the same hand. I would, over and over, till infinity come crushing down."

"By God. She runs both you and them dogs."

"Daylight through dark."

Hubbard's visitors got to their feet. "I'll take these empties inside and git me my deposit back," Plunket said. He went. Stonewall beat his hat against one leg. "Looks like that dang picture show is about to start." He scented the air, next saying to Hubbard's nodding head: "Rain tomorrow."

The Dinette owner's large frame filled the doorway.

"If a woman might git a word in edgewise," she said, "you might like to know the governor called."

"Now, Daisy, is that any business of mine?" Hubbard said.

Daisy ventured outside, shielding her eyes from the sun. Her reddened arms were dripping soap suds. "He's hauling ass in here on Sunday. He wants twelve of our Sabbath Holy Plate Specials with all the fixins."

"Good lord! You'll have to shoot three pigs!"

"Pork don't go in the Sabbath plate, honey. Seeing as how you've dined on the dish through the decades, you oughten to know that."

"What in thunder goes in it?"

Daisy shook her head in disbelief at his and the world's stupidity.

Now and then Governor Cherry did come. He came in a motorcade of crying sirens, whirling lights, an endless train of shiny automobiles and state motorcycle cops. The governor was as big on show as his long-dead mentor compatriot in Baton Rouge, Huey Long, had been.

"That's it?"

"He wants his special advisor on human relations made available."

"Amarantha? Be a dog!"

Cherry was good. He paved roads, opposed lynching, chewed tobacco, was favorable to drink, and routinely kicked the butt of that young Dixiecrat pea-brain governor down in South Carolina, Strom Thurmond. Farmers, teachers, and Republicans didn't like Cherry. He'd moved the mandatory schooling age up from fourteen to sixteen. Education, the governor said, was the precious ticket to progress. He was finding the bold initiative unenforceable.

"What else?"

"He specifies Hubbard, Esquire, is to be at the table. In a fresh shirt and sober."

"Rats!"

"He says we can forgit ice tea, he'll be bringing his own jugs."

"That's good."

"He don't want those Greys hollering at each other. He gits enough of that at home, he says."

"Is the wife coming?"

"You bet. He says Mildred would walk here from Kingdom Come for our Sabbath Holy Plate Special."

"An admirable woman, to be sure."

The minutes played on, tedious as a waltz. The sun hovered overhead, spilled egg-white on a blue plate, bathing one and all under a rinse of light and shadow. In the street two skinny dogs, mindless of traffic, were sniffing each other, taking pause to monitor the skirt of a young woman just then crossing, the woman igniting a burst of shrieks and a quick splay of legs, this catching the attention of several other dogs, all soon rutting under the whirling skirt.

Mr. Varner, wife to his rear, appeared in a wheezing shuffle, powered by rough-hewn crutches high under the arms, their visage similar, in cold fact one a hardened duplication of the other, conveying no warrant for which was the original, yet unalike otherwise as two erratic dogs following the one scent.

It was that homicidal Grey did this to him, he was telling those interested few parties stepping aside in his wake. He meant to git that boy locked up before nightfall, he said. Then he meant to bring personal injury suit against the vile pus, and against any sorry Grey relative who had a hand in raising the loudmouth Charles Atlas muscle-fit bastard. He'd git his Omaha insurance company on the case, which had cost him an arm and a leg over the decades, with not one cent accruing into his pockets, not even when half his roof swooped into far away counties during the '44 hurricane. It was the insurance would be forking over greenbacks in payment for his split lip, his busted kneecap, for Dottie's pulled hair, his broke railings, plus anything else occurring to him. "Everybody saw how I whupped Grey's butt good. He won't be spoiling for no nother fight soon. I give him a nose limber as a squirrel's tail. He was like a rat in boiling grease fat. He was mine to rend into pork chops."

At the same time Dottie was saying to her friends, "No, by God no, we don't aim to see this picture show.

We've seen about as much of Viota Bee as we can stand. She's making all this money on the picture—strumpety as a wildcat—but not delivered to us one red cent. Like Varden says, we have cast her out. Now she's bedded with outlaws, what no good bozo will she bed next? She was a thoughtless—"

"Now Dottie, don't beat a dead dog," Varner warned.

"—vain impossible child, wanting everything her way. Bitching daylight through dark. Bossie Britches, we called her. We had to tie her to the bed or none of us got any sleep. A polecat she was. Language as would tire an ape. We had to lock her in the pantry, I'd say frequently. Then me to come into that pantry to find my every canning jar dumped to the floor. Trampled, flung each which way. Peaches, fig, blackberry, apricot. My dandelion wine. I tell you. How I slaved in that canning. Heavens to Betsy! What parent could put up with the like? We built a shed out back. Locked her up. Chained the door. This'll teach you, we said. In two days she'd dug out the same as would a manic dog. Gone sixteen days. Sixteen! Doing what? Come to find out the vixen been sleeping under Grey's bed, the two not nine years old. Which goes to show you—"

"Spoiled that child to kingdom come we did," Varner put in. "See where it got us."

"—goes to show you a trollop nature will—"

"Whereas little Cindy has been sweet as a tamed rabbit. Already a twelve-year-old boy done offered his hand in marriage."

"—will sooner or later reveal itself, as God's my judge."

"Now you mention little Cindy, where is she? I'd think she's a bit young to be left alone."

"She's been bad. Bit off her best doll's head."

"So she's got housework to do."

They trundled onward, renewed by spleen. One of the usherettes come out, flashlight in hand, to inform the throng the next show would start a few minutes late—five or ten. Because before the start of the feature presentation the Buster Crabbe serial—chapter nine, Buck Rogers vs. Mad Killer Kane—had jumped the sprocket and got banged up when the projection boy stepped on it. The usherette was a cute tow-haired, trim-ankled girl living out on Primebeef Road near the french-fry place you had to have transport to git to. Where the auto junk yard is. Best french-fry night spot in the state. But can you git to it? Not if your car is rusting in the junkyard, how Essie's is. Rita is the usherette's name. No, she didn't have no particular boyfriend now. No special one. No, she didn't want no date, she said. Not especially. She wasn't in the mood right now. No, her old boyfriends had treated her fine, she just wasn't in the mood right now. Not especially, she just wasn't in—. No, she didn't want no drive home after work. Well thank you, yes, Sally Forth had done a 'specially good job on her tresses. It hadn't set her back but two dollars, the Tuesday Special Sally said it was. No, she won't but sixteen. Why thank you, that's awful nice of you to say so, I do try to keep myself fit. No, I don't run or do push-ups, I can't say I 'specially do anything. No, that wasn't me you saw swimming naked in the river. I don't swim. No, she won't be in school now, she had quit. Half her class had quit, she couldn't exactly say why, they just had. "Hidy, Walter," she said.

"Hidy, Rita," Walter said. He was passing under the marquee, toting a five-gallon gasoline can. It could be he was one of the usherette's old boyfriends because he next said to her with no mild irritation, "Every time I see you you got a bunch of nasty, grinning vultures grazing your elbow. And you cutting up, pretending you've got not a care in the world and don't have no inkling of the gutter where these skunks' mind is."

She said, "Whatever I do is none of your bees-wax, Walter Ullrich, so you can take your vain, ugly, pig-shouldered self straight out of my sight."

And there, instead, she went out of sight, stepping pretty as anything you'd ever hope to see.

Walter Ullrich halted beside Grey Junior and his gang and looked stomped on. He looked like he wanted to run Rita down and tackle her and propose marriage if she didn't try too fast to git up.

"What's that gas can for?" was the question Junior put to him.

"Them stumps," Ullrich said.

"What stumps?"

"Them stumps down there."

"Down where?"

"Down there, goddammit. Where you see that smoke."

"What smoke? Why's they burning stumps? Who is burning them stumps?"

"It's me for one burning them, you forward bastard."

"Why?"

"Do I know? I'm doing what I'm told, which was to git this gas."

"Well, don't slosh it on us."

"As I'm employed by civic authorities I guess it could be said them goddamn stumps are burning at the behest of the town."

"We got no civic authorities."

"Then by God they are self-appointed."

"Why burn them stumps?"

"Do I know? I got me a handful to set fire to so I best git on."

"Maybe you best put out that cigarette."

"Did I ask you mawkish, back-stabbing fiends for advice?"

"No. So truck along then."

"I aim to. Why you pulling that Red Ryder wagon? Did you lose what little sense you had?"

"We got business with a mule, if you must know. Now listen, Ullrich. I got me a collection of five hundred matchbooks from all over the nation I'm willing to let go at a good price. Most still have matches. I got a ball of tinfoil soon to be the biggest such tinfoil ball in the entire nation. I'm thinking tourist attraction. We could install that tinfoil on your stump field and charge an ungodly admission."

"How big is that ball now?"

"About your size."

"Then it don't interest me. I like matches, though."

Another couple, by Carol Bly's booth, stooped down to talk through the little window cut in the fly-smeared glass. They'd bussed in from Jackson, they were telling her. They were asking the precise minute the feature show let out since they had a bus to catch to git back to Jackson, where twelve folks were hoping to be fed. They ran the boarding house next to the Jackson pool hall, one of a half-dozen business empires in Jackson, that locale being about the size of a lean man's thumb. They were a pair known to Junior,

Daddy Grey having run the Jackson pool hall during a tender year, and lodging in the couple's home, at times taking Junior along. Junior approached them with a smiling hello and the woman rewarded him with shrieks, while her husband clapped his backside. They served ample, nourishing food, had soft clean beds, a sink in each room, and you could git along with them. Junior had been impressed by the people coming through: Moon Pie drummers, the Singer Sewing Machine sales force, bible thumpers, lightning rod crews, a man one-time selling exotic birds, Fullerettes and Fuller Brush men hawking Fuller Brush doodads, the Watkins Man, the odd Jewel Tea man flogging soaps, sauces, percolators, weed killer, roach balm, mouse traps, hole diggers, mule harness, nails, fire retardants, baking soda, and iron skillets guaranteed resistant to wear and tear.

Junior was at a dead end when it came to recalling their names. They were a dumpy, well-dressed pair, the man in new gabardine, the woman in hat and brown hose sliding into brown shoes with bows on top, shoulders draped in a grandmotherly fichu. A teensy peach-pit hat.

"I want one down front and a cheaper one in the balcony for Dilsey here," the man was saying. "Too close to the screen and Dee she gits neck spasms."

Dilsey and John Spring, those the names.

"We can't have that, now can we," Carol told them. "We have open seating. Balcony costs the same."

"Why, that does not make good business sense!" John Spring said.

"You and Dilsey just look to see where you find two good seats together."

"I be dogged if we won't do just that. Be dogged if we won't. Do we pay for treats to you or in there?"

A maze of sparrows hurtled in from the street's northern end, paused momentarily, then swooped up the street in a line straight enough to have been drawn by a ruler. Smoke wafted in alongside and behind them, fuelled by a burst of wind transporting still-flaring cinders. A mule pulling a weathered wagon, on the slat of which sat a similarly weathered, hatted man, hove into view, the wagon heaped with watermelons. The driver, like his mule, seemingly unaware of where it was he was or intended going, not answering or even turning his head when a Dinette figure blasted from the door, running fast, blowing leaves upon Hubbard's waking form, shouting, "Hey! Slow down! How much for one of them melons?" The wagon rattled on, the Dinette figure—Daisy, in fact—following in a siege of clumsy stumbles, in aggrieved disgust hollering, "All right, Eddie, goddammit, how much for ten of those damn melons?" At that, the driver Eddie uncoiled his frame, softly lay down the reins, the mule's head in the same second drooping in surprised revelation of its instantly stilled hooves. The wagon man hopped down over a wheel, dusting and balling up his hat before returning it to his head. "Four dollars," he said.

Hubbard got to his feet. He took pleasure in observing Daisy's business negotiations.

Daisy, breathing hard, came forward a pace.

"Three. The last batch you sprung on me weren't even pink."

"Four. And I ain't plugging nary a one," Eddie said. "They's guaranteed ripe as heaven allows."

"You know I can't turn no profit at four."

"Nor me at three."

"Three, and I throw in a RC Cola and my coconut cake to go with it."

"Don't hanker for coconut. What other flavour you pushing?"

"Apple. Butterscotch. Pecan. Cherry rhubarb. Pies. Not cake."

"Four. And I buy my own pie."

"You're a mean man would rob a blind woman of her eyes."

"You got the wit of a fencepost."

They strolled together to the Dinette, Eddie saying, "I'll have my RC and butterscotch out here with this old tramp. 'How you, Hubbard. You looking spry as a hob-nailed chicken.'" They watched, sullen and silent for the moment as Eddie's mule stared a long time at them, then pulled the wagon to the roadside and nibbled without relish a crop of crabgrass.

"I forget what you call that mule," Hubbard said.

"I don't. It calls me." Hubbard watched him reconsidering. "I'm giving thought to calling that mule Joe."

Hubbard hopped about in his seat. "I never saw such a damn fool as you, Edward."

"Edward, is it? Friends call me Eddie."

"I'd be surprised these so-called friends don't have a heap of other names for you."

"Like what?"

"Damn fool. Stubborn as molasses. Ornery. The brains of a stick in the mud. Hard-headed as a polecat."

"I hope for your continued good heath you're not saying I stink. In my opinion, skunks ain't hard-headed. They's quick to a decision."

"As you are, naming that mule Joe. Why don't you go whole hog and call it Joe Louis?"

"That's the name. Plain Joe's not good enough for my mule. That mule munching on town grass is Joe Louis, certified world champion by way of 52 professional knockouts, most ever in the ring."

"Now you get this straight, Edward. I—"

"You call me Edward again we going to have another knockout right here."

Eddie was standing now. He was limbering up, his fists punching the air. Hubbard stood also. Their chairs toppled over. Their faces were swollen with anger.

"I'm using your full name as a sign of respect," Hubbard said.

"It ain't a sign I'm agreeable with."

"So hit me."

"I'll tear you in two."

"You and what army."

They danced about, taking powder-puff swings at each other. Huffing and puffing. Daisy appeared, carrying a tray on which rode Eddie's pie and soda and a wedge for Hubbard. "You two stop that!" she said. "This minute! I swanee! Making a spectacle of yourself at your age. Sit down. I mean it. Sit!"

They sat.

"Eat your pie."

"Don't want no pie."

"So like children. I said: Eat it."

Each took a tentative morsel.

"Now what's this nonsense about? I've seen it simmering the last five to six years."

Neither spoke.

"Do I need to get a switch and beat the tar out of both of you? I swear to almighty hell I want to."

"Don't cuss," Hubbard said.

"Goes back to June 18, 1941," Eddie said.

"June," Hubbard said.

"We had us a bet."

"That dadgum title bout."

"My man the Brown Bomber versus his man the Pittsburgh Kid."

"A lie. I won't rooting for Billy."

"Was too. Skinny white man taking on ole' black Joe."

Daisy's head went back and forth. She seemed ready to find her switch. "Git on with this tale," she said. "I've cooking to get back to. As I recall, Joe won that match. I heard it on Mutual right here at the Dinette."

"Of course Joe won. But this lizard Hubbard claims—"

"I never claimed Billy Conn was better. What I said was what everybody says, that Billy was ahead on points when Joe knocked him flat in the tenth round."

"Thirteenth. You can't keep nothing straight."

"Didn't I pay you the dollar?"

"Not with good grace. You wanted that white boy to beat the nigger."

"Did not. And I don't allow that word in my presence."

"Only in the privacy of your little white heart, I guess."

They were all set to renew the battle when Daisy slammed her right fist into one shoulder and her left into the other.

"Let me attempt settling this quarrel in my own subtle manner. Hubbard was all over town taking bets on the bout of the century. He had it easy because every-body and his brother was rooting for Billy. How much did you win betting on Joe?"

"Near one hundred."

"And lost?"

"Just that dollar bet with this polecat. If we were to bet, I had no choice but to take Billy."

"That's the truth?"

"Damn so."

"It looks like five years ago I jumped the gun. You're not the racist pigshit I took you to be."

Daisy hastened away, singing

Patty cake, patty cake,
How do you do
My poor patty cake
She's down with the flu
Her nose does run
Her feet do too
My poor patty cake
She runs to you

For some minutes Grey Junior had been standing by. "Mr. Eddie, sir," he said. "I am prepared to remove those Dinette-bought melons to the desired location for a negotiable sum."

"Do it," Eddie said. "Hubbard makes me tired. We can negotiate later."

"I disapprove of that arrangement, sir. You are likely unaware I deliver the *Weekly Herald*. I can't express to you the difficulty I experience in collecting my five cent for that fine paper. I rap my knuckles raw, weekend and week out. Folks refuse to come to the door. I can see them hunched over at the kitchen table, not so much as bothering to look up. If by rare chance they do stumble to the door—usually it's the wife—she tells me to come back next week. 'Come back next week.' I've heard that 'next week' line 'til my ears has grown moldy. Next week it's the same story. It's contrary, wouldn't you say, sir, how much folks in Destiny hate parting with a nickel."

Eddie flipped Junior a coin.

"That's a half-dollar to shut you up," he said.

After listening to the ridiculous harangues issuing from Hubbard's mouth, Essie, working herself into a vile temper, spent ten minutes in the Dinette washroom untangling her hair. She acknowledged a deep distaste for what she saw in the mirror. She'd been a pretty girl once, pretty enough, now just look. No, she hadn't been no beauty queen, hadn't won no Miss Hotsy-Totsy contest like Viota Bee had, but, by the same token, boys hadn't taken to heel the second they saw her. Ridiculous. Quite the contrary, thank you. I had to beat them off with a stick. On me like flies, they were. She told herself this, another big lie, so ridiculous she was almost driven to spit at the ridiculous, concerned face looking back at her in the mirror with red swollen eyes on a long sorrowful neck. Well, thank you, face, feel free to go on with what you were doing.

She washed that face. She washed it good. Some women she knew never allowed soap, actual soap, to touch the precious skin, but she by God was not one of those oddballs. "Ridiculous, ridiculous," she kept saying, a word she now applied to any thought entering her head. The tap water ran hot one second, cold the next, which was ridiculous, but this she could at least blame on the idiot cooks in the kitchen running their own taps. This made her think of showers, baths, wrestling matches with Grey in mountain streams, various smooching sessions on high, low, or intermediate inclines, with or without water. How ridiculous. With sober dismay she contemplated fingernails, which in the frequent past had known the exquisite rapture of being tended to by the captivating ladies at Bon Vivant Hair (and Foot) Salon. The nails now had been chewed back a bit. They were poor and ragged specimens, too ridiculous to behold. Since reading in the *Herald's* asinine Soc(i.e.)ty column of Miss Hotsy-Totsy's going-away shenanigans at Bon Vivant she'd vowed never to return. They were fun girls, chattering magpies, gossip mongers par excellence, and, heavens to betsy, did they not know hair. It was thoroughly delightful to sit in a comfortable chair with a whirring helmet the size of a Ford coupe on your head while Sally Forth pranced about uttering her insane prattle, but Essie couldn't help feeling betrayed by Sally Forth's not inviting her to join in the celebration. Not, certainly, that she would have attended any shindig celebrating the marvels of Miss Hotsy-Totsy. But, still. Still, Sally should have granted her the pleasure of refusing. It ticked her off no end how those girls teased her about the long *friendship*— ha!—Grey and Viota enjoyed. Ridiculous.

Even more ridiculous was Hubbard, snagging her just as she was about to take off...well, somewhere. Maybe home.

"That injunction you got out on Grey isn't apt to smooth the marital waters," he said. "Any more than is that shapeless rag you have on and is calling a dress. Why did you git the law involved?"

"Because I wanted to."

"You Petersons always did what you wanted to rather than what was good for you and everybody else."

"I'll thank you to leave the Petersons out of this."

"I'd be happy to had they left me and the town out of it. Your ancestor rolls in here on a golden chariot, throws up four textile mills, a giant paper plant, throws up six hundred houses he calls Colonial Revival, each exactly alike down to the last nail—"

"Are you having one of your fits?"

"—builds his company store, hires his thousands at a dollar a day, six-year-olds at a penny an hour, rents his Colonial Revivals at fifty cents a day, sells his clothing and food at twenty-five cents a day, his power and water at another twenty cents, miscellaneous at ten, so these employees end the week owing the saintly bastard their souls and dollars. All with the collusion of—"

"Shut your mouth, please. I wasn't born then. The silver spoon eluded me."

"Then your vaunted grandpappy hustles his golden coach off to Asia and China once the union threatens, most of the town now boarded up. Small wonder Grey—"

"Grey don't hold against me my gravy birth."

"I reckon must be twenty bodies buried beneath that picture show house across the street your grandpappy put up in the Revivalist style to steal his worker's one last cent, now showing, 'The Picture They Dared Us to Make.' Plus, you got, or had before you took up the pool-hall life, more education than that fool has, which Grey can't like and no self-respecting man would. Plus you can't talk local no matter how hard you try."

"You're an old-fashioned crank. Are you done harassing me now? I come hoping you to cheer me up and—"

"You're cheered. I can see you got your spunk back. Anyway, I know you entered the public thoroughfare hoping to spot Grey before he spots you. Go home. He will likely be on your doorstep."

"I don't count for nothing to nobody. Even Junior can't stand me."

Hubbard laughed. "The absolute truth," he said. "Have some paregoric. It will sing to you like Lily Pons."

Daisy showed up. "You two take the cake," she said. "I may ban you both from the Dinette, you continue disturbing my peace. The industrial revolution has been long afoot, Hubbard. You might ask yourself what people in these parts had before them mills skipped in."

"Nothing," Hubbard said. "Upended by worse."

*

The picture show was letting out—a whole gang, like in a cattle drive. Some stranger said, "Viota Bee was spectacular. Her bazooms, headlights—whatever word you want—are a damn unnatural phenomenon. I near wet my pants when she slid in bed with poor shot-to-hell Jessie James."

"Billy, you mean. The Kid. Why'd she change her name?"

"Who?"

"What'shername."

"Who?"

"That Varner girl."

"Hollywood can't have any old Betsy Blue on the marquee."

"Now she's in pictures Grey ain't never to unhitch hisself. It's love with bluebells tied to it."

"Uh-huh. She'd melt fire hydrants. I'm plumb disoriented by the sexual fantasy preying on—"

"Though Grey swears he never once thought of gitting into her pants."

"A sick man, if so."

"Fidelity to the loved one is a trial every minute of the day."

"As the Good Book says, a thought cemented in the head is sin equal to the actual deed."

"We are all in apprenticeship to love, a workshop of ungodly hours and merciless futility. It is the rare party graduates."

The throng was mostly men, mostly men alone, all smiling, walking with springy shoes. The few women with men were smiling a different smile, like they had done something they were quite proud of or soon hoped to accomplish.

All right, let's move on, or, come to think of it, let's not for here comes, in becoming wedge, the scintillating Bon Vivant bunch, all whooping it up, Sally Forth in dancing lead, followed by Jean, Judy, Bertha Bell and like-minded camp followers, the shining faces made diminutive by wondrous towers of beehive hair in luxurious variety of tints and shades as only Bon Vivant can. They are shellacked almost to the point of non-recognition, their faces denuded, then masterfully restored, beatified and beautified, each in ballooning mannish pants and translucent shirts showcasing exquisite breastwork exemplified by brassieres of uncanny design as can be seen, Sally Forth would aver, only in the sub-tropics. Their fine hips shift like boats rocking in billowing oceanic waves, highlighting the magical association such divine movement these hips have with jewellery-encrusted, gravity-defying high heels.

"Why, it's Grey's little rooster!" says Sally Forth to Junior. "How yawl doing? Those lashes you're flashing will have us girls swooning one day. Look at me, girls, I'm about to fall into underage arms! I'm in panic-satanic, smitten by a kitten! Easy to see our Junior is soon to be a rover in clover! Let's kiss him all over! How you, how you, how are all of you grinning boys! Come to see our gal Viota crawl in the sack with Billy, have you?"

She goes on crooning the greetings, Jean, Joan, and Bertha Bell throwing in their equally abundant salutation to a sea of admirers, paying scant attention to the odd outlaw hand slithering round one and the other's waist. Passing out cards, *Tuesday Special Wash Cut & Trim 2 Smackers, Thursday Hallelujah Hours, the "Whole Shebang," no checks please.* And here arrives J. Scruggs, pigtails slicked down, mandolin not in sight, thank God.

"Where's Grey?" he says, tousling into Junior, "Hot damn, I'm 'sposed to have succotash with that conniving daddy of yourn. Or is that scrupulous bastard supping with you and Mother Essie tonight? Well, Holy Jesus, how is that loving souped-up hot mama Essie? Say, didn't you think Viota Bee owned that fil'um? Wasn't she the total essence of blessed femininity? What gumption she had! It was a disappointment however Viota don't show up 'til sixteen cotton-pickin' minutes into the show, coming at Billy with pistol, pitchfork, and bosom, I'm tellin' you."

"That there show," one of the girls, Jean, puts in, "ain't about Viota and Billy and Pat Garrett and Doc Holliday. It's about that strawberry roan."

"The horse? Now you hold on," Joan says.

"You hold on," Jean says back.

"Viota was smashing but who's to wind up with that cute horse, that's the whole picture."

"You got the brains a billy goat has. True love's the issue."

"Yes. Who gits the horse."

"A certain snowflake I know can shut her mouth."

"Make me, you stuffed field rat whore."

"Now girls, don't spat," laughing Sally Forth tells them.

They laugh too, being bumped into by Bertha Bell, sore "as a mummy's hind leg," Bertha says, because she's being left out of the fun. But here arrives an arm around her shoulder, a soldier boy's sweet breath in one ear, to which, not whom, Bertha say's, "Now, we're cookin'."

But there they go, as if in jaunty springtime when the sun's rays first fall, Jean and Joan hooking happy arms with Scruggs, dainty slim vermillion fingertips raking his spine and posterior, inasmuch as it's generally conceded both are in adoration of Scrugg's steady loom-fixer employment, the dapper musician's smidgen of talent with strings, with his scrawny neck, his wide shoulders and adorable bum, his strong chin, his wide ears, his unwed status and unremitting love of women, his sparkling repartee, his sometimes hilarious panama hat, his string tie and freckled nose and sockless feet, with his Brilliantine-pomaded pigtails which any day soon they will suds up, bouffant, beehive, colourize or chop off.

Unless.

Unless like others in this garrulous troupe they are merely bringing a spigot's infinitesimal worth of joy to the gruelling lifespan of a mill-worker town's deferred paradise—moment of amusement, appeasement, mercy—to uplift, titillate, hopefully horrify the greater beady-eyed republic which in a moment of laxity has, as the *Weekly Herald* put it, *"unleashed the horrors of unabashed sexuality upon our town's treasured inhabitants."*

But, but, but, what did these ignorant sod-busters have before we came! Else it is skilful play-acting of the Bon Vivant crew enacting the role of someone other than themselves, in opposition to stern reality, as Grey was earlier, according to Tillich, theorizing. Why not, when the Bon Vivant future is a lifetime of clipping; buffing; fumigating finger, toenail, and heel; washing; scenting; bee-hiving and spraying; dyeing, endless heads of hair, for godsake. That or badgering husbands, drooling babies, never-ending housework, bitter ridicule and heartache, poverty the giant shadow hovering at the door, sickness, accident, impediment the interminable rockslide as your once-young body breathes *at last,* at last becoming what was there all the while in hungry wait. Nothing. All upended, promised replacement worse for evil-doers. If Grey ever had a thought to git into his friend's pants, he's sunk.

Meanwhile, thank heaven, all picture-goers in apparent aghast amazement at the show already witnessed or soon to be seen: voluptuous Rio, whether Viota Bee or Jane Russell or an as yet unknown or one-millionth party slipping wilfully dutifully in full decadent decency into the outlaw's bed—which we might remember is Rio's own and only and sacrificed bed—with the justified calm of a woman you could tell had done the same a thousand times before and would do the same a thousand times more, even *if* Pat Garrett and Doc Holliday and a thousand Mescaleros and whomever else were blazing away beyond a door so pathetic as barrier anybody on earth may enter at the drop of a hat.

And will, so Essie and Grey have often exclaimed. You don't even have to drop the hat.

We were in St. Louis, she sometimes remembers, *having won a pot. These gangsters rope me to the motel bed. It was like the money wasn't even important to them.* "Cover your naked self," *they say. It was humiliating.*

At the Dinette across the street, Daisy and Amarantha have joined Hubbard's watch of the exiting crowd. For some minutes Amarantha has been scorching their ears with scorn and fury. They haven't yet unravelled what prompts this rage. "It's unholy," she's been saying. "Unholy and disgusting and plumb unnatural. It's heathenish and barbaric and I couldn't be more riled if Jesus showed up wearing a red hat."

"What's set you on edge, Mandy? Git a hold of yourself."

They've had clues. Her ailment has something to do with the Bon Vivant bunch, that's clear.

"Disgusting," she says again. "Makes me want to spew up."

Daisy is beginning to get irritated. She's filled today's quota of bad behaviour.

"Explain yourself or go home," she tells Mandy. "It's on the tip of my tongue to say you are beginning to disgust me."

Hubbard has decided he had best keep out of this developing fray.

"Pants! *Men's* trousers!" Mandy says. "Those Vivant hussies! They ought to be in a lunatic asylum. The day you see me in long trousers will be the day we bring back green cheese from the moon."

Oh. All has become clear. It's true: the Bon Vivant women have recently taken to wearing long pants. The *Herald* has been waving red flags over the issue. *Women, whether in the home or workplace, have no business being seen, in public or privately, in long pants. Some might argue World War fabric shortages has brought this sad spectacle to our shores. We don't. We advise apparel shops, and our readers, to avoid pandering to this highly indecent fashion craze imported, like many another, from the insidious north. Such can only lead to moral turpitude. To misadventure. We cite Deuteronomy 22:5. The woman shall not wear that which pertaineth unto a man.*

To Hubbard, also, the fashion smacks a trifle of the unholy. He likes it.

At this time, Jim Talley the younger, age seven, more or less of sufficient intellect to roam the street, heir apparent of Mercantile Dynamics, son of the self-same Jim who had the good fortune of accompanying Viota Bee to renowned Far Portsmouth—he bikes along, dusty-haired and eager, wanting to show Junior and his gang his skint knee.

"Where is Grey?" Junior asks him.

"Who?" he says back. Then he relents. "Your poppa Grey give me fifty cent and a swack on the noggin not to tattle his whereabouts even to The Lone Ranger."

"On Mutual, owned by William Randolph Hearst. Grey said that?"

"And swacked me."

"Who? The Lone Ranger?"

"Is Grey the Lone Ranger?"

"He is my own daddy. Git tuned in, buddyrole."

"Your daddy Grey says your mama Essie has come to her senses, found a gun, and means to splatter his butt with buckshot."

"Shotguns don't shoot buckshot."

"He says you may be in on it. What does 'on it' mean? Are you 'on it'?"

"Nope. But I may might be."

"It took me a while to recognize your poppa. He is some banged-up."

"Sure. From that Vardin fight."

"What Vardin fight?"

"This a.m."

"Excuse me?"

"Varden."

"Oh, you mean the Vardiers. What it looked like to me was Grey had fell into a firepit. He's singed tip to toe. He's hardly identifiable coming or going. He's got a bloated foot from, he says, from kicking the door."

"What door? You are making no sense."

"Sure I am. I am making top-notch sense."

"Just tell us where you seen him last. Meaning to find from that where he might be now."

"There is that fifty cent he give me. I'm a man of my word. If I'm to break my word I've got to see a whole dollar."

"A whole dollar?"

"That's my price."

"You crooked sidewinder, you know well and good I don't have no dollar."

"How much you got?"

"Nothing?"

"No? In that case, you can owe me. No interest because of my sympathy for broken-home, sorry-ass turds like you. Grey was at the drug store seeking burn ointment. Then he was to catch a bite to eat at the Dinette. Brunswick stew, hush puppies and such. Then he might—"

"Hope not. Essie was at the Dinette."

"Don't I know it? Then he wants to sleep awhile, he can find a safe bed. Which he won't, out of fear he won't not wake up. 'Sleep is what got me in this predicament,' he told me. 'Beware of sleep,' he said, 'and never take up the weed if you got an ounce of sense.'"

"What weed? You mean a plain, old, harmless cigarette?"

"Then Grey says he's likely to be where any fool might expect him to be: in the cemetery, the ABC liquor store, the pool hall, or at home."

"*Whose* home? *My* home? Mother Essie's habitat?"

"You can't git no more from me on credit. Now excuse the higher agency, I got to plug along."

"Git, then. You're useless as jackrabbits in a snowstorm."

"Don't forgit my dollar."

He hops on the seat, kicks up the stand, does his Indian yell, and off he wheels.

Junior shouts after him, "Did your Daddy sell those two bull cows? Did he git anywhere with Viota Bee on that Portsmouth trip?"

But those Talleys hear only what they want to hear.

Junior has his accounting to do. He wets the pencil on his tongue and writes in his tablet the new dollar owed. He enters several other figures. He adds and subtracts. Then he smiles: he's got a good bit ahead today on the financial front. Moreover, he has high expectations for the governor's visit. The governor likes a chaw, so every patrolman and officer of the law wants theirs, too. Which requires a deep personal investment. Junior figures a few dozen Grizzly Long Cuts, the guv's brand, a sack of Blood Brother Plugs, a few Cannonballs, and a handful of ordinary Beech-Nuts for the know-nothings ought to do it.

That runt Jim Talley has reminded Junior that time is the beast at his back. At five he must be home by the radio. The Lone Ranger comes on. Then The Shadow. Next, The Green Hornet. After those gems it's a whirlpool of nothing until the next day. Even Essie will listen to The Shadow. She drives him crazy, romping from one room to another, screaming, *"Who knows what evil lurks? De Shadow know! De Shadow know! Indeed de Shadow do!"*

Never since drawing human breath has he got one shade of respect from either of them.

*

Here now festooned upon the blighted thoroughfare was a parade of undernourished girls and boys barely old enough to walk. Preschoolers with pale, studious, business-like faces, stringy hair, the girls in washed-out dresses too long or too short or hardly there, mostly with bare, dirty feet, and boys in hand-me-down spewed-upon vestments and bowl-cut hair cropped high above snot-encrusted nostrils in white-ringed cheeks, indicative of ringworm, jaundice, pellagra, the absence of any breakfast or lunch ever, dinner likely not prevailing—all staggering hypnotically along in unwieldy fashion, led by Miss Izzard the wizard, limping on a swollen foot. Miss Wizard, our ancient redeemer. If you lived in this black-foot town you had to have had Miss Izzard—her smacks, hair-pulling, her strident blessing.

Junior presents himself. "Hi you, Miss Issy? How you hurt that foot, Miss Issy? Where you going with them young'uns, Miss Issy?"

The children had voted as one democratic entity, this aged mentor explained, to flee their school encampment for a sighting of the photographs of the inimical sole person in this town, through heinous decades, who had made a success of herself against all godly odds, and that in Hollywood, no less, pivotal successful applicant to the American dream of becoming president one day of the fated land. Is it Tyrone Power playing opposite Viota Bee, Miss Issy wanted to know. Is it James Fenimore Cooper or Johnny Weissmuller or Basil Rathbone or "my personal favourite, Franchot Tone?"

"I do hope dear Martha Rutherford has a part—or that sibilant toothy fella who was the fat man's savant in *The Maltese Falcon*, 1941. Peter Lorre? Or is it *Boots in Boot Heel* I am trying to recall? Surely a best-ever picture show beyond compare, no matter how good our local girl is. Viota was in my classes, so lovely, so smart, judicious in all undertakings though rarely in attendance, those Varmeers, you know. The Varmeers tend to regard education for females unfavourably. Education for anyone, I suppose. I confess moments occur when I can hardly blame them. Do you know Viota Bee, young man? It is Grey, isn't it? Is your father still among us? I am told he is a devout rake. Viota, I remember by her feet in the aisle. If an aisle existed, her feet would be in it. Quite pretty feet, actually. And her nose-picking. I have heard this *Outlaw*, if that's the title, is a picture show of exalted rank. But now listen close. Closely. I have brought along this tape roll, kindly do give attention. You are to apply—economically please, because I have need of that tape—a strip to the pertinent part or parts of our starlet's frame—breasts, derriere, knees, elbows, fingernails if in colour—since it is desirable that—Well, how nice of you to understand! Now go ahead and have your peek, children, and mind you my taboos—you are not to witness any one anatomical part for overlong seconds, as it will vex me considerably and git your bottoms smacked…Yes, darlings, do hold your nice flags high. Stand erect. Do not fiddle with your organs. Thank you. Such dear pilgrims they are. Afterward it is my intention to convoy my sweet barnacles into the woods to observe what Slick on WCBT informs me are a plethora of burning stumps, divinely ignited, so it has been suggested, of which I have no doubt. I quote you, I forget, which Bible text. After that, a nature prowl, if you please, though I am aware little is to be seen save nettles, briars, animal droppings, long-leaf pine—a tickle of honeysuckle mayhaps. I shall compel them to sit on their heels, boys and girls alike, in a study of bug life. They will execute artistic creations in these drawing pads I have with foresight attached to my person. They have given me, in the past, excellent bug renderings."

*

Little Dibs and Big Dabs, preacher folks, both plump-to-well-rounded fellows—fecund butterballs, some describe them—"Spheres of ballooning waste, a maggots' broth," Hubbard says they are—today attired in form-fitting and deeply wrinkled searsucker suits. "Straight from the clothesline," some said. They'd been coming and going all morning-long. A petition wanting signatures, the bed-ridden to call upon, pretty housewives to entertain, a free lunch and what-else if God so stipulated. Now they were back with folding chairs to sit on, not that they were sitting yet. They were up at the ticket booth telling Carol Bly why the bloodthirsty inferno was her next stop. "That skirt don't cover your knees, sweet child," Dabs told her. "That groove, or rut, or ditch, or crevasse or valley between your two unharnessed mountain tops, needs flattening out, though it will take a strong hand to flatten chest work, sweet child, of your magnificent magnitude." Carol didn't appear to mind. Her chest even seemed to expand a bit in gratitude even as her stubby fingers fluttered away their foolishness. The activity made selling tickets, usually not many, more interesting.

Dibs and Dabs sat down in their chairs, resting homemade placards against their fat knees. SEE THIS PICTURE SHOW the one said; FRY IN HELL said the other.

Seated, "How many women you laid?" Dibs inquires of Dabs.

"Consensually or otherwise?" asks Dabs. Crackpots of a common sort these two were; picturesque buffoons offering local colour to these unoffending byways, roles they specialized in and dutifully accepted, daily honing the chosen mantle and willing themselves most dangerous only on precious Sundays.

"Words don't rule the world," Dibs said. "Words don't have airy thing to do with it, not even the beginning words of the first seven days."

"Yours don't," Dabs said. "But neither of us was there so I reckon we are not the final authority."

"That Grey boy claims he was. He claims he saw the whole marvel unfolding."

"Yes, well he's about as full of shit as most others in these parts."

"So how many?"

"Many as were willing."

"Acquiescence. Give that ye be given to."

"Amen. 'A tiskit, a taskit,' here they come hopping along. What's a man to do? He gits wore out, I tell you."

"'I dropt it, I dropt it.' Into one and another."

"Hallelujah. Nine in one day. How many you?"

"If nothing existed before God in seven days created the world, does that mean prior to the creation God was the God of nothing? And if He was the God of nothing that seems to ask the question, *Why?*"

"Why what?"

"Why was He Himself created to rule over something that was nothing?"

"If you are all-powerful you can do what you want even if that's holding dominion over squat."

"Over squat?"

"Squat."

"Well, if squat was there what was the need for Him?"

"Swirling planets."

"I'm not following you."

"The Good Book is short on that."

"Scratch of the brow."

"And we've got swirling planets far as…far as what?"

"His eye can see."

"The heavens, check."

"But not *the* heaven yet."

"Why not? Maybe within all these swirling planets *the* heaven had what may be called a pre-existence."

"Not if there was squat. If heaven did pre-exist it was empty. There were no swirling planets midst what we've agreed was a long-standing squat."

"Right."

"Right. These are the conundrums I like providing my flock."

"Me too. Keep them baffled and the donation plates overflow."

"Knock on wood."

"Knock on wood."

"So… How many?"

*

An old blind man drifted up. He was known as Mr. Rainbow and lived in a backroom at UltraFine Funeral Home on Enfield Road in River Flats. "I'll pay any upstanding young boy ten cent to escort me to that picture show and describe to me every salacious activity transpiring."

"The pictures got sound, Mr. Rainbow," Carol Bly told him. "Use your imagination." He thumbed away his Chesterfield, plucked a crumpled dollar from the sack around his neck, paid the twenty-four cent adult fee, doffed his knitted cap, and plodded inside with the determination of a man on his way to the gallows.

In the tall weeds of the vacant lot beside McCrory's five and dime, a woman named Hattie Johnson, retired now after thirty-eight years a spinner on the third shift at Peterson's No. 2 mill, was supplementing her nine dollar a month pension by daily stringing up a clothes-line between two stunted trees, on which shortly would appear some of the dresses, undergarments, blouses and now shapeless, ragged hosiery it had been her ill fortune to throw upon herself through that interminable time. Assisting her for an interim period today is Junior, who has run out of other souls to pester.

"These here mason jars filled with buttons we can surely sell," he tells Hattie. "And this black coat with not that many moth holes. That junk box filled with dobbins, shuttles, spindles, valves, jennies I'd peg at a dollar reduced to twenty cents, and some of those cankered shoes will go once we scrape off mold."

"I'm obliged. Grey he sometimes auctions off my pieces, but I reckon he's not available today."

"I don't know the gentleman."

"Shoosh, Junior, surely you know your own daddy. Gracious me, you're inviting God's wrath to say such a thing."

"Wait! Hattie! What's this?"

Junior held aloft a capped jar filled with a clear liquid in which swam a bone-like specimen the colour of rust.

"Quick. Tell me."

"I—well, golly gee, I hardly know—know where to begin."

Hattie was flustered. Her face went red in embarrassment.

"Speak!"

"It was the end of World War I. The men folk were coming home and I had just turned fourteen."

"Forgit that. I want to know what's in this jar."

"I was going out with—was to marry—a man named Charlie Templeton. I don't believe you ever knew the Templetons."

"Hattie!"

"No, you wouldn't have. Your daddy wasn't even born then, and Essie—"

"Hattie!"

"Where we're standing was no more than a scraggly field. Everything was. Scraggly fields unto eternity.

The cotton mills hadn't yet come in. You asked us, we wouldn't of known what a paper mill was."

"The jar, Hattie!"

"And boys were coming back from the war. Did I tell you I was fourteen? That's what I tell folks, but it's a little white lie."

"How old were you?"

"Twelve. Close to twelve. Just standing here in this scraggly field."

"When your man Templeton returns from the war."

"That's so. It was somewhat surprising. Folks figured few would. Return, I mean. But Charles wasn't my man then. I had to win him."

"How'd you manage that?"

"You are of prying nature, young man. I hope your prying nature will not be your downfall. It often is. You were asking of that jar? He give it to me."

"What's in it?"

"I have you know that's not water that thing is in. I remember Charlie telling me that."

"It's likely formaldehyde. But what is it?"

"He was practically tearing my clothes off. I didn't see how I could marry him after *that* display. Me oh my… Not that he wasn't apologetic afterward. And he had my concern. He'd lost a foot, you see. In the war."

"Poor Charlie. I'm right sorry, Hattie."

"Poor? You don't know the like. We'd eat shoe leather, if we had any. You're a lucky boy to have parents can gallivant all over the country and always have change in the pocket."

"Grey and Essie don't git along."

"Oh, shoosh! Just shoosh about that. Them two are like crocodiles thrashing over invisible bones."

"I've got to have this jar, Hattie. Do you know what's in it?"

"Charlie said... he was right specific in claiming it was the forearm of Judas. Judas Iscariot. He'd picked it up... over there."

"Ten dollars. More tomorrow."

*

From the high upstairs window Essie has a sweeping view of the town, the wide river, the long, clattering board bridge so narrow one scrapes the paint of any passing automobile. She has clear discernment of the sprawling mills by the river midst layered green woodland and even has intermittent sighting of the first of two entities of historic interest the region may claim: the now dry overgrown channel through which deep canal waters once flowed and over which ships of regulated size in bygone days with regularity steamed. The other moment of earlier times she cannot envisage, given that it is nine miles removed from her favourite perch. But she knows of it just the same, and has made with her son a single patriotic pilgrimage to the site: the sway-back, one-room, dirt-floored log cabin known as the Bennett Place, where in April, 1865, General William Tecumseh Sherman and General Joseph E. Johnston—"That traitor ought to be strung up by the hind legs and shot, then hung from a sour apple tree," Jeff Davis said—signed to the surrender of the last barrier to sanity, some 87,000 confederate troops in five states, thus effectively concluding the Civil War. That canal also, she's been told, serving as one in a multitude of routes of the Underground Railroad, though Essie

81

does not consign to her beating heart every rumour heard. Hattie, the ex-spinner, looking better today after a life-sentence since age twelve bearing up to insufferable mill heat, clamouring noise and cotton dust resulting in brown lung, is stringing the familiar clothesline.

Lo! Can that possibly be Junior helping out Hattie? Oh, Junior, how you break my heart. There goes the postman, Freddy Reeks, bald pate glistening under hot sun, bent like a fish hook by his bad back; the bookmobile will soon be pulling away for there goes the strange little boy on the long walk to wherever it is he lives. The Dinette roof is in view, along with a scattering of garbage cans and a lone man by a burning barrel smoking a cigarette. Looks like Finn, still on Mandy's leash. Hubbard she can't spot. There, going into the drug store for his monthly prophylactic, is Hubbard's old friend Owen Myles. Dogs are out in force. From this window she can see and in part identify those assembled at the movie palace, those stationary as stone and those bobbing and swaying like jack-o'lanterns freed from the box. The glass windows of the pool room, of McCrory's dumb department store, periodically—blinding to her eyes—sparkle in the sun, and it is to the pool-room glare that her eyes each second return because sooner or later, perhaps in the next second, this feckless husband and father, though seceded from wedlock and fatherhood like a rat escaping a cage, will reveal himself. He will. If it's a pool room, the lanky senseless scoundrel will be making either entry or exit, since his life's ambition is not to be husband, lover, and father, the pearl of a wife's denied adoration, but gadabout pool hustler put on earth to whip into dust any and every other staunch son of a bitch has the gumption

to think he can beat Grey. Grey don't lose. With a deadly smile whips the balls into the designated pocket like a strike of lightning, ten or hundred dollars to the ball, the cash in sight on the table for him to scoop up. No, you can't beat Grey. Not even she often can, and she's no pokey herself when it comes to mastering the felt. Luther the Booster, Minnesota Fats, Greasy Cue Curly McCauley: of that league. She glimpses a form passing a mirror, a thin laugh escapes her lips. Her hair's stringy, a mess, her skin is dry, you could sandpaper a table with that flesh; she's not applied cream, rarely a washcloth, to her face in months. Pallid, eviscerated flesh, dry lips, a chipped tooth, chipped nails, flab, more flab, yet more flab, scaly feet, elongated toes, diarrhea likely presaged. Probably she smells. Yes, now she mentions it, she does—woo, how rank! Lunacy, that's today's tune. Where went her girlhood grace, dear unsullied wanton ebbing springtime youth, the joyous cries of yesteryear? Laborious breathing, a reliable sign she's about to flip. In a minute she'll be cackling like witches at a barn dance. Lower the hatch, torpedoes full speed ahead, all women on deck. A nunnery git to. Tote dat barge, lif dat pail, thow dat tar baby woman in de briar patch. Git out the hatchet, chase a chicken, wring its neck. Cluck cluck cluck oh drats did I miss the neck   lookkk lookkk
      at that dead bird frittering the
  dappling the   escaping the yard.
  Fa fuck's sake, Essie!—
  Calm down …

From time to time Essie's sight veers back—riding a wave of repressed but valiant hysteria—to the burning field. Over recent days she's watched workmen with axe and two-man crosscut saws take down upwards of thirty full-grown trees. Why? The purpose of this no one seems to know. The *Herald* has made no mention nor has the radio. The part-time mayor has remained mum, and mum as well on who exactly owns the land, whether legal permission was necessary and if so obtained. Is another mill to go up when those existent are in disrepair, crumbling, moving piece by piece to distant continents, India, China, where else? Area population dwindling day by day? Now several men will occasionally splash onto the thirty thick stumps, onto the piles of brush, kerosene, gasoline, jumping back as leaping flames erupt with a booming sound. Essie has yet to observe the smallest success. The fire rages, sputters, cinder and ash carpet the area: an expanse of softly flickering flames rise and perish in seconds, then another and another ignite, forming an ascending cloud that hovers grandly over the darkened town as fireflies take to the river, as the habitual drone of frog and cricket fade into silence. Essie now had the spyglasses out. She'd hunted high and low for those glasses, emptying several closets. Feeling a growing panic. Finally, she'd found them in a shoe box behind a jangle of Grey's rods and reels, and another box filled with flimsy, tangled-up tackle. One of his hooks had snagged skin. She'd had to hunt here and there for Band-aids, for mercurochrome. So, all right, she was not the world's best housekeeper. The binoculars turned out to be in a shoe box containing never-worn, open-toed, open-heeled shoes of softest leather. Nicest lavender. Strumpet shoes, three-inch heels. When, why, had she bought those shoes? Box upon box of objects not seen in years: fancy dresses, high fashion scarves, blouses, underwear, she barely recalled. Why hadn't she remained on the family compound in beautiful fucked-up Bel Harbour surrounded by masses of Peterson industrialists, bankers, lawyers, importers, exporters, joke-cracking playboys saying, "These heady times call for another gin fizz, genteel whisky sour, a gimlet may very well heighten my *drab sister's mood.*" But, no, the little fresh-faced runt had to hop on the train, conjure herself upon the sleek Silver Meteor, head off into the fabled land of magnolia, jasmine, apple blossom and apple pie, partake of hominy and sordid grits. Hear actual music at the source. She had to see Naw Awleans, Savannah, Charleston, Memphis, the Delta. She had to git her hot little opinionated, arrogant, blissfully ignorant fanny out into the sundry, bustling, hopped-up, gaudy world. Only to end up in this one-horse dump with a crazy man. With insufferable Grey? Who's this Grey, they'd asked, are you out of your mind? Yes, yes, I was. I was, I was out of my my…

…my mind.

So she was thinking as she rushed to the window with these spyglasses. To see, first of all, who but her own messed-up skin-and-bones son, shed of Hattie, seated on his haunches at the movie house among droves of honest, despairing, temporarily festive citizens, pouring salted peanuts into Royal Crown Cola's gigantic bottle. Another hick, her own eccentric hound dog son—how to explain it? He knows he's not to drink that sugar-loaded beverage. But it's the drink of local choice, RC is cold and tasty, delicious, why not? *Why in the world not, RC is the ultimate refreshment, I tell you we like it.* Peanuts, too, the jaunty cur. He wants to fit in, who doesn't, doesn't she herself want to? Damn right,

I'll fit in, I will, never mind the…never mind the…
well, just never mind. Which brings me with scope to
this hot air, cinder bespattered window, a stark-eyed
floosy whose marvellous shoes of old no longer fit the
deformed feet…Miss Nervous Nellie, Miss Can-Hardly-
Breathe, Miss Dropped-the-Ball, Miss Loser, Miss Has-
Lost-Her-Mind…to catch sight of one fleeting eyeful
of a demented, yellow-belly husband who has survived
car conflagration, battled a tribe of zany Varners, no
doubt had a drink with that foul-mouth radioman Slick,
no doubt consorted with a fleet of State Line whores,
taken time out for an alley crap game with rabid like-
minded rot-tooth ruffians, certainly has taken time to
hail his vaunted pals in the spit-speckled pool hall but
has lacked the wherewithal, gumption, courage, stat-
ure, bravado to call at the door of his lamented wife.
Injunction? It might be a small irritation to his mind,
about on the scale of a mosquito bite, but a big laugh
otherwise. Humiliating, yes, in this burg where everybody knew everybody's business and can't wait to tell
you what that business is. Even the sheriff, roly-poly
son of a bitch, had laughed: *Honey, you taking out this
paper on Grey is like twinkling your fingers at a moccasin
snake. It's a sure-fire guarantee he'll fly like Jupiter's arrow
to your door.* And she had known that, known it, had
banked on that result. Humiliating, that even the most
brainless creatures in town could read her mind. Even
her son could: "Now Essie! Oh Essie! Poor mother
Essie. It's a consternation. It's pitiful. You are pitiful.
That injunction you're so fired up about is an expression of unremitting love. Unremitting, unimpeachable,
ponderous, powerful, impossible love. Which is surely
how my daddy Grey, no slouch on the mental frontier,

will himself see it. Such a sad, sorrowful, wasting case, the two of you. I expect I'll go through the whole of my formative boyhood years bringing light into your four stupid eyes."

Freak! Cesspool! You dare speak to your own mother that way! You dare!

There Essie hangs, spyglass raking the town.

Wait, by God. Who can that possibly be knocking at my door?

"Mandy?"

"How yawl? How yawl cuttin' it, Essie?"

"Doin' fine."

"I can't say you look it. Take this."

"What is it?"

"Sassafras greens with red beets. Hoecakes. And what Daisy calls her *coup de gashe*—that's my French—sweet potato, chicken, orange dumplings. She sent this over for you and the boy. She says you're too pretty to be running around like a skinny beat-up stick."

"A stick am I? You can thank her for me. Have you come across Junior?"

"I seen him at Willie's Place buying a mighty load of chewing tobacco."

"He's *chewing* now!"

"You're the mother. Don't ask me."

*

Hubbard is tired of sitting. He's feeling cranky and fed up with himself. The leg cramps are troublesome today. His feet are hot in the boots. Why he is clunking about in hot boots is a question worth considering. He crosses the street. Then crosses back. Then goes and stands in the street middle just for the hell of it. Owen Myles has sent him a wave. Owen apparently has no time for him today. Owen has hooked up with Thelma Bitch, who rents two rooms above the drugstore and hires herself out as an untrained nurse, tending old people. Owen has said Thelma is all right. He says she gives him back-rubs. Well, that's good. Old Owen has been alone a long time. Thelma has invited him to move in with her, and he's cogitating on it, though probably won't, being worried about what people will say. They never eat together at the Dinette, out of the same worry. Thelma takes one wall, Owen another. She always has fried chicken and string beans, while Owen is more experimental. She leaves first. He will shortly follow, taking the alley, and entering her building by the back door.

Hubbard says to him, "Owen, you're a citizen of some repute. Thelma is of age. She's respectable. Everybody within fifty miles knows of the relationship. Why sneak around like goddamn fools?"

"Her daughter," Owen explains. "Her daughter thinks it wouldn't be proper."

"Why, then, it's she who's the godamn fool."

"She says we're too old."

Hubbard still stands in the street middle. He can't decide which way to go.

Talk in the *Herald* was that a traffic light was to be hung and parking meters soon to brighten the economical view. Farmers coming into town were taking up all the spaces and spending what few dollars they had only at the Mercantile. The county, conniving with Gov. Cherry, was mapping out a new roadway system which would put 301 in the dust and deliver a party from New York City to Miami in no more than scant hours.

Travellers wanting to stop to eat at the Dinette or to rest their heels at The Only Motel would be spinning their wheels into these parking slots, it being well-known that northern money was the best money on earth.

The sorry ministerial duo has returned with their placards. Hubbard decides he'll take another gander at the picture show exhibit.

"…was a mirror in the hallway—we had that minute been blowed in by wind. I was pleading a nail in my tire, needing her phone. She said, 'You and the deacon know I has no phone but you wipe your feet and come right in. Maybe you can save me like the deacon didn't. I'm ripe for saving any hour now.' No, I'll not reveal her name because you'd know her well as you know your own sister—"

"Then what?"

"And she said, 'Here at this hall mirror is good enough. Standing is the best you deserve. I'm not about to mess up the bed which twice this month I've already aired."

"Clean sheets. That's class."

"Class is class."

"A man of the cloth, they feed on him like gobbling piranhas."

"God's truth."

"*Fry in hell!*" the one shouted.

"*Baste yeself and roast yeself in hell!*" crowed the other.

"God a'mercy, 'a tisket a taskit,' here the womenfolk come with they's abiding need."

"Well. Wives aside."

"Don't tell me."

"I've partaken of the flesh, sayeth the Lord at the well, and my ardour has cooled."

89

"And to give the redeemed jezebel final satisfaction."

"How I feel is sometimes your smallest malfeasance outweighs your whole noble achievements and you're left waiting for the gate to lift and lions to roar in. That's my sense of my life since birth and I thank the Lord he showed me his rainbow."

"Amen. His spirit draws us fit and screaming to the rainbow."

"In his image he made us tough nuts to crack, like the black walnut."

"Damn so."

"Fry in hell!

"Baste yeself and roast yeself in hell!"

A few minutes before this, the Acorn Bros. tow-truck pulled slowly in and parked. The brothers had the garage and junkyard eight miles out on Deep Ditch Road, close by Dibs' Tabernacle of the True Light and Dabs' Sun of the World Temple. Ralph and Jaylene alighted, stepping over to greet Hubbard, each boasting weathered features above clean checkerboard shirts, pitch-black hair smartly duck-tailed. Every automobile Hubbard had ever owned had been surrendered to the Acorns for repairs and upkeep, dating back before the brothers were born, when the shop was simply Acorn Lube Motor & Tire. Hubbard asked the brothers had they received a call about a Ford mishap out on State Line.

"Grey's, you mean?" Jaylene said. "Ralphie and me were off to pick up that buggy this hour. But then, cruising by, we see these two peckerheads."

"We got unfinished business with them," Ralph said.

Jaylene took a seat on a tow-truck fender, Ralph on the running board, both chewing Beech-nut tobacco and frequently spitting gobs through muddy steel-toed brogans while maintaining a steady eye on the preachers, who had fallen into sullen, wary silence.

"Looks like you boys have something in mind," Hubbard said.

"We got reasons," Ralph said.

"Good reasons," Jayleen said.

"I'd be appreciative if you limited the violence."

"By how much?" Ralph said.

"Modestly?"

"Hubbard, you always been one we could rely on for the level head."

Both preachers stood up to remove their black suit jackets, then sat back down. From the pockets they extracted fold-up fish knives, with which they set to pantomiming the cleaning of their nails. Neither party seemed particularly worried. The animosity between all was of old, brewing hotter in recent times. Over recent weeks the brothers nightly hurled beer cans into the temple yards; the preachers retaliated with open paint cans sloshed against the Acorn façade. A shotgun blast took out windows in the Sun Temple. The guard dog at the junkyard experienced a sudden demise.

Hubbard said to the foursome, "I ask you to take into account children are watching."

All nodded. Along the street the odd person stood, stilled and watchful, like sheep in a drizzle. A marquee light bulb suddenly popped like a gunshot, scattering thin glass shards about. Carol Bly left her booth and went inside the theatre, returning a moment later with broom and dustpan. She moved among the five as if oblivious of their presence. Dibs lifted a slither of glass from his hat brim, dropping it into the offered pan as

Dabs searched his own hat. The brothers scrambled to get feet clear when she came their way with the swinging broom.

"I never!" she declared, swatting at their brogans. "And you," she said, turning upon Hubbard with a fierce scowl. "Here goading everybody on. I never!"

The warring parties at once took leave, the Acorns in the tow truck, the preachers back to their citadels. Hubbard ambled down to view the burning, now unattended, stumps. It was an extended field of stumps, the grass blackened all the way up to the ringed treeline on the north side, the whole of this line singed, the smaller trees sagging, and the string of clapboard houses to the south caked in grey ash. He spotted the Ullrich boy hiding among a clump of dead bushes, smoking a cigarette and pretending not to be watching him. Hubbard could see from here, between the rich green fall of kudzu, the flow of the river rapids, white waves crashing. It was a fine wide river, brimming with eel, catfish, and slumbering moccasins. If you saw one of those moccasin heads peep out of the water and tried smacking that snake with a stick, you'd quickly regret it, for that snake would slide onto land and chase you here to kingdom come. On another day Hubbard might have trod down to and along the bank, but today he didn't quite feel up to it. That girl—woman—Carol Bly had put him in his place, sure enough, and it tickled him no end that a pretty thing less than a third his age, one he'd seen scrambling about in diapers, had scolded him. It had been thirty to forty years since he'd seen men having a good scrap. He and Eddie had gone at it a few times for the fun of it, throwing no punches and mostly rolling on the ground in search of a killer head-hold. He guessed they'd come out about even, though that isn't what they'd say to each other or to anyone asking.

The smoke was stinging Hubbard's eyes. He turned about, destination undecided upon.

Those Acorn boys might one day kill the reverends or the reverends do in them, but in the meantime they were doing right well for themselves and had good hearts. The last thing Jaylene had said to him, pulling away in the truck to pick up Grey's wreck, was how unforgiveable it was those jackals dishonouring glorious Viota Bee, a woman they'd done their durn-level best to git a date with since she'd turned sixteen. Until Essie high-stepped in, that damn Grey always seemed to have the upper hand.

*

What has been confirmed by now is that Grey's Ford out by State Line, burnt to its very frame, had not him inside. He was smoking, he's been heard saying, and fell asleep after untold hours behind the wheel—a mere six hours down from the Quaker City, Philli-town, easy-peasy but for the fourteen hours previous working the tables, hustling the rubes. *I was the eight ball in the wrong pocket after riding the bronco all night of many all nights.* Engulfed by flames! Came awake to the smoking lap, fiery thighs as the tires rumbled over stones, dawn's first light, which I thought of as a false light, dark light if you want to call it that. My arm out the window doing its best to catch fire, the seat then catching, still I'm thinking *It can't be morning yet, that's a false light, Essie won't like this, she'll blow a...well, blow a gasket, highly unlikely she'll know what a gasket is. The boy will tell her, I am sure dear precious anonymous will.* Flames by that minute everywhere. The wheel given up, ditch awaiting. Damn door windows resisting every kick. God have mercy! Help me Jesus, I repent!

But if so, how is it Grey is come to be found in the poolroom dressed in what clearly is a new suit. A new suit, we are told, and shiny shoes to match. A new suit, naturally, since he is a man taking notice of his appearance, a man with suits in closets spread around town, five or six in wife Essie's hideaway, shoes replete with fancy wood inserts he insists upon. He's made a call to some unknown party—not with any success to Viota Bee, she as we know is in greener pastures, certainly he has not walked—and sweet-talked this pliant sacrificing unknown soul into motoring secret desperate miles—best the town not to git wind of it, surely not boyfriend, husband, bossy parents, anybody with eye to the knothole, "which in this town every eye is"—with fresh duds and maybe a clean washcloth. "Something, hope to God, to ease the ache of body and mind: honey, vinegar, towel of cracked ice, witch hazel is said to be helpful with burns. A handful of BC Headache Powders, a dozen or so those beautiful Bromo Selzer bottles since you could say a hangover knocked me half-dead before fire tried finishing the job." Maybe this phantom woman has taken time to prettify her face, dab on Evening in Paris, to bob her hair, to slip fresh petal-pushers over her fanny, not having yet the courage to descend into slacks. Surely the druggist will want to know what in fire she wants with all that BC Headache Powder, all that Bromo Selzer— "when I know to a caution your folks don't eat fish on a Friday, don't drink or cuss or even spit out the back door, for fear of burning in hell." So maybe Grey called no one. How many had phones in the first place when your net annual income didn't hit four hundred dollars and Peterson got that? So let's admit in all probability Grey footed it into town. Let's assume he come across a puddle of ditch water and cleaned himself up as best he was able. Or drew up a bucket of water from a farm well, borrowed shirt and pants from a clothesline or talked farm wife or hand into doing what they could. Then along comes an old grouch hauling a load of melons to market and he hitches a ride. "Nome. You owe me nary a gibbet. Seen you trudging. Thought my eyes were seeing a dead black man. Said to myself, 'That won't be the first one I've rid beside. Itter'd be Grey, you claim? Then you must be that pool-hall slicker WCBT gabs on about. Got a wife, I believe. A son, too. Doubtful you to be welcomed in your current state." Essie he has not dropped in on yet, possibly because of the injunction allowing him to stray no closer than one hundred feet to her doorway. Or more likely because he wants time to recover his wits, git his juice back, bemoan cash consumed in the burning wreck, such an albatross that wreck has been. Too cheap to buy new transport, don't want the Feds breathing down his neck. Or maybe simply wants to git back to State Line, favoured hunting ground for those fated for violent dispatch to unknown worlds, a lawless domain through untold decades currently presided over by three long-necked northern university educated radical wildcats, shows nightly featuring unbelievable bosoms, long legs, harum-scarum outfits, salty songs, terribly crude jokes. A live slide-guitar—plucking mouth harp, longhair traditionalist musical genius come weekend nights—

I'm bringing home the bacon tonight
gonna eat no mo' poke and beans
gonna rally with my sally tonight
in my land of dreams
gonna shilly and shally my sally on the floor and door
gonna eat no mo' poke and beans
gonna fly naked birds in the mighy tree
me on top or otherwise she—

why, because, well, you might say

In the beginning of time
Was nothing but soup
You couldn't walk upright
You couldn't stoop
There weren't no heaven
There weren't no hell
Black moon ruled the black moon light
You had no speech, you had no sight
Woke up a creature of primitive size
It was off to the Kingdom where no one lives
And no one dies
No mo' poke, we only got beans

An auction house on the premises for the selling off of goods in payment of gamblers' debt: jewelled trinkets snitched from home, snitched from the wife's very make-up table as she executes mind-numbing, hot stand-up work over the clattering looms of the mill's third shift—not to mention the auctioneering of the family dog, of the farmer's livestock, the one cow that provides milk, the mule that pulls the plow, the chickens that supply eggs, the very title to land and home.

Everything is up for grabs at State Line where bootleg liquor flows, punchboards in every room to relieve you of your hard-earned cash. Tiered bedrooms wallpapered, so they say, in cat fur. Beds to rent by the hour, the day, the month. Companionship, as desired. No, no peace and quiet for anyone within shouting distance. But a fine place to sleep off a long hangover, as good in that regard as the hut headquarters of the vets of foreign wars. How many husbands, husbands-to-be, grieving teen youngsters and old alike, claimed by those educated fleshpots whose every advanced degree—sigma cum laude every one—hung in faux-gold frames against that cat fur. In dawn's misty light, come the bright sunny new day, witless abandoned wives, unwilling to reconcile themselves to the humdrum doormat times set down for them, the cards dealt by solemn fate, eased by in ratty trucks or derelict coughing vehicles bearing wide-eyed open-mouthed children—firing off shotguns at an assortment of obscene doors. Well, hell's bells, why not? Let's assume these women's private advanced thought. There comes a time when bad luck grinds the whetstone: what was piss-poor is like a new divinity on the doorstep, God's hot hand layering your brow and the only way to remove that hand is to shoot something. Shoot at the barn door, at a tree, knowing fullwell the bastard had done it to you is behind what it is you did, will and will again shoot at. Here's for the barefoot children you gave me! you might say. Here's what I ought to have done the first time I set eyes on your hide! Boom, boom. Then more boom over everything perused by naked eye, could your trembling fingers stop dropping the buckshot. Down on your knees grubbing for ammo, riling these unloved, said to be domesticated women and girls all the more. You have done your best to trod me into oblivion, into darkest corner, now you gonna git what's been coming to you since your first breath. Snake! Weasel! Vermin of the lowest depths!

Grey was bad and gitting worse, though thus far he had been spared such humiliation. Essie had been known to come at him with a bullwhip, knives churning in both hands, this behaviour, however, being confined to the golden days of courtship when bouts of thunderous loving stirred the pot. Because she knew he would never be true to her. She knew that. She knew no man could be, not one had it in him to be, no matter how often he told his lies to your face or how hard you pulled his hair or how tenacious you were in catching him at his lies. Meanness is what it was. They were mean and conniving to the core. Else they were a sweet tooth mama's boy lacking any shred of backbone, and what woman would choose that? So you took the meanness into your own self and once in a blue moon shook that lowdowness into something you could tolerate on worse days, on spiritless days when you flung up your hands in acknowledgement of blind fate. Because you have his self-same image underfoot night and day, an image bearing even his same name, Grey Jr., goddamn it, and that image ever telling you what it wants: food, shelter, wantwantwantneedneedneed. If only it would shut up but it's a boy and what boy will?

"All I am saying…all I am saying is, Junior, that raising a jerk like you is a labourious undertaking."

"It's good I have a damn good sense of humour, otherwise I'd have to take you seriously."

"No cussing in this house, damn you!"

"Fuckfuckfuck."

"Fuckfuckfuck."

"If you'd take on a little help in the raising, then both of us might have it a shade easier."

"I'll not take the wretch back."

"What if he promises to be good?"

"Promises don't wash dishes. He wants Viota Bee. He can have her."

"She's spoken for. They were flames in grade school, that's all. People say she's dynamite in that show."

"This town excels in the ludicrous proposition. Viota Bee wore a dunce cap throughout her school years. She stumbles over *Little Red Riding Hood* and the *Big Bad Wolf*. I had to write her Homecoming Queen speech for her."

"Wish I could read it."

"Wayward skirts are Grey's franchise. He fancies he's the good Samaritan to any woman hard up."

"Rubbish and you know it. He beats you at pool. That's what you can't forgive."

"The few times he's beat me I have allowed it so he could keep his pride."

"Is that true?"

"A good mother never lies to her witless brat."

"I thought you said I was switched in the cradle."

"Damn so. Ten in the nursery and I had to pick you up. Grey is behind three months' payments on your upkeep."

"Show me the books."

"He says we eat too much."

*

Essie had the radio tuned to the local station, WCBT, as it was near time *for de Shadow know indeed he do.* She loved shouting out these and other such words, since so little else she did seemed to have any effect at all on Junior. But *de Shadow do* made him grind his teeth, sulk and yell and finally spring up and chase her from room to room or even outside and up and down the street. Then he'd hightail it back, shaking his fists and throwing up his puny insults before again gluing himself to the radio. Whereupon she'd start it all over again.

The volume was low. She turned the Philco lower yet because, to her surprise, she was herself on the air. Slick Jess Helms, months back, ran an interview show called "Your Town Dime." The show had been cancelled due, she supposed, to lack of interest. But now Slick had been hired as "The Editorial Voice of Free Enterprise" at a station "broadcasting on 50,000 watts" in the state capital, in combat against "creeping socialism." In consequence WCBT had pulled from the depths Slick's "golden oldies," a series in which he and guests expounded on local hot topics.

Slick: Today on Your Town Dime we are discussing teen unwed mothers and are happy to have with us Essie V. Grey, a young woman who herself underwent a teen preg—

Essie: I was nineteen and quite mature.

Slick: Look here, Essie: It seems every day we have another unwed teen mother having a baby. Whose fault is it?"

Essie: I don't know. Yours?

Slick: Ha-ha. Then months go by and here the little gal sues for non-support. How much should the poor chump pay?

Essie: I don't know. How much do *you* not pay?

Slick: Ha-ha! What a card! I expect you folks out there in radio land know this fine lady is kidding.

They had been seated face to face sharing a single mike. His hand had been drifting to and from her knee. Finally, she had smacked his face.

The station had edited out that part.

That show was what, that night, got the loudmouth his arm broke.

*

A peculiar emotion took hold of Essie. It was extraordinarily strange, strong, and uniquely unfamiliar; it left her dumbfounded. What on earth!

It was an unreasonable urge to clean: herself, the house—*inside and out*—by God, everything! The thought made her shudder; it made her go weak in the knees. It brought tears to her eyes. But *look*! Just take a gander *at this filth!* Grit on the floor. Cobwebs, dustballs, dirt-dauber hulls, mouse droppings, food spills, flat-out *garbage*—yes, garbage, no other word for it—all over. Disgusting. Greasy, fly-specked windows obstructing anything that might be called natural light. Drab, ugly walls—*time to paint!* Ugly green war-time shades still hanging. Spring clean-up had just passed this house by. How many springs, that was the question. Scrunched-up, spider-webbed paper, lint, under every chair. Sticks!—how in heck did *sticks* get in? Did trash just walk right in? Heavens to Betsy, give me a break. And look here in the bedroom. When was that bed last made? Let me smell those sheets. *Ooof!* Those carpets—mud, cat hair, cotton fluff, peanut shells! Are those *fish scales*? Dingy, my word! Smelly, my word! The air in here, how could one breath? Well, mother in hell, there's the earring I lost three years ago! Oh God, don't make me look at the kitchen. A Mack truck couldn't make a path

101

through this muck. Don't anyone ever wash a dish, scrub a pot and pan, in this house? What's that sticky stuff all over? Jeepers, the rust! Who emptied coffee grounds over the Dinette? Did someone dump a bag of sand over the radio? No more de Shadow, de Lone Ranger, Our Miss Brooks, de Sam Spade hour, de Philip Marlowe, Amos 'n' Andy—no more Slick for this house!

She didn't dare open the door to what both she and Grey referred to as the Business Room. That room hadn't been entered in months. No way was she going in there.

OK, filth. Put your dukes up. Your goose is cooked. Then to bring a pumice stone to my own black heels.

She assembled the supplies. She got down—down on her knees—to it.

In Junior's room she had a fright. What's this? Where did this big jar come from? Did the little beast come home, then sneak out again? What, pray tell, is that *in* the jar? *Horrible.* Excuse me, is that a ...a *human arm!*

Where on earth does he find these things?

She knows about the treasure box he keeps, locked, under his bed. The crafty weasel is unaware she has a key. De Shadow must know. She peeps inside. Good. It's still there: the four small snaps of herself and Grey taken years ago in a photo booth. She sits a moment on Junior's bed, catching her breath. Wiping her eyes.

But what's this? Way at the bottom of his box. All these scribbled pages. Midgets? Showgirls? *Corn Flakes*? Is the little twerp writing a book?

*

Hours later Essie is still hard at work. She's moved outside now. The yard is a disgrace. Weeds, when not dead, a mile high. Dandelions up to her elbow. But she can't concern herself with such just now. Small wonder neighbours have been sticking notes to the front door. She has thick windowpane grime to think about. An aggressive assault is deemed necessary. With that in mind she's mixed vinegar with water and searched the house for old newspapers. In Junior's room she's found a closet stacked high with old newspapers, magazines: *Heralds, Grits, True Detective, Black Book Detective, Thrilling Detective, Phantom Detective, Spot-On Detective Tales, Dime Mystery.* The *Police Gazette* appears to be a favourite: *3 Million Female Teachers Utterly Insane! Four Hundred Nude Strippers Invade White House! Crotch Blow Floors Champ in Title Fight! Scientific Proof Women Escapees From Mars. Pentothal in Buttocks: Four Million Wives Confess.*

Who *is* that boy?

*

For some time Essie's been aware of moody little Cindy Varner standing on one leg in a patch of the yard's dying grass. In silent watch of her. Essie likes Cindy.

"Make yourself useful," Essie tells her. "Rake those leaves."

"I don't believe so," Cindy says. "I've got lots else to do."

"Like what?"

"I'm going to where Viota is. I'm running away."

"Where is she?"

"She's at the picture show house. Everybody says so."

"Those are not real people. It's like I git out my Kodak and take a string of pictures of you, then make them move."

"I don't believe so."

"It's how they do it."

"I don't believe so."

"Your sister's not at the movie house."

"She's not?"

"I don't believe so."

"You don't?"

After a while little Cindy picked up the rake. She began raking leaves and dying grass.

"I like raking," she said. "You've got tons of leaves. What's that burning over there?"

"Stumps."

"Why?"

"I don't know."

"If you got out your Kodak and took a string of shots would those stumps move?"

Essie saw her son turning the corner, in the company of a gang of chattering boys. He spotted her and ran fast.

"Two little Bo-Peeps," he said. "Hey, what you doing with my *Gazettes!*"

"Improving your mind."

The twerp turned snotty. "Don't think I don't know why you've rolled up your sleeves," he said. "You're hoping to impress Grey."

"I don't believe so," Cindy said. "It's because this yard is rat-putrid."

*

Afterward, who rolls up in a black Chevy, honking the horn, but Wimpy Lassiter, greatest nine-baller ever. Wimpy lived not two hours away, in E City, bustling burg butting up against Albemarle Sound. He was about thirty, with a severe night watchman's face, longish limbs, small hands and feet, and a build so slim he appeared to totter. At the table he was magnificent. His kind, compressed eyes possessed the visual acuity of a bald eagle. He called his favourite cue stick Delilah and treated her the way a Delilah would desire. With that stick he could criss-cross, circle, leap over, and seemingly burrow under any spread of balls interrupting his projected path. He had the binocular vision of a speeding Cooper hawk chasing prey in rainfall on a dark night through thickest forest. He was Grey and Essie's nemesis and idol. Heaven-sent. He was no one's pigeon. He was the one hustler in the entire southeast neither Essie nor Grey had ever beaten. He put them in the shade.

Such a nice man.

"Heard Grey was in town," Wimpy said through the open window. "Heard he was in a car crash but don't look to me like you're in mourning. You've not had another one have you?"

"Another one what?"

"That little cutie with the big eyes holding the rake. Nah, she can't be yours." He whipped his sight onto the girl. "You theirs, honey?"

"I don't believe so," Cindy said.

"Speak up, honey. My motor's running."

Essie was looking hard at Wimpy. Since boyhood he'd suffered a curious affliction. Whenever he found himself in the vicinity of an attractive woman his eyes went blood-red and his lips swelled to grapefruit size. The cleaning must have taken something out of her. He wasn't swelling one tick. She told him what she could think to tell him of Grey's condition: Grey was fine; he was the same old bad news, the same old hardheaded nutcracker.

"Glad to hear it," Wimpy said. "A party tinkling the ivories got to have good fingers same as us. The steady grip. We can git by with the mended shoulder, the bad back and knees, one good eye, the broken thumb, so long as the cue stick knows the score. Ain't that so? Now I'm off for a round-robin git-up tourney in sailor-boy land. Hitching up with Broadway Fats, Mosconi, some others. In the port city, tidewater-central. Norfolk's still the sucker pool cap even with the war done over and much of the Navy gone to home-bivouac."

Essie patiently waited to hear him rattle off the dime. She was often lifted out of her boots, hearing pool talk.

"What we got when night befalls the horizon: seven ball set four game rush nine ball set four to the floor eight ball set three to the door. Ten in touchline set high to low. Just to apprenticeship the pigeons, learners, and gawkers. Then the biz. Ten grand moolah, which I aim to bring home to mama. Sure to, if Willie's gone blind. Mama's aching, wants her moolah. Like to come? Grey and his Missus? That little missy with the rake if she's got shoes. You and Pretty Boy Grey OK? I hear the lovebirds been out of the frolic. Off the royal road, off the merry-go-round. Glad to hear it. Can't stand yappy dogs lapping at my heels. You privy to this tale? Last I seen Grey he said to me if you miss one shot in the next two hours you are done, shut out, nailed to the door. I got past one hour, two hundred orbs dropped, when his hums reach my ears. He's humming some Lena Horne number. So low under the breath a man must crawl on knees to hear it. He knows my feeling for Lena. So I'm looking at him, I'm lining up my shot and he's doing Lena real swell, but when he busts in with Big Joe Williams my spine shivers. I scratch. Not since I was ten years old have I scratched."

"Then what? I know you got'm."

"I tenderized his hot ass with my own shank. He's running the racks, he's down to the acy-ducey, he's got the prize ball rail-pinned for a cushion-roll drop. A crying baby could make that shot. But I've had the mouth harp going. So down-low mean I'm coming from underground, coming in like tugboats from the deep. Each time his ball hits the pocket, I raise the pitch a notch. I've gone past the lyrical hayride of Little Walter, the vibrato of Sonny Boy. He says, 'Bud, look at me. Another five Ben Franklins on the table, and I'll bypass the obvious, plunk that bastard off three rails, jump the florescent, careen it off the Dew Right sign, have it dribble down your coattail and pocket it square-dab here on the chalk hole whereas both chalk and ball will die in the corner pocket where I'm standing, all to be done shooting left-handed from my backside.' I just yawn. Some bystander says, 'I'll cover Bud's Franklins and raise you two.'

"I say, 'Grey, since you're singing, I hope you don't mind I accompany you with a tune.'

"'Damn no,' he says.

"Well, as the cue ball is about to kiss the target my mouth harp shrieks like a gang of banshees riz naked from the grave. Cue ball stops in a dead-flat spin, the target ball flies a hundred yards off the table, leaps the florescent, rebounds off the Dew Rite, dribbles down my coattail, whirls back to the table where it plops like a fried egg on top of the chalk. It teeters there a minute before rolling for the pocket, the chalk comes chasing after the ball. Plop falls the ball. The chalk rocks on the pocket edge like a lady in a rocking chair shelling Sunday beans. Rock rock rock. Ain't none of us taking a breath. I felt I could of walked to Ohio in the ten seconds that little cube hung there. I pocketed sixteen hundred. Remember that story?"

"You took him to the cleaners. I remember that."

"Gave maestro the shank, yes I did. Well, if you're not coming I'm going."

"Come anytime...hello to Fats, to Mosconi. They have up there what they call Pizza Pies. Bring Junior back one."

But Wimpy had his horn in continuous bleep and did not hear. He was gone.

*

Essie did miss the pool-hall life. What was most mesmerizing to her mind was the frequency with which, to her mind, Grey would opt for the wrong shot, or the wrong English for the right shot, or his fondness for zingers utilizing the collision of several balls in liberation of the one pursued. Which did, she supposed, ally itself somewhat with his views on marriage. It wasn't that his decisions were wrong, just that she would have gone about it differently. He was a show-off, wanting to impress himself, his opponent, and all observing. Same with this union. That he'd do it, make the unsound choice of shot, then bring it off, made her feel foolish. She was his shank. She might git a pinched face over some near-to-impossible shot. She walked around the table, appraising matters, more than he did. Neither broke into a sweat, not at any rate so it could be seen.

Such were her thoughts, walking little Cindy home. Ashamed of herself, Essie asked, "Did you ever see Grey and your sister kissing?"

"Kissing what?"

"Did Viota Bee git herself a four-poster?"

Cindy said, "I don't believe so. What is it? I'm a Problem Child. Did you know that?"

*

Grey's burnt-out vehicle had been towed to the brothers' wrecking yard. The state and the county would argue about who would pay the two dollar tow charge, the one dollar permanent space fee, the two dollar crush fee, the guard dog fee, if the brothers could stick them for it. Certainly Grey was not on the hook for these charges, any more than he was for littering the road or igniting a grass fire consuming twenty prime acres owned by God knows who. This info came Junior's way when he intercepted Oleander Driscal on his way to the Dinette. Oleander was part-owner of the pool hall. He was sick and tired, Oleander told Junior, of gitting by on peanut butter nabs, moon pies, pigs' knuckles, and RC Cola. His gullet demanded something more substantial, so he'd left the business in the hands of Royston Clay who was only good for sweeping floors, and did a bum job even on that.

"Hire me," Junior said.

The vehicle registration number, Oleander further said, had been tracked to a man in Omagosh, Michigan named Joshua Tulip.

"Tulip. Is that a good name?"

"Beats me. Mr. Tulip says that brush-beater of his was scooted away from his front yard four years ago by unknown hands while him, his wife Thurma June Tulip, and little Betsy Blue Tulip were watching the Indy 500 on their new Muntz TV."

"Grey *stole* it?"

"Don't put words in my mouth. Grey and Essie were on a hustling trip. Tulip oversubscribed at the tables. Grey and Essie got the Ford, the Muntz, and could have got Betsy Blue Tulip if they'd wanted another scrub child."

"I could have had a sister?"

"You might have one yet."

"I would of bet they stole that Ford."

"Yes, well, about thievery I'd like to have a talk with you sometime."

"Do? Thievery is a heavy burden to carry, I'm told."

"I wasn't thinking of myself. I had in mind certain disappearances from my paperback racks."

"Be doggone. Probably ole' Hubbard. Or that Tillich skunk. I hardly never read, myself."

"Uh-huh."

*

Oleander moved along, leaving Junior to his own questionable pursuits. Oleander observed that the tree stump field had been newly doused with gasoline, the green treeline smoking, the odd leaf and branch flaring off into the heavens. There would be hell to pay if the wind picked up, though he didn't suppose it was any of his business. Carol Bly was up ahead, huddled with a bunch of sailors, each trying to outdo the other for her attention. The odd auto passed, sometimes beeping, mostly not. The ice truck puttered by, water dripping from the tailgate, turning onto the lane leading to the ice house where a group of boys were kicking a tin can, girls dourly watching. A younger group playing Jacks ignored everyone. The nurse woman, Owen's new friend, at her window above the drug store, looked out at him with an expression of vague discontent, then disappeared, to be replaced by Owen, sending him a snappy salute. Two men he didn't know were just then entering the store, as Viota Bee's little sister Cindy was coming out, slurping at something in a paper cup, probably a cherry soda. Way up the street where the business district abruptly terminated and the byway became rutted, man or woman could be seen pushing either a wheelbarrow or a baby carriage, no way to tell which at this distance. The pretty usher at the Imperial, name unknown to Oleander, hobbled out struggling with a heavy wooden ladder, the sailors hurrying to assist, Carol Bly looking surprised to find herself suddenly abandoned. Then the pretty usher was climbing the ladder to the marquee, net bag of light bulbs dangling, the sailors begging to accomplish the task, but then pleased enough to arrange themselves around the ladder, not exactly maneuvering to look up her dress but not avoiding the pleasure either. Whatever it was they saw or did not see elicited a round of shrill whistles, much to Carol Bly's amusement and bringing a brief smile to Oleander's face.

Oleander stopped yet again to study the star's face on the poster. He was not among those subscribing to the notion it was Viota Bee in the picture. In fact, for twenty dollars cash paid to the manager, along with a ten dollar J.C. Penney suit, he, with Grey, had been witness to a midnight showing at Norfolk's Byrd Theatre, to satisfy themselves on that issue. As then, Oleander now concluded Viota Bee's lips were somehow less ripe than Jane's, the eyes kinder, the voice less harsh. She possessed an aura, a definition of—he hesitated to call it small-town *goodness,* not being a legitimate small-town boy himself—something intangible but worthy the other in his opinion lacked.

One of the sailors thumped him.

"My friend over there was saying you looked like a 4-F type guy."

"What do you say?"

"I'd say the same. You got the look of a draft dodger."

"Do I? What do you propose doing about it?"

"Hit you?"

Carol Bly came between them.

"Quit that," she told the sailor, touching a hand to Oleander's cheek. "Oleander served in the Aleutian Islands."

"A real war zone," Oleander said. "We got to the Aleutians, finding the enemy had... Every one slipped away."

"He got trench foot from the cold after the battle of Attu," Carol Bly said in correction, obviously quite proud of Oleander's suffering and savouring her knowledge of the skimpy details.

"I be dang. Well, shake my hand," the sailor said, afterwards turning to remark to Carol, "I take it you are romancing this man?"

"He got snake-bit too," she said.

*

Hubbard's chair outside the Dinette was vacant, which likely meant the geezer was out back having a pick-me-up with the usual crew or had merely gone inside to escape the sun. Or maybe he'd faltered and gone home. The fellow was hunching these days, shoulders sliding down his backbone unless Amarantha or Daisy reminded him to ship his shoulders back. Amarantha said she wouldn't marry a man who couldn't stand upright, to which Hubbard said, "I believe you married that fool," pointing to Finn. Finn said, "I resent aspersions cast upon my character over the whole of my years in this humbug town saved from mediocrity by—"

"By he forgets what," finished Amarantha, rising from the table. "I'm going off soon. Can I brang you applejacks anything?"

Oleander joined them, and all immediate questions had to do with Grey.

Oleander reminded them the Ford was not the first auto Grey had sat in smoking and falling asleep in while plugging along at a legal fifty-five an hour. The others he'd only hit a tree with, or straddled a ditch bank, and once a haystack a good three minutes off the road. No harm, Oleander said, since Grey's never seriously maimed himself or driven anyone off the road. Excepting the school bus that one time, forty youngsters flung on top of each other, which sooner or later, Grey said, they would have been anyway.

"Yes, yes," Oleander said. "I can confirm Grey escaped in one piece. He told me he crawled about thirty feet from the fire and when he could stand up that's what he did. He wanted a cigarette and there in what was left of his chest pocket was nothing but a scrap of tinfoil. He was worried his road earnings had gone up in smoke, but there in the pant pockets left him were wads of rolled bills. The field had caught fire so he had to scramble again. He could see Nitespot showgirls running to the blaze, many with water buckets, in night shirts, skivvies and birthday suits, like a celestial brigade, a sweep of jouncing warriors, most beautiful sight ever witnessed, short of the time he saw Essie walking toward him off the landing strip in San Antonio. He thinks he might have passed out. His hands were black and he reckoned his pecker would be the same for another century or two. He wanted to know what no-good business Essie and the boy had been up to during his absence, and I told him best I could. Essie's injunction, manifold threats made against his person, I didn't pass on."

"You're a good man," various table partners said. "Someone pass his flask to that man."

All did.

"That Junior," Oleander said, "I don't mind saying, is a riddle to me. The spitting image of Grey and Essie. He sneaks into my establishment when he hopes I'm not looking. He empties my paperback rack. He storms my magazine spread. His favourites seem to be this Fu Manchu character, and two top-notch guys, one named Fred—Fredric, it would be—Fredric Brown and Jack D'Arcy. Out of curiosity I read one of those D'Arcys. It's about this midget private investigator who takes no bull from anyone, solves the case, and has a hundred dames flocking to hear his every word. Not that the midget talks that much, except to give these broads a hard time. Every month I turn over the purloined book bill to Grey, who pays up without a flinch. I'm talking money here. Usually in the twenty to thirty dollar category, which, at twenty-five to thirty-five cent a copy, works out at about thirty books a month the little bastard has filched. Not counting the detective mags. And the little hotshot not an hour ago dares telling me he don't read.

What does Grey say? He taps his brow. He reminds me Essie is an educated woman. He tells me he is himself a dedicated book man. What a liar! It would shame him to be seen picking up a book.

"As for Essie, what can you say? She's got a mouth on her that won't quit. When Grey's gone she turns overnight into a hundred-year-old hag. I sometimes spot her at that upstairs window and all I can do is shudder, thinking any minute she's going to throw herself out. The suicidal impulse runs in the family, so I've heard. A sister did it to herself with a rope in Mexico when her bullfighter lover dumped her. Another sister—it's said she jumped off a cruise ship sailing to some goddamn place. Though that's not verified and Grey claims Essie only had the one sister. He says if Essie ever jumped from a window he or some bewitched angel would be there to catch her. He furthermore insists she speaks six languages, could have married the Kublai Khan, lived in an aerie in a fabled kingdom anywhere in the world but prefers it down here in this hellhole where honest, deluded people struggle in the land God was indifferent to in the first place."

"Hubbard, are you going to sit there and let this carpetbagger knock our town like he's doing?"

"I'm giving him the sporting edge," Hubbard said. "Sooner than later a talkative man's own words will hang himself."

"That don't make no sense, Hubbard."

The table was quiet awhile, then Oleander went on.

"I reckon Essie's right about that last. This town's citizens are amazingly good at impersonating the dead. Myself included. You get the impression that most people have some strange sense they've been wronged. Patriotic boasting is only heard from officially elected voices. Or Slick. They invariably sound more stupid than the rest of us. The Editorial Voice of Free Enterprise, Slimy Jess at WCBT, has designs on a Senate seat, and I'll wager he gits in. Setting us back another hundred years… I been in this town two decades and have never known anyone other than family invited over for so much as a glass of iced tea. But Essie. I don't know how she expects to git away with her sappy story of somebody else being that boy's pappy. She wants us to think she's hopped into the sack with every man who's got two legs when we know at base she's of prudish nature and upright as a Christmas turkey.

"I mean, the boy *does* look like Grey. Now Grey don't have no eyebrows. You could say that fire gave him a piss-poor haircut. He wobbles, walking, like a crow on one leg. The accident has affected his mind a good bit."

Hubbard speaks: "That could be a salvation."

Oleander wasn't to be stopped. He's sure it isn't the flasks stopping by. It has more to do with Carol Bly telling a sailor about his time in the Aleutians while punching her hips against his. What was she up to? They'd had a thing, wasn't it over?

"This burg spends its waking hours asleep. Then Grey comes to town, all goes haywire. Houses git broken into, Acorn's gas gits robbed, somebody hating somebody all his life suddenly picks up a crowbar and goes after that somebody. Sex gits in the air and suddenly some straitlaced sourpuss vegetarian suddenly decides to eat raw meat and jump in the hay with—well, it don't matter who. The robbers think the law will decide it's Grey the guilty party. Sam in the wee hours gits his store window hit with mallets. For nothing more than a pair of lace-up Thom McAn's. Mrs. Pickens, that saintly old slug who sludges about like

Jesus through a cemetery now lays claim to affliction of
the spine caused by Mr. Picken's whopping her beside the
head with a shovel when she wanted the window raised, in
combat with his desire to have it shut. Why? She wanted
the window open in case Grey dropped by. He usually
does, she says. Brings her these nice souvenirs of places
visited: Rock City, Chimney Rock, Luray Caverns, Nags
Head, Rooster Hill, distant places like that. Quite a collection I'm told she has. You'd think she'd given birth to Grey,
how she goes on. A French woman—"

"Heloise."

"—a soldier bride, sees a peeping Tom face at her
bedroom window, thinks it must be that demon she's
heard so much about."

"Grey."

"Turns out it was her dog wanting inside. There's
another itch. Those State Line vixens mean to harpoon
Grey. They mean to share him among themselves the
way you would Sunday dinner."

"That'll git Essie gyrating."

"She gyrates on principle."

"Grey has never give her reason to fuss on that
score."

"She fusses out of general principle. Can't live with,
can't live without."

"They're a truck with tow tongue at both ends. She
pulls, he pulls, then they fetch about."

"Gitting no place fast. Even the dogs behave peculiarly when Grey hits town. Excuse me now. Now I've
got to goddamn eat."

"Et, please. Fancy language is frowned on here."

*

117

A man with a big gut walked into the Dinette. "Any of you sad sacks got a drink?" he asked. The Dinette crowd threw up hands but otherwise did not respond. "Stuff you," the man said, going on: Bibbs was the man's name. The town drunk. A while back, Bibbs had lost his only son in the war. The same day this message was received, his wife went to her second shift job and lost her hand in a loom.

Rita the usherette's head was seen poking out between the picture show's doors, then was gone.

"It's that Ullrich boy," someone said. "She might as well tattoo his name on her behind."

"They've had a falling out."

"She's fastidious. A Junior WAC."

"Women got no business in a war alongside men."

"You think?"

"Ullrich must wise up if he hopes to win her."

"'Specially now with sailor boys hot on her tail."

"Those Ullriches don't have much between the ears."

"Thick as a salt block."

"There you go."

"There you go."

"Them stumps flamed all last night. More trees to come down."

"Think?"

Daisy chalked in a sign: ICE COLD WATERMELON 1O CENTS.

"Were they ripe?" she was asked.

"You old boys wear me out," she said.

*

Anytime now, the eight 'til four first shift and four 'til midnight second shift would be hitting the street, the one coming from, the other going to. Billows of smoke churned along, mixing with a sullen cloud cover, all in all, Hubbard timidly observed, looking like overweight birds in sorrowful flight.

*

Essie is grinding away at the washboard. "Bless my hide," she says, "it not yet dark and the little squirt is home."

"I'll thank you in future to keep your hands off my goods."

"You poor sap."

"For wickedness those Fu Manchu women got nothing on you."

"My goodness, have you learned to read? Your face is red. You mind that sun. My hands are raw from this washboard. I'd sooner be down with colic than do sheets. Before that was mice I had to chase. They got holt of corncobs from somewhere. I got a scalp itch I hope is not fleas and better not be lice. Here, take this tub outside and hang those sheets on the line."

"I can't reach that high."

"Stand on a bucket. I'm not in this mothering business to raise a useless child."

"You ought to crimp that hair. Are those Grey's trousers you got on?"

"That's my business."

"In training for spinsterhood and you not yet—how old are you?"

"Twenty-nine, thirty next week, thank you very much."

"That's awfully old."

The wash got hung. Then Junior to sit on a kitchen chair chomping on Velveeta melted in a fry pan between gummy slices of Merita white bread. The little squirt wanted pickles but pickles had taken flight. Wanted Coca-Cola, RC or Grapette, but the icebox lacked that. It lacked most things. It lacked ice, too, since the ice had melted, dribbling through to the holding pan on the floor, which sloshed over to wet the feet when pulled forth. The local ice truck surged through town daily, dripping water. Someone had not been alert and they had missed today's delivery. To learn the ropes, the squirt had recently worked three days, free of charge, riding the truck's open back. Twenty pounds carriage was his capacity. At day's end he could barely lift the tongs or his own feet. He hoped Grey never heard of this. It seemed to him that he had been stuck at seventy-eight pounds for the past five years. Even so, you wouldn't think hauling a twenty-pound block up and down streets, up and down stairs, would give a seventy-eight-pound boy that much trouble.

"What are you doing?" Essie asked the treasured son.

"Thinking."

"Woopty-doo."

Moments later, Junior was behind locked door, filling the bare pages of a writing tablet with his latest monumental epic. He'd appropriated, days ago, D'Arcy's midget detective, and had the character, this very second, hauling a hundred-pound block of ice to an upstairs business establishment called E & G Imports & Exports. Here, the midget was about to discover a dead man crammed into the overhead compartment meant to contain ice...*He paused at the unexpected sight, contemplating a parallel between melting ice and declining human life*... The corpse wore striped blue Bermuda shorts, knee-high green socks, and soft crepe shoes...Each item wet to the touch and still cold...He had a wicked grey moustache...Carefully groomed, much to the midget's admiration. The midget had been thinking about growing such a moustache himself: with a moustache and Sam Foster sunshades, a new wing hat, he could stroll the city streets unrecognized and therefore undisturbed by the herd of patootzies ever at his heels. Nice enough tootzies but always gumming the works.

Above the blue eyes was a fine black hole the size of a suit button. The midget was studying the bright jewel affixed to the dead man's left ear when a beefy flat-footed bozo in a black hat lumbered in with bullets blazing. Ice chips flew. The midget, dodging one way and another, sought escape through the open window; he leapt thirty feet onto a pile of boxes. He'd had the presence of mind to drop the ice, kick it at the gunman, then blindly fling the tongs. The tactic worked because here through the window came the gun, here came chips of ice and the gunman preceded by the tongs embedded in his forehead—about to land on top of him. "Jumpin' Jackspit!" the midget exclaimed, hurling himself aside. Only to find he'd rolled into another dead man stuffed inside a huge Kellogg's Corn Flakes box.

Such not being the midget's immediate worry, for here running up the alley toward him, with heaters blazing, were two tough nuts in wide striped suits, one wearing a black eyepatch, homburgs bouncing on their overlarge heads. But there was the fallen tough nut's bean-spitter within arm's length; he snatched it up, darting behind the Kellogg box just as the corpse inside the box jiggled from receipt of a half-dozen rounds. The midget was beginning to lose his temper. His borrowed pea-shooter got the front-runner square in the eyepatch. Down the fat fellow went. The second tough nut flopped over the first, and the midget's bean caught that one in the buttocks. He wasn't dead yet. For reasons inexplicable to the midget, the goon was reaching for his homburg, which wind was trying its best to claim. "Pop goes the weasel," the midget said under his breath, and there went the man's hand. *Now for the kneecap.* The midget didn't like killing people without being provided a better reason than this. Two other hotshots were crowding the window the midget had jumped through. Wowsie, am I popular today, thought the midget, waving the gat. That they were not shooting at him lifted his spirits somewhat. They were saying, "Jeepers, boss! Let's scram!"

"Me, you, and Descartes," the midget said, wiping, then ditching the hot pistol—reclaiming the ice tongs. The company would dock him if he lost it.

That evening three of the leggy blondes who adored the midget showed up uninvited: to soothe his scarred face, bath him in a doe-footed washtub, and cook him a succulent beef stroganoff. "Leave me alone!" he told them. "You patooties are dumb as breadsticks. Get out of my sight! No, I don't want my back scrubbed! I don't want my head washed! Get your naked bodies out of my tub! Damn de-icers, cover those tits!" The dolls said, "Don't you like us? Don't you find us pretty?" The midget said, "Go away! I'm indifferent to the beauty of the female form. Your perfume assails me, your long legs poke me in the night, your protuberances tire my mouth." The dolls went wild. "He loves us!" they shouted. "He has declared his love!" They swaddled him with embraces, one and another protuberance found a path into his mouth. *"Rock the cradle,"* they sang, *"Rock-a-bye baby in the cradle!"* Their long limbs, curves, protuberances, and perfumes wafted him into bed, whereupon, in multiplying numbers, they sang and danced for him the way they did for big spending gangsters in unmarked clubs selling illegal hooch down unlit streets and alleys in the city. He said, "Cease with that racket. I got to think." "Quiet!" the molls shouted. "The guru is thinking!"

"All that time," he said, "the torpedos' guns blazing, your maestro limping away, I never heard a single siren. No coppers in souped-up black and whites. So that means the law is in on whatever fiddle is going down. You pistachios take over the ice-truck deliveries tomorrow. No tough nut is taking potshots at me without paying a price. I'm taking on the gumshoe job. I'm calling this the Kellogg Case."

"We like Corn Flakes," the girls said in frenzied delight. "We'll help you!"

"I have to hotfoot it to Bermuda," the midget complained. "It comes to me the corpse in the Kellogg box was wearing the same type Brit outfit the ice box corpse wore. And the man in the window the other man in the window called 'Boss' had on his head a fine straw hat

I'd liken to a panama. They cleap to that jive down in Bermuda. Time to hop a freight."

"Kool!" the patooties said. "We're smackers for Bermuda. Now that you're doctored, may we all crawl in bed with you?"

"One at a time, goddammit. I'm only flesh and blood."

*

Gritty linoleum demonstrated Mother Essie's white-faced lie. She'd done no charwoman's hand-and-knee scrubbing in here. Junior was seated at the kitchen table, making another of what he called his motorized tractors, now and then, to Essie's dismay, singing

> *Way down here in the land of cotton*
> *my feet stink and yours are rotten*
> *look away, look away, Dixieland*

For the tractor all that was needed was a wooden spool of thread, a few short sticks, and a good rubber band, wound up tight. One stick went through the spool hole, another kept it to your ready surface, and as the rubber unwound the tractor chugged along with breathtaking fortitude. He could sell these any day, he told Essie, to any dumb child coming along.

Essie said, "So that's where my thread has been disappearing to."

Then a worried look crossed her face and she said, "You look tired. A mite peaked, as they say around here."

Junior got off another verse.

Way down here in the land of cotton
your lips are red but your breath is sodden
look away, Dixieland

"Stop singing that stupid song."

It was God's truth that Junior was feeling plain give-out. It had been, one, a strenuous day, and, two, he had been up near the whole of the previous night unable to unshackle himself from D'Arcy's midget. The midget was like Daddy Grey: uncompromising, diligent, inventive, and unpredictable. He was like Junior hoped to be—cooking with gas, a knuckle-buster, divine lulu-belles his eternal province. On previous nights, the culprit keeping the light lit into early morn had been Fredric Brown, world's trailblazing page-enabler. *The Screaming Mimi, Here Comes a Candle, The Fabulous Clipjoint*—each twenty-five to thirty-five cent at Rexall Drugs and free of charge off the pool hall rack if steely-eyed Oleander's back was turned. But Junior wouldn't steal, would he, he wouldn't, no, never, not Grey and Mother Essie's upstanding boy, flesh of their flesh, he wouldn't, that boy would sooner choke a monkey than allow a cuss word to depart his mouth, a bad thought to enter his noggin, to purloin precious reading matter—yikes! no! never!—as de Shadow know and indeed de Shadow do know! In de heart and de mind of dis boy lurks no evil. And not to think that Junior, son of lauded parents way down here in de land of cotton, feet stinking and other parts rotten, forsook the enduring classics.

There was then, for instance, *at Sicca in Numidia a golden temple in which persevered, midst gnawing delirium, the girl-child Nadeir, known to her subjects as Princess of the Heavens, and rightful sovereign of lands stretching under glowing sun past the glades of Infinity. And there lived then also evil Pantanimous, Sovereign of the Depths, who hungered to have Nadeir as his child bride, naked and yielding, and calling forth his tide of rapiers and dragones and haughty wyverns whose every thought was to deliver Pantanimous this rightful treasure. And furthermore this deed must be accomplished before the rising sun went to its next demise, for Pantanimous was old and decrepit and so chewed by desolation now that he might very well fall head-first into oblivion without he had for renewal beauteous Nadeir of Sicca in Namidia on the pillowed bed beneath him and his shaft to plummet her and his dark soul to bestir her and his lips to devour her, and her womb to deliver, and all into the very recesses of these Depths to rejoice with a resounding Hail Mary, and the walls of Sicca in Namidis to crumble into dust and lay inert throughout the full measure of Infinity.*

So what, wonders the little squirt, if arriving in the first rays of sunlight leaking into this far realm, on a two-wheeled chariot catapulted by the thundering hooves of a mighty roan mare stolen from the very stables of Zeus, is none other than our old friend the midget, and the Princess of the Heavens, bolting from window to window in the golden tower wrapped in beclouded mist, perceives this zealous little fellow thumping aside, as would a grinning spectre with scythe in hand cutting flax in a field, the fearsome wyverns, dragones, and rapiers, to stand finally before the verymost evil one ever known to mankind: Pantanimous the Terrible, Pantanimous the Invincible, the All-Powerful Rector of the Depths, known to dine on upstart midgets at breakfast, lunch, and dinner...Alas, alas. *Heavens help me!* cries the child-princess, *His evil shaft shall plummet me, His dark soul bestir me, His putrid lips devour me, my child's womb shall deliver His obscene product and every star in this ringed firmament whose brightness stretches into the unheralded Otherlands of Infinity shall perish in the instant and Darkness shall reign forever and ever and ever!*

Poor lost baby.

Dear mother, dear Grey, someone you know has fallen prey to the *Screaming Mimis.*

Junior stretched out on the pool table in the Business Room off the kitchen, a restored 1920 Brunswick Isabella, arrival of which had come at great cost to the parental character, for two walls had to come down and the ceiling lifted into the rafters. Then the table had to be removed because after the table's settling a correct level could not be achieved unless first the flooring was reinforced. Which meant earth had to be removed before the foundation could be brought up to specification. Electrical rewiring was required. Their private sticks also proved inadequate. Their balls were defined as inferior. True Belgium balls were a necessity. These must be calibrated to perfection, boast matchless sphericity, possess rewarding balance, demonstrate superb rebounding integrity, display radial tolerance, be impact-proof, weigh the regulated six ounces, manifest a refined eager appearance, and, of course, be made of phenolic resin and not that cheap stuff so detrimental to the reputation of your common nickel and dime establishment. So, too, did new racks have to be ordered because the Isabella would find offensive anything not equal to its glorious personality.

Junior was not yet born, thank God, when these hassles erupted. To finance the new mansion, Grey and Essie had to take to the sticks. They took to the road in separate vehicles, hustling the rubes; then, those ranks depleted, onward to large and larger cities where star material was reputed to hang out. The scam was to begin an evening combatting each other, winning and losing, combining excellence with inconsistency, brilliance with eccentricity, thus gradually summoning to the table vain-stricken deluded hopefuls and finally, often enough, the truly exceptional—near dead ringers of themselves, the purified, who actually stood a chance at winning, much resting on the perfection or imperfection of the break shot and who owned the cue stick thereafter. Essie liked the soft kiss, anchoring the cue ball snug against the tight-racked point ball, while Grey most often exploded the triangle, if triangle is what the game called for, three to four balls unfailingly finding a pocket. His games were often over in three minutes, a set in ten, stick never relinquished, unbroken strides around the table in soul-defying concentration. Then arrogantly mouthy, injudicious comment, as the final ball fell. Whereas trim Essie with tightened lips and furrowed brow spent endless minutes studying the layout, computing the mathematics, learning the cushions, fabric-wear, soft-spots, the firmness of tits, chalking the stick, appraising possibilities, psychoanalyzing the opponent. He was perhaps superior with the eagle flight, with top, side, and bottom spin, the cue aligned, then the jaunty bastard not even looking as he floated, rammed, speared or whispered the prize shot home. He was a natural; she reached her plateau by plodding application beginning at age six on the dumb table in the sea-side manse—fabled home!—a servant trucking the Egyptian-jewelled stool to and fro about the table that her smarmy fatted baby limbs might bridge the rails and poke the green. Worthy competition gave Grey buoyancy, he practically bounced on his heels, a repulsive sight. Then he'd drop an unmakeable shot that made her swoon. Owning the table herself, she ever felt sweat dripping between her breasts, heating her thighs. Even her feet dampened. He favoured the twenty-ounce cue, she the sixteen with dime tip, screw-on barrel for added zing. Their win-loss record when in serious play against each other lent Grey the edge, a topic for fraught discussion during which gender insults abounded, old wounds, both the real and the imagined, resurfaced. Each proficient in giving these the surprising spin, the belly thrust, the hatchet between the eyes. Mom and Pop theatricals, prelude to week-long sulks, silences, the hooded, accusing eye. Pride, ambition, low blows, wore them out; mattress time, one beside the other, plummeted, often weeks passing when they refused to so much as acknowledge the other's presence. In one short period during which nights blended into one and afternoons faded into pledged recovery from alcohol, cigarettes, trash food, and exhaustion, they claimed to have taken in more than forty-thousand dollars, a mammoth sum good enough to buy seaside mansions.

At St. Louis, Mo., dawn beginning to stir against the night that was to terminate their sojourn, they had between them five tables running simultaneously, the walls lined with gangster types whose sullen eyes under caps and felt hats followed their every move, no sound but the clacking of the cue ball dropping one upon the other ball in the called pocket. The clock nudging six a.m., Essie unscrewed her stick, slid the tooled parts inside the leathered tube bearing her name, and crunched fistfuls of dollars into her pockets.

"I'm wrung out," she said. "Better luck next time."

"The dough Cinderella won," someone said, "she ought to bed all of us."

"Maybe next time," Essie said, putting on her smart sharkskin coat.

The shark they had been alternately playing was from Dayton, Ohio. He was heading back tonight after a long road trip, he said. Call me Dayton. Dayton had kids and a wife he missed, he said laughing. He was a laugher even as he was dropping a tidy sum closing upon four thousand dollars.

"Which means," he said, "after three road months and two thousand miles I've cleared no more than about eight cents a mile."

That was when Essie made her first mistake.

"That's more than us," she said. All movement stopped. For a moment the one sound heard was the ticking eight-ball wall clock, heretofore unheard. Until that moment the "us" had not existed. Her second mistake was to say to the Dayton man, "Maybe I could flag a ride with you part way." That raised a few brows. Grey returned from the men's room to hear the mullet saying, "What? You aim to leave your rusted '34 DeSoto Airflow Coupe round the corner in the parking lot? Next to where Ace has his Ford?"

Their mullet did not lack admirers. He had the best rep in the Corn Belt and a sweet mama mistress in St. Louis, Mo. So Dayton had roots and was more one of them than these southern greasers. Certain private citizens of unalloyed integrity in St. Louis, Mo. had stakes in him. The Corn Belt king of the cloth came to town, he was assured a loyal audience. Still, no need yet, on this busy street, to get out the brass knucks, the shooters.

Pulling yet another fat roll from a pocket, shouting, "Rack the pills, Demitri!" Then to die again after five minutes, his stick barely touched. Dayton no longer laughing, the roll thinned to nothing.

Close to breakfast time, Essie and Grey, tired and not thinking straight, saw another of the now familiar St. Louis road signs posted along state route 64—naked female form in red silhouette: *St. Louis …Yours to discover!*—and not far along an intersection dominated by a stand of blackjack oaks and shagbark hickory trees, a tide of dusty shrubs… in the centre of which beckoned a decomposing Red Dot Inn, not too steep at $8.88 the night. They pulled in, promptly registered as man and wife. Breakfast? Walking toward the adjacent Bob Evans restaurant, a newish chain they liked for its farm ambiance, Essie complained of paralysis in the right hand, tired feet, a stiff neck, a sore back, and too much cigarette smoke inhaled over the past eight hours. "Puny," Grey said. "What else is eating at you?" She laughed, turning about, saying she wanted a hot bath and to jump into bed between clean sheets.

"You go get your Bob Evans while I hobble into dreamland."

He did so, feeling more than a little pooped himself. Looking for the room, he was dimly aware of two heavy-set, jowly men advancing his way and another looming behind him, but gave them little thought as the morning was clear and bright and the motel was bound to have a good many people beginning the day. A second later he was pitched headfirst through an open door, pinned to a red carpet with someone's foot lodged at his throat. Essie was stark naked on the bed, legs and hands strapped, welts on her face.

"They want our earnings," Grey heard her say.

The man's shoe was grinding into Grey's head. They were working fast. A slip-knot secured one ankle, the rope wrapping around the other, and now the rope slid behind his head, looping his neck. Someone yanked the rope. Grey found he couldn't breathe. The Dayton man they had fleeced was bent at the waist, looking into his eyes. He was smiling. "I'd wager St. Louis is wide of your usual turf," he said.

"Let him go," Essie said. With her teeth she'd been pulling the red bedspread up over herself. The man watching her do this flapped the cover away. "You're quite pretty," he told her in a flat voice. "Rape is a distinct possibility."

"Although," said the Dayton man, "as a general rule we abhor violence."

"Except sometimes," said the other, "when the woman is a looker we tend to disregard the general rule."

"Well, we throw the subject up for discussion," Dayton said.

"I don't doubt such is how you get all your women."

The man by the bed tweaked her nipples. He was so gentle about it that Essie almost smiled.

"She likes it," the man said.

Grey wallowed about. The shoe returned to his head.

"So where is your stash? We've searched your transport."

"Relax the rope," Essie said. "A dead husband will not be much use to me."

The rope tightened. Grey emitted a strangled cry. For a full minute they watched him roll and flip about like a fish. Then the foot was back on his chest.

"Untie me," Essie said. "I'll get you the dough."

"Already?" said Dayton. "I thought we might have a smoke, bring in a bottle, chew the fat. You can see how enjoyable this is for us."

"I'm cold," she said. "Please cover me."

The Dayton character nodded and the man by the bed flipped the spread over her. He pinched the cover under her shoulders and swept a tangle of hair from her face.

"In St. Louis politeness does not go unrecognized," he said.

"We beat the shit out of you," Essie said. "We did it fair and square."

"True," the Dayton man said.

"So what's your beef?"

"I don't quite know how to state it. They have a saying here in the Mo which goes something like this: what's yours is mine. It's served the city right well." He was busy unroping Grey, saying this. He was helping him up. Essie was also free. "Get the money," he said. "Then one of the boys will bring in a bottle—coffee, if you prefer—and we can talk pool. You're both good. Damn few of us left around these days." He laughed heartily. "No hard feelings? The same—worse, to be truthful—has happened to me. Fact is I've been off my game lately. My divorce, probably. Otherwise I'd of trampled your butts."

Later in the day, a long way from the Red Spot Inn, stopping for late lunch at a rustic Hideway in Tennessee's portion of the Great Smokies, she said, "They were nice as pie."

Nursing grievances, Grey had little to say.

"Did I tell you I am pregnant?"

That lifted him from his seat.

*

Junior was born.

*

Now Grey will be sauntering into Stark's Pool Emporium. Dick Stark is thirty years past his prime, diabetic, rheumatic, and nursing an ulcer. Owner and proprietor in name only. Oleander is the party keeping the business afloat. Oleander is viewed as a newcomer to the town; he has been in these environs more than twenty years and is aware that if he remained another twenty he still would be considered a newcomer. This does not disturb him, in fact cheers him. It allows him to continue believing he is different— more unique and smarter—than the dumb lot usually around him. All that is true, which also cheers him. He offsets these nasty truisms by practice of a humility which, over the years, has accumulated until it has become truth. Such is his view, anyway, and one with which Grey, being much the same, concurs. The two have often discussed such matters and along the way Oleander has admitted his crush on Grey's friend Viota Bee. "I've had the hots for Viota," he said, "for what seems a thousand years. Since I saw her riding a rusty Schwinn bike to and from school when she was about twelve. She's why I've never left this dead place."

"That wasn't a genuine Schwinn," Grey said. "It was a salvage of other graveyard bikes. Terrible machine. Always falling apart."

"So was I. Totally smitten."

"I know all about it, Oleander."

"You do?"

"Who doesn't?"

"She'd slip away at midnight and we'd motor to the gravel pit and enjoy nude swims."

"I know about the swims, Oleander."

"Always dark as thunder at that pit. Never a moon. Drove me crazy that I never got to see her naked."

"She's said the same about you. A loss, I admit. But one, as I understand matters, soon rectified."

"Rectified? That hardly encompasses the—"

"Go right ahead. Encompass it."

"Never you mind. I can't believe she told you all this."

"Why not? I was and remain Viota's best friend. I'd probably kill for her. I'd certainly knock out a few teeth."

"Not mine, I hope."

"No, not yours."

"Since you're so understanding maybe you can tell me what to do about that Mercantile Dynamics idiot she apparently intends marrying. When I heard that I dropped into a deep hole. It was like hitting one of those air pockets in the sky. Down, down you go."

"What causes those air pockets? Do you know?"

"Fatigue. Taking things for granted. Letting love's rope go slack."

"Yours slackened when you secretly cuddled one night with Carol Bly."

"Jesus Christ!"

"You hurt Viota's pride. It also made Carol twitch. She'd been happy in the arms of the Dynamics idiot before you scooped her up."

"Carol's a whiz. She's got soldier and sailor boys in her scoop this minute. You might like to know your robber-baron son is coming of age. He's been giving the eye to little Cindy. She already has the long legs. Before we blink she'll have the rest. It is amazing that witless parents can produce such fireball children. You are yourself a prime example. At least in your case the son has a divine mother in Essie."

"That divine woman would like to chop off my head."

"That's what I'm saying: she loves you."

Royston Clay is attempting to sweep the pool room floor. He is studying the broom as though it is an object his hands have never held. Royston wants to know what to do with the trash after he has it piled.

"Where do you usually stash it?"

"Different places."

"How much do we pay you, Royston?"

"Not enough."

"Go home," Oleander tells Grey.

*

Make no noise in the dark. Grey's good at that. At the foot of the bed he will say, "Now about that injunction…" Essie will say, "Oh hush. Get in. But don't move until I say you can."

"…Now?"

"No."

"…Now?"

"No."

"…When?"

"Now."

They will not be seen for days.

Sooner or later, the squirt son will hear the door-knob rattle. Essie or Grey will be heard shouting, "Bring your parents a glass of water."

*

Come another day he will most likely hear the clack of balls from the Business Room.

"This is no way to raise a child," he will say to them.

*

The *Soc(i.e.)ty* column, March 7 (1947)—Spring rolled in this week with Psyche's sweet breath, balmy skies expected summer-long. Kicking up her heels in a return to town was celebrity star Viota Bee after joyous nuptials galvanizing wedded partnership with Oleander Driscal, recent arrivee to these parts. An invitation-only shindig held at Chochyatte Ball Park witnessed "Hula Dance Warfare," an inspiration of Sally Forth of Bon Vivant Hair (Joan, Jean, and Bessie Belle clogging)… The Imperial picture show announced its "best year ever," thanks to the extended showing of the formidable classic, *The Outlaw. Variety*, the showbiz periodical, neglected to report that the engaging actress will reprise this role in a local dramatic production this fall… In other developments word has reached Soc(i.e.)ty that poolshot exemplars Grey and Essie have resolved difficulties pursuant of them through a decade of strife. We have it from the horse's mouth that a second child is on the way. Let us weep. Famed town leader and eccentric nobleman Hubbard, wearing the same old suit, was feted by dozens of thrill-seekers at his 88th birthday bash at the Dinette, during which the governor passed out free tobacco plugs to adherents of this vile habit. The midget detective many will have seen striding our fair ramparts, in company with a slew of winsome beauties, is said to be here investigating the strange disappearance of two hundred "rare" Reader's Digest book condensations from the county Bookmobile while said vehicle was here on a recent visit. In sadder news, town stumps enhancing our thoroughfare continue to blaze. Several nearby abodes have been abandoned. As elders sleep, a cadre of children nightly patrol the smoking inferno with filled water buckets.

It is with profound sorrow that we announce, as of this date, Soc(i.e.)ty will be no more. Without pay or a nod of appreciation, we have been terminated. Adios to the fine town, Destiny. Thus do we say *thirty*, a journalistic word meaning *the end*.

*

Let us now ring in the attendant; she will show you to the door. There the footman awaits. He will escort you to the carriage, whereupon the coachman will hurry you away.

*

In the middle of the boy's eating from a plate of canned pork and beans, the old Duke of Bologna muttered through the hallways into the kitchen, utterly naked except for patchwork slippers on his gnarled blue feet, the ermine robe in slipshod fold over one frightfully thin arm. "The midget wants his soup," his frail voice lamented. "He wants that soup now and no more high talk about it!" Echoing through the myriad chambers of the ancient castle clinging to its promontory above the roaring sea in this enclave of the damned arose the midget's enraged baritone: "Not soup, you lusting idiot!"

Eighty years come and gone.

SARA MAGO ET AL

A FAT MAN and a thin man and a woman who was in between came into the café, in the afternoon this was, around three, with another hour left in the day shift. They passed up the cleared tables in front, and sat—odd, I thought, but live and let live—at the unwiped end booth where the staff and the regulars, what few there are, sometimes assemble, all the cups and crumbs and crumpled napkins still on the table, along with a deep spread of salt in which Sara Mago, now dozing at a counter stool, had fingered in her name down to the yellow top, and the words "Hereby Looms A Tale," with cartoon balloons dripping from the letters that were meant to represent her tears, all her morbid life up until this hour. And mine, I guess, as well. All our fallen yesterdays, our gloomy tomorrows, no relief in sight, not today, not ever—though let's not be overly dramatic, if you don't mind.

Not a word, not a nod from these three as they entered, the woman who was in between sitting between the other two, all on one cramped side—odd, I thought, but live and learn—and moving aside coffee mugs and the like to make room for their elbows, then all three solemnly studying the vista, although no news there. This vista being a seamless vista, the same desert scrub through two days journey, coming or going, until you hit the rugged Pecos on the one side or scaled Edward's Plateau for Austin on the drab other.

I said, "What will you have?" calling this out to them from my spot at the cash register—"What'll it be?"—as I rung up a No Sale on this ancient chatterbox just to see if it was still into free enterprise. "A cold drink," I said, "a menu, a meal, a snack? Here at Doc's Place we aim to please, service like a shot, reasonable prices too, check and compare."

Their three heads turned as one and regarded me warily, defeated by the heat, I would guess, not so much as a nod of civility in the way they kept looking, as I hit the keys I like to hit on the old machine and rang up 999 dollars and 99 cents—the most you can ever buy at Doc's Place, according to the old machine.

"Soup du jour?" I said. "Vichyssoise, special today only? Ice water, beer, our number one deluxe milkshake?"

Outside I could see tumbleweed skittering along all in the one direction like squat little musical signatures, emblems of runaway time midst the rueful space, a thick scrim of ashen dust coiling four or five feet above the desert, and above that layer upon layer of rubescent haze stretching far as the eye could determine, the sky crowning this wizardry an endless stretch of limpid blue, which would be the colour of Sara Mago's eyes, of Sara Mago down at the counter end if ever again she opened them. Sara's love had run out, leaving only the last vestiges of charity to limp about on hobbled legs. She's endured the daily broken heart, the breakfast jeers, met death face to face, yet retains the innocence of a starved child, all of which combines to make her sleep-headed daylight through dark. That white uniform she was wearing, why am I only now mentioning this? To begin with, it was dirty. I mean, before all the savagery started, or perhaps before it was so much as thought about, that uniform was filthy. She has two. The other was torn, likely in a fight. She had not yet had time to sew up the bodice, nor yet time to wash its replacement. So the soiled one was the necessity. And that one had not survived the ordeal without becoming—what might be the word?—besmirched. More besmirched, in that it was now spotted, smeared, with Doc's blood. She'd fainted, or fallen, slipped, maybe wallowed in his spewing— would I know? She claimed his last words were *I don't know you!* but who this *you* might be is up for conjecture and, in any event, she could not have heard his last words, being elsewhere, and I have serious doubts that old Doc, a man of unsound mind so solidly entrenched such had become his vocation, would have thought any act, final or otherwise, deserving of last words.

"Highly recommended, homemade," I said to the three sojourners, "best you'll find any place on this road, good for what ails you, that's our soup du jour." They shook their heads, these three sojourners did, each in slow and considered denial of need, the woman hunched low between the men, her spine curved, chin all but resting on the table, their shoulders overlapping hers, one bent finger poised above Sara Mago's name engraved there in salt, as though she would smooth out the grains and exchange a stranger's name for her own, though let's hope for her sake she imbibes not one dram of old Sara Mago's morbid news. I set the tape going, not the

143

Brahms, not the Chopin, but a yippieayeoh cowpoke tune, with a Ry Cooder man stroking the backup strings.

The woman's eyes momentarily locked with mine and what you saw there, in the livid aftermath of her musical distaste and before some residue of inherited politeness made her swallow it back, was melancholia deep as a fever, the way the heart works from within to burn its insignia upon your face as resolutely as hot iron on the skin of a yowling calf.

She then took to picking up the coffee mugs, glancing into them, sloshing the leftover liquid around, and speaking in some secret code to the other two, a quiet drone of observation perhaps, with no particular expression of grievance or sorrow in her expression, commenting, perhaps, on nothing more consequential than the shade of lipstick smears on the cup rims, the cigarettes heaped in the ashtrays, the tattered, crumpled field of napkins, messages you might compose in salt the way you scribbled a name in sand on a lonely beach—and the two with her whispering back their odd consent or notice of same, nodding, and looking away at this and that, yes, at this and that, the lean one by the window now saying with crisp authority to her, "Don't go haywire on us, Dobe."

Don't go haywire on us Dobe.

Though I could have got that bit wrong: not Dobe, could be, but not Dale or Doll or Dole, only something within that range of sound, the woman at that point snapping out a quick beat of code, spoon rapping the table, spitting out a quick response—"...haywire dotdot haywire your dotdot self!"—as she squirmed her shoulders clear, her head darting up like a chipmunk from its catacombed depths—"dotdot your frigging dotdot asshole self..."—before subsiding with a deep pull of breath, her shoulders now further sagging, curve and slide of backbone, and clasping her hands and fluttering them restlessly over the table, just one eye and the top of her head about all that was visible now, as my yippieayeoh cowpoke mounted his mustang and clippityclopped off into yippieayeoh land.

"Why isn't she here?" the woman moaned. "What time is it?"—and all of us, Sara Mago excluded, slammed our eyes onto the remorseless clock.

No movement there, nothing going on with that clock, that clock gone into other zeniths of being. New batteries required, that clock no longer bound to its earthly quest.

"She'll be here. Said she would. Just hang on."

Sara Mago groaned, brushing at her rear end as if to disrupt the flight plan of swarming bees.

I put on the Brahms and watched to see would the woman in the booth unclench her fists, lose her grimace, make peace with the world.

Outside, the tumbleweed continued its pilgrimage. The dust field was lifting, allowing the yucca, creosote, mesquite, and like plumage to say hello, we are back from our vacation, hope you did not miss us too much, it's a bit dry out here, for God's sake could you not grant us a nice rain.

"Look," the older man said to me as I arrived with a wiping cloth, and glasses of water. "Flap on off, okay? We've been cooking in the car all day, we want to sit here for a few minutes undisturbed, family matters to discuss, okay?"

Hoekay, I thought, by your leave, amen, let's put the working man in his place.

"No charge for that water," I said. "Though it might interest you to know we had to drill through hard rock to get that water, an aquifer, you know, yes, by God, a giant ocean exists mere miles beneath your feet."

"Buzz off," the older man said. "Hoof brain," added the other.

I looped back into the hanging cove off the kitchen, a warren of rooms each the size of tea biscuits—warped floors and joists, cracked low ceilings, a leaning, afflicted place, with doors that opened to other doors, windows that opened to walls. A dark, rustic, unswept maze, our No Where place, its Fixit times come and gone. Sara Mago and me, come and gone, yet holding on, God must wonder why.

Because who else will keep the vigil, command the post?

The air conditioning didn't reach back here and the heat was breathtaking, lapping at my face the way would a eudemonic dog. I sat down on the creaking bed. An eye for an eye, I thought. A tooth for a tooth. I could smell the burn in the thin, gloopy mattress, a charred black bowl where a thousand buttocks over the years had tossed and turned. Scant nights ago, under the flatiron hand of drink and swimming in the afterglow of good times, Sara Mago had leapt from the perils of restless sleep, banging her head on the ceiling, screaming, *"Oboe, you dumb fuck!"* Rousting me from the flaming mattress with a bucket of cold water over my flanks. *"Now move, you sonofabitch!"* Up on the wall, a defaced yippieayeoh calendar marked the year, but which year?

I peered at my face in the broken mirror over the rickety sink. You could see the years, that was about all there was to be said. Where had my dimples gone? My rosy cheeks? The throbbing halo this young fellow used to wear?

Okay, I said. Flap, flap, flap.

As a crow would flap. As a lone, scheming vulture might.

I took the back way out. Up the path to the ancient trailer sitting in warped disarray on rotted tires. Scene of the crime. Home sweet home. The screen door was still on the ground, kicked aside and trampled, the lock on the main door wrenched loose of its screws, a jagged hole and peeling slivers in the weathered surface where Doc had put his boot through the flimsy wood. A patient man would have mounted the single step, turned the knob and entered, to be greeted by an empty nest.

A radio was playing somewhere, static mostly, a blur of Wichita country and distant *espagnol*.

> *Olé, olé*
> *Love came through my door*
> *And I did not know her name*

I upended the mangled bed and removed the blood-stained sheets before heaving the hinged side back into the wall. I plopped the seatside back to its favoured position. Shattered vases, tables, glassware. The radio under the bed.

> *Olé, olé*
> *I was your Mr. Right*
> *Who could do you no wrong*

I yanked the plug and the static died. The pole lamp in which one bulb yet flickered was overturned, that bulb ghoulishly illuminating the trampled pages of Sara Mago's slew of books, *The History of the Siege of Lisbon*, *Baltasar and Blimunda*, *The Year of the Death of Ricardo*

Reis, etc. etc., wherefrom Sara Mago had petitioned for and secured her name change with a total no-hassle outlay of $29.95, not including postage and the wrath of a newly-minted Poppa Doc.

The sheriff's crew had removed the knives, the pistols, the rope, the body. They'd left behind the suicidal chair, surmising that it had splintered under his weight, "well, my gosh!" perhaps being his final thought.

I opened the small, thumping refrigerator and guzzled back a spot of whole milk. I looked in the aged freezer to see if she still had it there: the tight wad of dollar bills bound by rubber bands and encrusted with ice inches thick, as everything in the unit, and the unit itself, was. Sara Mago's secret *bicycling through Portugal* stash.

Sara Mago had come howling through the trailer door after discovering Doc's body. She'd trampled daisies and thrown pots down the well. Then she'd flung herself into a zigzag course onto the highway with me trailing. Don't ask why. Do not ask why.

In the sky, two white lines were soundlessly writing themselves, miles up from the floating horizon. And through all of this the heat rippling like the flesh of horses on a race course.

The highway, for the whole of its dusty, wavering length, coiled through the plains like snakes climbing a frazzled rope.

Perched on a leaning saguaro, a hawk squared off in contemplation of its sunbaked kingdom.

Sara Mago's head remained on the counter, not much to see except a pile of honeystrewn hair, pale, thin arms encircling her head and one tight fist marooned over a sugar bowl.

The woman was looking at the twin jet streams up in the sky, her eyes hard, more than a little mean, feet pressing the booth's opposite seat, the muscles straining in her legs, her throat thickened, too, a whole heap of knots up in her brow, and all the while addressing her companions in some code hard as timber.

I went over to their booth with my wiping cloth and cleared their table, saving the salt for last, scooping that into the palm of my hand, scattering the salt over the floor and wiping my palm against the apron.

"We close in fifteen minutes," I said, an outright lie.

"Creep," she said.

Sara Mago stirred. The older man turned to regard her, not overly interested, the younger one staring out the window and muttering "Jesus Christ" under his breath with a look on his face that asked why in God's name would anyone choose to live out here. Sara Mago looked like she'd been walking too many fathoms on blistered feet with a noose around her neck waiting for someone to hang her. In a slurring voice she said, "I think I took too many pills, I feel birds have been nesting in my hair, in my mouth, watch your language, you," she says, and her head plops back down.

About this time the door swings open and in stride two officers of the law, johnnies-come-lately to the desert patrol. One carries the wreath he's lifted from the front door. "Surprises me," he says, "to see you'd put up a wreath for that miserable bastard."

"That's the Eternal Wreath," I tell him. "It gets passed along."

"Seen any suspicious characters today?" the one says, and I think about that as I'm watching the other one down beside Sara Mago, stroking her hair, his face up at her ear and her hair half-covering his face, patting his holstered pistol, too. "Nothing today," I said. "Not a peeping soul, nada, no suspicious persons crossing our parameters today." The one I'm saying this to squints at me, wrenching his head, squinting all over, a small welt of pink skin in that fresh cut beneath his left eye.

They settle onto stools a space removed from Sara Mago, giving her serious study, the one saying, "I see old Katsky's taking it hard," the second one saying, "Two to go, we're onto something hot now, no time to chitty-chat."

"Water," the other says, the one with the cut under his eye. "For the fire-eater in the cruiser. Fact is, you could take it to her, she's not going anywhere without that dog."

"That damn dog," the first one says, and the two of them smile, obviously sitting on a story they are eager to tell.

Over at the booth the woman is trying to wedge herself free, she's flapping an arm at the lawmen, but there's a hand clamped over her mouth, both men are pressing against her, pressing her flat, or so it seems, she's fenced in so all to be seen of her is a pile of hair, one eye, the nose, that big hand over her mouth. You'd almost call it assault, a trespass of the living temple, someone should intervene, but this is yippie-aye-oh country, maybe Dobe has gone haywire again, could be such is her natural state, maybe she's only saying hello, what business is this of mine, there's such a thing as an entitlement to privacy.

And the troopers are telling their tale.

"It's like you say it was with Betsky running wild on the highway after she finds Doc jiggling from a rope off that hotshot chair, except this was daylight not an hour ago, we spot this figure weaving on the road. I'd say not exactly running, going in circles, more like, thrashing this stick, which turns out to be a walking stick, except not exactly a regular walking stick, laminated tip, you know. She's screeching to high heaven, drugs, we figure, alcohol, a runaway war bride, another one of those. But it turns out she's blind, a legitimate one-hundred per cent blind person, a teenager for God sake, and she's lost her Seeing Eye dog. Some sonofabitch, you could say, has struck her dog with his automobile, probably intentionally, she thinks. She's berserk, it takes us a while to learn that. Yes, so she thinks. Though, now listen to this, an accident or intentional, this didn't kill the dog. She hears the *blam*, all these sundry noises, maybe she even heard a blaring horn, tires chewing on gravel, then *blam*, *crunch*, *crunch*, *crunch*, that dog whining. Whining. Moans. She hears that. Then nothing. Silence. Silence like the universe has ceased operation, has closed down. Her dog. Where has her dog got to? So what we compute is that wounded dog, delirious, has dragged herself off. That Seeing Eye dog's mind is not functioning. She's out in the scrub dead or dying. We harness the girl, we zigzag each which way over the terrain, miles and miles, the binoculars busy. We search high and low for that goddamn irreplaceable dog, well, insofar as there is a high out here in this goddamn place which I for one wish the Mexicans had retained."

Maybe you guys hit that damn dog your own selves is what I'm thinking.

Outside, in blinding sun, a jeep and two trucks lumber by, digging for the army depot fifty miles up the line. The girl in the Dodge Charger is maybe thirteen, sitting bunched up, a dusty, shrivelled rag, like she's been rolled in prickly pear, has wrestled with cacti, her face and arms spotted with dried blood, though what I mostly notice are her eyes, those sightless eyes, she's looking somewhere else, she's blind, no doubt about that. "Who's there?" she asks, a stricken voice, "Did you find my dog, those troopers, they said they were looking for my dog, who are you, are you looking for my dog? Something happened to my dog, a car hit her, I think it must have swerved right into her because Pozzo would never never have walked on the road, Pozzo is an exceedingly bright dog." She would not shut up about that dog, Pozzo had the heart of ten thousand dogs, she was a dog of priceless merit, a saint was dear Pozzo, I was getting nowhere at all with my questions, What were you doing walking that road, where were you going, where do you live, only drunken idiots and hapless soldiers ply that highway, here, drink this water, it's a furnace out here, forget that damn dog, How dare you say that, go away…

The vehicle the trio inside had arrived in, boasting Oklahoma plates, was a tired-looking heap with little to say for itself. It was pocked with rust, dotted with dirt and insects, but I didn't see anything indicating that it had slammed into a dog. Boxes on the backseat seemed packed with baby clothes.

The troopers were leaving. It's *vamanos* time, they said, another search for that dog and we are done around here. As for Doc, they say, his body is ready for release, you can pick up and bury the bastard anytime you like.

The sky is a stagnant, unknowable blue.

Sara Mago, waking up, groans, "I dreamt someone nuzzling me." She stretches those arms, "The men in my life," she says. "Beepbeep, and they're gone. After I've drunk all the liquor in this world, after I've smoked all the cigarettes, after I've gone to bed with all the men in the world, then maybe I'll be happy. I dreamed I was in a big field containing nothing but empty sacks. I opened one of those sacks and a dead man jumped out shouting in a strange language. Then all the other sacks opened and out jumped..."

"Don't tell me," I said.

Sara Mago can feel in her haunches the smallest shudder in the earth's core, the smallest shift, plates rubbing together, teensy ruptures fifty miles beneath the earth's crust.

"I need to wash my face," she says.

Beep, beep, she's gone.

"We will have that soup now," the booth woman says. Her voice is bright and cheerful, a marvel to behold.

Out in the desert wastelands, a solitary figure was on the move. Not fast, and not without difficulty. It seemed to be coming our way on three legs. Now and then for long moments it tumbled over and disappeared, becoming as one with the rippling heat.

A dog. It would be needing water.

SLAIN BY A MADMAN

HE WAS SLAIN by a madman. He was slain once, and the madman wasn't done. He did him a second time, top to bottom. I won't say it was not deserved. We all might have slain him, if we'd known we could get away with it. The whole town contemplated the act a thousand times, daylight through dark.

A day pass! They had let him out on a day pass. Who could have imagined such! That institution was asking for trouble. And where does he go on this day pass? He comes here. Of course he does. He comes home.

So the actual hard-nosed slaying of him by the madman brought some easement to the local situation. But process and accomplishment are two different experiences. They are hardly even related. Like you have three sisters totally in disagreement as to character and dimension, and their mother in far orbit and the father so different from those others he's hardly worth mentioning.

The madman, who can talk a blue streak when he wants to, isn't saying much. What he did say, in a chillingly calm voice, was he didn't do it. "Affliction's giant foot is ever stomping down," he said. "You want to know what marks humankind? That foot. The giant behe-moth." The next second he clammed up. "Now I'm going silent as the little lamb who made me" were his actual words to the authorities, by which I mean me. I'm the law around here. I run a pretty tight ship. Such is what I told this person when she came in, looking all fidgety and run down—*strung out!*—claiming the madman could not, could not, *could not possibly!* be the guilty party.

Did I know at that point she was the madman's sweetheart? No, I did not.

What I said was, "Delores, dear little sister, why in God's name are you here?"

She said, "Because the party you've got locked up back there could not possibly be the guilty party."

I laughed. Delores is always eager-beaver about something.

"Why not?" I said.

"On account of his having been in my arms at The Only Motel when said deed was said to have been accomplished." She sat right down in my chair, in that thigh-high red polka dot dress, saying this. Drinking this Slurpee drink through a straw. "He may well be a madman," she said, "and I suppose he is in the minds of some individuals, but no way would he pass up a good time with me to wreak what havoc you say he wrought on that other fella."

I said, "Now come on."

She said, "You come on."

I said, "Honey, you are a lying cockroach. At the time of the deed you were teaching your six-year-olds how to hop, skip, and jump, and not at no motel."

She said, "Every Wednesday at two p.m. for the past two years I been hopping on my bike and meeting my madman at The Only Motel. I give my little serpents the *Bad Frog Book* to play out."

"Not the Bad Frog!"

"People wanting to git that book banned left town. It's back on the curriculum, hot as potatoes."

"Damn," I said.

She scowled. She has always hated cussing.

I said, "All right. You can go on home now. But don't say nothing to your mother about no motel."

"Oh, poor mother! It's her wash day," she said.

She went.

But first she said, "I know my man is no Goody Two Shoes and that he seduced a nun in the long ago. It's jealousy is what it is. All you randy he-hunks want to seduce a nun. Don't try telling me different."

"Now hold your horses," I said.

"He is the apple of my eye, my solace in the crippling storm, and I am up to here with certain people casting aspersions on his character. Just because he once made out with a dumb nun."

She sliced a hand up by her chin, saying that. The little polka dots bounced all over.

Then she went.

I sat a long time mulling over her words. He-hunk? But "havoc wrought upon *that other fella*" gave me pause. Did she not know this *other fella* bore her identical name? That, biologically speaking, he was family? Or was she, like the rest of us, bound to deny such until our dying day?

Here he came on his day pass. Spotted the instant he stepped off the bus. Baggy suit. Emaciated. Good. May he expire on the spot, we thought. Shoot him. Knife him. Next, he's seen peering into the new Subway. He's gauging the changes since his departure ages ago. What is that he is carrying in the left hand? Is that a gasoline can? Is that a cigarette between his lips? Yes.

Yes, yes, yes.

I went, too. I got the lights spinning and the siren churning, and I juiced right over. I went to The Only Motel.

A short minute before arriving, I passed the family ruins and the glistening enmity of Mink Lake. How I hated that lake. But the road was straight and I could close my eyes.

A toxic wasteland, the sky ever smoking black above it.

A poetic line occurred to me: *May the tears of ravaged angels cleanse my cheeks.*

"Explain your needs," Ms. Fixit said to me. Ms. Fixit, what I call her, is one of three sisters running the place.

She said, "It's not Tuesday, why are you here?" She said, "Your usual room is occupied, and anyway Vivian is in Buffalo."

"Shopping," she said.

"You look terrible," she said. "You need a good mudpack ointment on that flesh."

Vivian is one of the three sisters. She doesn't get along that well with the other two. What I say to that is who can.

Me and Vivian, to make no bones about it, have a thing going. She was supposed to keep her trap shut about it, but, women, what can you say.

"She's buying a new mattress," sister Fixit said. "A new man, a new mattress. Every time. It sure beats me."

"Never mind that," I said. "I seek confirmation on a love tryst involving the madman and a certain redhead named—"

"Yes, yes, yes!" is what I got in return. "I can set my clock by that pair. Dee zips in on that yellow bike, he zooms in on that red truck. Then you don't hear a peep from in there until the six o'clock news."

"Damn," I said.

"You might as well face it. Those two are practically wed."

"No way am I welcoming another madman into the family."

"Another would hardly be noticed," she said.

"Now hold on."

"You hold on."

Her hands and hips were covered in mud. So, too, her naked feet and her hair.

Smoke was rising from a barrel out back. "What are you burning out there?" I asked.

"Your bed sheets?" Ms. Fixit said. She was a smart-mouthed, big-knuckled woman known far and wide. The black folds of history had not obscured her light, to hear her tell it. It seemed to me the flesh darkened under her eyes each time she spoke to me. I could remember holding her down when we were little. Maybe she remembered, too. Although Vivian said neither of her sisters remembered last week. You never know. I had held her down and got in a good bite on her neck. Then everybody else had piled on. The adults hadn't minded. They thought we were having fun. What she had said was I had a teensy weenie and only fruitcakes would ever look at me. She deserved those bites.

This, of course, was before the mayhem.

"Where's Marlene?" I asked. Marlene was third in the sister trio and way older. Miss Moneybags they called her, on account of her being the bookkeeper and payroll mistress and hard-nosed tyrant yard-boss who every day strode about in logging boots with her white mane flying.

"In town getting her shots," I was told.

Shots?

"Yes, shots, by God. One shoots off to Buffalo to buy a mattress, the other shoots into town to get her fanny pumped up with shots. Who by God is left here to do all the work?"She went red in the face, saying that.

"Well," I said, "you'd best get at it."

"I don't like your tone," she said. "I don't like your tone one teensy bit."

The Only Motel dogs were snarling in a distant field.

"Those dogs," I said.

She said, "Yep. Dogs." And strode off to the lean-to where she makes her mud pots. Not mud, I've been told, but clay from the good earth. Sometimes, when they are talking to each other, you see the three sisters out there shovelling ivory-tinted clay into buckets, milky lumps from the high walls of the small stream quietly flowing behind The Only Motel. Mink Lake the wellspring. My water, in other words. It has taken, I'm told, ten thousand years for that clay to form. They slip and slide, they tumble, they swat at each other. Always one or the other, sooner or later, will throw down her shovel and crawl miserably from the ditch, shouting nastiness at the others and at any lodger who chances to be on hand.

At times, the water in that stream runs the colour of blood, who knows why. Blood shades the favoured glaze.

"This is pre-literate clay!" storms Viv when in one of her fits. "This is pre-agriculture clay! This clay predates the Age of Reason by 30,000 years! All they needed was a big bonfire! While we're at it, throw in a virgin child, why not!"

"Oh, come on."

"You come on."

Way off there, in a grove of warped trees, sits the familial home, parents abiding mysteriously within, a chain fence in surround of this, No Trespassing signs dotting your every step. Keep Out. Keep Out. Mind the dogs.

"They are perfectly normal," Viv has said. "You ought not broadcast these erroneous details."

Erroneous, my word! Meanwhile, drone planes fly invisibly overhead. Our nation's on the watch.

They've got suspicions, too, about those nuns.

Sisters and parents had been visiting the day hell broke loose. Dinner! Ice cream! Dee, playing in a sandbox—chasing a cow?—had been spared. She was what? Two? I was eight. Nine? Did I yet know my arithmetic tables? No I didn't.

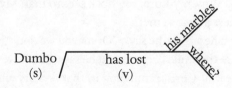

Dumbo (s) / has lost (v) his marbles where?

Is that right? In this backwoods hole, before the nuns, did we diagram a sentence that way? Yes we did.

It was a woman's shoe the dogs were arguing over. A black pump. Well, once black. Now it was mostly slobber. Slime. Grit. One dog had the toe, the other the heel.

161

They were pulling and twisting, having a dandy time. What that shoe reminded me of was the madman's befouled nun. In her nunnery period she had worn a man's black, clumpy shoe. My men had done a lot of snooping on that nun. We knew everything about her except why she'd give up her virtue to a madman. Although that did, looked at in a certain way, make sense. She was still around, that nun. She had wanted to marry the madman back then, and have his children. She could be very specific about it, if you ran into her at the Easy-Go or Abe's Drugs. "By God, I still do," she'd say. "I'd toss up Chuck and my current crop of sweet babies for five minutes with that madman." Chuck, he pulls on his suspenders, he laughs. "My simple tool," she calls Chuck.

Once, I was eating a foot-long at our splendid new Subway and her boss shoves into my booth. I'm looking at his white collar the whole time he's talking to me. Finally, I have to ask him, "How do you birds keep those white collars so clean? Never a smudge. Nothing. Me, a dirty collar-ring the minute I don a shirt." He looks surprised. "Why, my Lord, my flock sees to that! My nuns! Goodness gracious me!"

Then he smiles, he says, "Or maybe we don't sweat."

Next, the smile deepens and he says. "Or if we do it's the sweat of Christ reminding us that divinity and hard work are soul brothers making our day."

What he'd been complaining about prior to that was his shrinking population. He'd lost three nuns—"*Three!*"—in the past year. What was it? Was it the air people breathed in this town? Was it creeping socialist criminalization of a disengaged citizenry? Was there a sex club afoot, their whole goal the claiming of his nuns? I tell no lie, they catch sight of the madman, they go giddy. They waddle about like cracked eggs. They'd die to ride in his truck."

What could I say? The madman's a handful. He's no picnic.

I thought about having me a slug from the bottle in the glove compartment when I got back to the cruiser.

I could see Ms. Fixit working at her wheel was giving me long looks. The V in the neon over The Only Motel office was blinking. It had been blinking for about six months now. It couldn't seem to make up its mind about giving up the ghost.

I decided I really wanted that drink. I had enjoyed me a few on the drive out. Then pitch in the Dentyne, which I could get wholesale any day of the week through my friendship with Big Fred at the Easy-Go. Fred was doing okay now. He'd survived the institutions. He was giving the nun battalion the same deals he gave me. Our families had been tight all the way back to our grandparents, which was as far back as anyone dared remember. There hadn't been any nuns around here in those days. There hadn't been much of anything, truth be told. Just endless, soggy fields and a horizon so low you could pitch up a hand and feel moisture dripping down the wrist.

I was back in the car by this while, having that drink. Drinks.

The scarecrows, I noticed, had come down. Now I thought about it, it seemed to me a long time since I'd seen one. Used to be soybeans growing out here. Corn. Beans. Grazing livestock. Then a new season and flat uninterrupted land stretching to distant wood lines. Now we had houses and town and highways and Subway and The Only Motel. Oh, my!

Our cherished Days of Yore. Such was the phrase occurring to me. My eyes wet, though don't get the idea sentimentality had anything to do with this onrush of tears. You could say any fondness I had for those olden days was in relapse. In disrepair. I still wanted to chomp down on someone's neck.

I had the dog's chewed shoe on the seat beside me. The tongue and heel was likely inside one of those dogs' bellies. In my line, you never know when you'll be needing evidence or how that evidence ought to constitute itself. I could look at that shoe and see CRIME written all over it. Which crime? What? Where? My evidence room was stacked with such as that.

The V, Vacancy sign, was making spitting noises. The word, in big orange letters, was spaced all along The Only Motel's nine shed-like rooms. $19.95 the night. Hours negotiated. Wind had blown rags and fluff and plastic bags up there.

My Daddy and Big Fred had burnt down the other motel. That project had been the bright idea of some guy from Ohio. Bar, restaurant, disco, pool, fountains! Up in smoke, I tell you! Three days it took our volunteers to smother those flames.

About the same time in come three Greyhounds hauling those nuns. Into the lumberyard now known as the Olde Abby they move.

The dogs were back, scratching at my doors, licking my windows, showing me their teeth. George and Martha, if you want me to give those dogs a name.

I gave some thought to Viv in Buffalo buying that mattress. She liked firm, I liked soft.

I was exhausted, watching her sister throw those plates. I had to eat off those plates at home plus at Big

Fred's, everywhere, don't ask me why. Dinnerware kept those girls afloat.

I had me a madman to nail, and somehow I knew that shoe on my seat featured in the crime. Anyway, my bottle was empty and I needed a bathroom.

I had a bit of the shakes but I was composed. Don't go thinking otherwise.

Now it was back to the lock-up to chat with the madman.

But a detour was mandated. Today was payday for the caregivers. This little ditty popped into my head:

> *Sex was on a rampage*
> *whence it lay*
> *with love*
> *in dewy glen…*
> *Or could be plot*
> *took each the other's way*
> *(So they say.)*

Such foolishness had lately been coming to me.

Sleeping Estella, dear Mum, had been bedridden through driven years. First the fire, then sickness slouching in. She'd been out of bed once in the past year, that time to see Christmas lights at the Olde Abby. The crèche. She had looked but hadn't seen. But she was pleased. Dee claimed she heard rumblings in her chest. We tried feeding her ice cream. Which was a mistake. Two churns were going the day hell broke loose.

Today was bath day. The caregivers had her in the shower stall, propped up on a stool. They had wrapped themselves in black garbage bags. Estelle seemed to be smiling. Perhaps she retained a memory of what water was.

I watched them carefully wash, rinse, and dry her hair. She had fine, lovely snow-white hair—the part that had grown back.

Later on, they would dress the bed, salve the roughened skin, powder her. They would ever be talking to her. They delighted in thinking sometimes she laughed. They were good at their job. They had the expertise.

"You drink that coffee," they kept telling me.

The madman had ordered in dinner. He was sitting at a table with a red-checkered cloth, in the company of a few of my boys. They were all chomping down on something I soon learned was duckling a la chipolata. Or *Caneton a la Chipolata*, as he called it. "Here's how Delores and I compose this dish," he was saying. "I quote to you from the sixth printing, 1961 edition, of *Larousse Gastronomique*. "Braise the duckling in the usual manner. When nearly done, drain and remove the trussing string. Return said duckling to the casserole, adding a chipolata garnish composed of ten braised chestnuts, ten glazed onions of rudimentary appearance, ten lean rashers of bacon, and eighteen lovely carrots diced to olive size. Boil down, please. Strain and pour. Over the duckling, of course. Cook. At the last moment add exactly ten chipolata sausages."

He paused. He smiled. He was utterly mad.

He swung around. "Isn't that how you would do it, Racine?"

Racine was my hired help. She was on probation, coming three days a week to sweep and answer the phone. Her face was up between the bars, worshipful, it looked to me.

"More or less," she said. "It's the leftover lard gives me the headache."

"You're right," he said. "That precious lard! Duels have been fought over that lard."

The next minute the conversation had gone on to something else. The madman seemed intent on telling the gang how he and Delores had initial inspiration for the *Bad Frog Book*.

"We were strolling arm-in-arm through Jardins de l'avenue Foch, in Paris, when this bad frog hopped right between the legs of a passing nun. Wasn't that where it happened, Racine? In Foch? That startled nun?"

Racine had her body glued to the bars. "That's how I heard it," she said. "The whole thing is to my mind so-so like a thrilling movie."

I was in shock. My little sister had been to France? When? On her salary? How?

There you have it: a madman's world.

I had to take hold of myself. Thank God one of my boys had a pocket flask.

What I said to the madman was, "What are your intentions?"

He said, "With regard to what?"

"Those Wednesdays."

"Those Wednesdays are privileged," he said.

"Delores is practically underage," I said.

"She's older than a pile of monkeys," he said.

I thought about hitting him but was restrained by his bulk.

He went reflective. "It started with that *Frog* book," he said. "Red had the idea my part of that book was biographical. Autobiographical, I mean. All that ridiculous business about my seduction of a nun. I asked her to name one instance when that book was such. She turned to page one. She read a few lines. 'Here you have this nun. Which nun, is what I want to know.' I was watching her eyes, how they skipped on ahead of what she was reciting. Then I watched her lips. I was hoping she'd recite the whole damn draft. So, in a manner of speaking, it was dating from those early precious seconds that *Frog* turned biographical. From that moment our lives were interwoven. Thus, the initiation of our Wednesdays. That's where our book was written, you know. Our Wednesdays at The Only Motel. Here," he said. "Have some duck."

"You're a madman," I said.

Some of the boys had to restrain me. I told him I meant siccing my dogs on him and if those dogs suffered mange and malaria and hydrophobia, if they foamed white at the mouth, then so much the better.

"You don't have dogs," he said. "Those dogs may run through your mind just the way you describe them, but those dogs were your crazy daddy's dogs and the whole kit and caboodle died ages ago, about the same time you were a barefoot boy limping around in barbed wire on a broken toe."

I tried choking him but we all know you can't shut up a madman. He was correct about the toe, the wire. He had neglected to mention the burnt hair, the boiling flesh.

"Yes," he said. "Yes. Your burns. Your father's lamp through the kitchen window just as the lot of you are pulling out your chairs to sit down to Sunday dinner. Grown-ups and children flying off every which way in their burning clothes. Thank God, Delores and I were still in the sandbox. We will never know why your father decided to incinerate everyone. And it is perhaps true I was overzealous in my response to the current situation.

An assault and battery charge might well be justified. I roughened him up a bit. I ripped up his day pass, took away the gas can, goose-stepped him back to the bus station. All right, maybe I singed his hair a little. Maybe— what is the phrase?—I employed 'excessive force.' After all, not for nothing am I known as a madman."

What shall we eat, what may we drink, where shall we run when every river is on fire and toxic fumes haunt every breath?

Whose hands ply these oars? Who is that burning boy? Say you're into construction, reconstruction, resurrection, the pliable self-redirected, improved, your body must be redesigned, restrung, other flesh grafted onto your own, ears rebuilt, nose, mouth, your very breath a sleek silent machine. The idea of a coming Sunday dinner is afloat, who is to sit down to that dinner, where will they sit, what will they eat, who is to cook, who shall wash the dishes, mop the floor? Sunday every day arrives, Glory Be To God, we are famished, hearth and hearty thanks to thee for this nourishment we now receive, sisters, please do sit down, will someone kindly call those lovely children in to dinner.

> *Nothing so firmly holds*
> *to truth*
> *as the boughs beyond*
> *my window*
> *swaying in wind*
> *Look how those leaves*
> *flutter each syllable*
> *not one among billions*
> *may comprehend.*

THE HISTORIAN

KARL OFTEN, AFTER his discovery, expected people he knew to come up to him and say something like, "How is Lasalle? How is that girl?" Something like that.

Or they would say, "You're a lucky so-and-so to have a woman in your life like that firecracker Lasalle. Why could I not have been that lucky?"

They would look at him with those slant eyes, while making deep-throated noises which anyone, not just Karl, would have found disturbing.

Today, he was in the Snack Parlour looking around for something interesting to look at or eat. Lots of yogurts in the fridge, a good many plastic bags containing one item or another. The owners' names written on the bags, as well as on many of the yogurt lids. Myrtle, Asiaga, Mary, Yolinda, and so forth, but no Lasalle. Not yet. Which meant that Lasalle wasn't sick like these others, or, if she was, then she was sick in another place. Not here. Wonder why not. What was she up to, that Lasalle?

A strange woman was poking his arm. Poke, poke.

No, not strange, not strange at all, now that he gave her face some thought.

Ruth, the nurse.

Ruth was speaking. She was saying, "We have told you and told you to stay out of those yogurts. Buy your own yogurts. You're not the frenzied yogurt-lover you make yourself out to be."

"I love those yogurt drinks, although those up here cost triple those down there,"—he was thinking Mexico—"and are not nearly as good."

"You mean in hell? What I'd like to know is when they dropped the h. Yog-hurt. I much preferred the word with an h. But now everything is like that. We're like a nation of zombies, desperately influenced by *Night of the Living Dead*. On the other hand, happily adjusted people are not among my favourites. Even rodents may be happily adjusted."

Karl laughed. Ruth was a guaranteed nursing fanatic. He liked her trim eyebrows and lustrous cheeks, which so well dressed up her generally trim frame. Generally trim, though not totally. Well, who in his right mind would want a totally trim woman in the first place? You could thread a needle with...fit in a key hole...

"Sorry, Ruth," Karl said. "You were saying?"

"Your daughter is here to see you."

"Who?"

"Don't play dumb with me. She's in the lounge. We've been looking all over for you."

"I'd better spruce up a bit," Karl said. "We can't be upsetting our visitors on a night like this."

"It's two in the afternoon, Karl. Try not leaping off the pier."

No one was in the lounge. The big TV was going and a bevy of new flowers, already shedding their petals, adorned the long windowsill. The window, which had a vista of practically nothing, was lit with fingerprints and loopy swirls. Someone had dribbled wet patches and a bit of scum on each of the three carpets. "Those TVs have only a certain number of hours to live," Karl said, addressing the room. "About four thousand, or so I have been informed. Then, like us, they go kaput."

He turned off the instrument and sat down contentedly in a red chair to watch it.

He awakened to find a wan, not quite wrinkled face staring into his own.

"You were making animal noises in your sleep," that person said. "I bet you fifty dollars I can tell you exactly what you were dreaming."

Karl said, "What I bet is that you are not on my visitors' list. This is a classy operation. They don't allow just anyone over the threshold, you know."

The person smiled. She looked, for a moment, radiantly happy.

"I love you, Daddy," she said. "You have ever been an instant joy to my eyes. You do not have any nice little contraband bottle secreted about your body, do you? Say yes, please! Are you aware that the identical cool medicinal aroma occupies every niche of this abode? It wafts through the vents, making those passing on the sidewalk wonderfully loopy. One acquires an immediate fix. I strolled endless corridors seeking you. The basement, I discovered, is in actuality an ancient, now long abandoned, subway stop. The line connects to countless other buildings. I walked the tracks. Morbid, I tell you! But what a complex! They are all hospitals. All are humming. I counted eight. All sharing the identical aroma, as though sprayed daily by a fleet of helicopters.

I peered into each of them. Barely any disarray perceived. *Impeccable*! Excusing, of course, extended nightmare in the emergency parlours. Saving lives: the last *art*! Are you delighted to see me?"

"Why exactly are you here?"

She tousled his hair, aligned his garment neatly, submitted him to prolonged scrutiny, and, a short while later, seemed to be gone.

"Did you enjoy your game?" Now it was nurse Ruth—provoking?—appraising him.

The visitor had been his daughter, Gayle, the youngest and dearest; he wasn't entirely flummoxed by a day's events. Let's put it this way: apparitions came and went. Gaylie—she had wanted to be called Zulu as a child—had brought along a chess set in an ornate onyx box—"Guatemalan," he told Ruth—the pieces so small they were hard to grasp.

"I beat her soundly," he said. "Mercilessly. I always do. Zulu lacks focus. She doesn't apply herself. Sometimes I see in her face the glassy eyes of those dolls she played with as a child. All my daughters possess that trait."

"Me too, after a long shift. She's like a ghost around here. The other day I found her in our linen room, sniffing the sheets. She settles rose petals on empty beds. She's nice, though a nuisance. She looks like you."

"I hope not. She's a helpless sojourner through unkempt fields, who ought to put on a few pounds."

"You noticed that? She can have mine."

"Go easy on yourself. I'm sure you have your pulchritudinous moments. Last night, about midnight, my telephone rang. It was the Police Auxiliary. The caller asked for a donation to help send young hoodlums to summer camp. Those were his exact words."

"Oh. Those calls. It could be the CIA, the Gnat Security Agency, one of those watchdogs, out to keep terrorists busy responding to trifles."

"Good grief!"

"You likely don't know this. That wayfaring daughter often overnights in your room. She sings you songs in a voice so faint and sweet we all weep. 'Little Girl Blue.' 'My Funny Valentine.'"

"Our favourites."

Karl ventured into the wrong room. It seemed to be filled to capacity with three obese girls who were of an age still to be considered children. "Someone, naming no names, has been foraging on my cupcakes," one of the girls said. The others showed a lot of teeth, laughing. Often these girls were seen hurling themselves up and down the corridors and riding the elevators. Banging on doors. They seemed not to know they were obese, or, if they did, this was something fated by life's prickly cauldron, to be worried about another day. Some while ago Karl had asked them their names. Zippo, the first said. Zappo, said the next. "Satchmo," cried the third. Then they laughed hysterically. "Got a fag? Smoking keeps oomph off the bones," continued the first. "After a fag we always like smooching a faggot."

The ringleader had said to Karl, "Zappo and Satchmo are structurally challenged. They are tormented by indecision, like that Hamlet poof. A heavy hand is obliged. A grizzly ramrod, lest they disappear within themselves like melting chocolate. I am the ramrod of this outfit. We are home on the range, rustling everyone's cattle. Sheep-keepers, beware." She compelled him to examine the peculiar watch adorning a

bulky left wrist. The watch had a colossally long tar-
nished silver band which wrapped like a snake up past
the elbow. "It's a cobra watch," she said. "A cobra on
a mission like those monks who throw themselves out
of windows. Defenestrate, that's the word. You'll see
tomorrow's date on the watch-face. This outfit prefers
to live entirely in the future. Everyone should, in my
opinion."

The two other girls practically wept with joy at these
pronouncements. They stomped their feet and jiggled
their hips, and the room appeared to tilt one way and
another. They cried out in unison, one going high, the
other low—the Raelettes, the Blossoms, the Cookies
came to Karl's mind:

> *we are ice-cold bitches*
> *when we cry*
> *ice cubes*
> *cascade from our eyes*
> *we are a weeping Gibraltar*
> *the melting north.*
> *your hereafter.*

"So you're the famous historian," the ramrod said.
"What period or realm or zone of being, life's hectic
traffic, do you or did you in your prime historicize?"

At this mention of his profession an immense variety
of cloudless memories zipped into and out of the many
rooms and closets and antechambers of Karl's mind,
like a thousand little mice desperately seeking shelter.

The ramrod smirked. Her feet were too large
for her canvas shoes, Karl noticed. Those shoes, of
Dollar Store design, were overburdened; they'd go

to their death inside the week. A sky-blue colour, matching her beautiful eyes. "What, professor," she was asking, "is the oldest fossil ever unearthed, since you're so hot-ass smart?"

These girls, obese nymphets, were a quixotic crew, Karl supposed. Even so, he would recommend a suicide watch with armed guards ever vigilant. He had convinced himself this was that kind of place. "Your views are utterly nonsensible," someone had told him. "Maybe so," he recalled replying, "but it is surely a sordid fact that one has to walk an honest mile from this place, through ruin and dilapidation, a festering city, in order to secure an alcoholic beverage."

"See me," a voice had whispered, but Karl, distressed, could not determine the origin.

The obese force kindly moved on to other prey.

"All you old goats in this place are illegal homesteaders. We mean to butcher your cattle, set ablaze your wagons, drive you out. We are obese renegade Indians intent on mayhem."

"We want pizza, we want pasta, we want heaping pie-à-la-mode," sang another…

Oldest *complete* fossil *Rugosodon eurasiaticus*, if you placed your truck on Zhe-Xi Luo. Karl hadn't remembered. He had stolen his way onto a chained computer on a vacated desk in the lower lobby. He had googled. Afterward, a tickled security man nudged him back upstairs. Before that, they had stood a good many minutes together in a doorway watching a parade of attractive women pass up and down the avenue.

Could the lost Lasalle be among them?

"In you go, professor. I were you, I'd forget that Lasalle."

"Chip—that's your name?—forgetting has become my problem."

Karl's deceased wife, Louisa, had liked saying to guests, "I do not always rise to my husband's expectation. I wither. He likes a saintly woman. The grandiose! Isn't that a remarkable characteristic?"

Oohs and ahhs often held sway those rare moments when Louisa elected to speak. Then a chorus would ring out: *Now for another martini!*

"It's like she's the hidden queen," Karl said.

"Who? This Lasalle?"

Karl was attempting to explain to three research pioneers—mere assistants—his Lasalle dilemma. They were in a panelled room behind closed doors. The trio had the look of people who had in their time experienced a good deal of grief. Their eyes were those of caged birds, beady and wary, their heads often tilted, causing Karl to think of Moby and Prelude, two of Zulu's pet parrots during her addled bird period. Eyes closed, he could see those parrots perched on Zulu's petite fingers, calling for watermelon. Smart birds constrained by tangled memory, always falling asleep precisely at seven p.m., six in winter.

"Louisa and I were forever having to douse iodine over those fingers."

"Sir? What? Pardon?"

Karl said, "It is, as you likely are aware, both treasure and burden to be equipped with potent memory. The condition neither foreshadows tranquility nor directly repulses it." Though they nodded it seemed to Karl they hardly recalled why they were here.

"Say you have before you a tuning fork that remembers not the tunes yet remains to all eyes the genuine article."

The three marvelled. Hmm, they said. I think you have lost us.

Karl, likewise, was lost. Tuning fork? Where had he been going? But by similar means had he formulated his best lectures, drafted his best papers, written his most enduring books.

The one with the cropped hair and wide mouth stood. He said he believed it had been forced upon him the necessity to amend his previous position, namely his analysis of... his analysis of... All waited. They waited through and past that moment when silence became an active, combative presence. Karl imagined waiting in cold night for heat from a disconnected furnace. To his knowledge this man had never offered an *analysis* of anything. This man harboured ludicrous bias against a certain obese gang. *Such commotion!* He expressed opposition to all "juvenile twaddle." Never would applaud the Raelettes. Tomb music would be his preference.

But be kind, Karl told himself. The engine of uniformity need not be invoked. The wrath of The Izarn need not apply; the laws of Hammurabi do not obtain. No need to rain down upon him my own bucket of abuse.

One of the women was up fanning the man's face with a bouquet of blue folders. "I think Robert has fallen asleep," she said. "He's always so intense."

A serenade of soft chuckles arose. Robert was the least intense man alive. His wife had left him. Parents refused him. What idiot had hired him? Soon he would be mistaken for dead.

The obese children could be heard running along the corridor. They were screeching, "I want my cupcake!" They were young and otherwise without purpose. Karl had never seen any cupcakes in the Snack Room. He'd seen crumbs in the lounge, some remains on chipped plates and whole ones thrown against the long vista-deprived window and in various beds belonging to whimpering adults. The girls, en masse, reminded Karl of those Henry Moore sculptures, shorn of beauty. He was about to give voice to this observation but then thought better of it. Some thoughts ought not to be put into words, although this one already had.

Snickers were heard outside the door. A note slowly surfaced on the floor.

PRE-PUBESCENT RALLY TONIGHT 8 P.M. IN B WING, TINKERBELL PRESIDING.

"Here's the thing about Lasalle," Karl said. "A while ago, clearing junk from the house, I came across this ratty old college yearbook. I thought I'd long ago thrown that business away. But there it was, the pages pretty much glued together. Sticky with age. Each page riddled with goodwill messages from hallowed classmates. Every one making reference to Lasalle. What a great girl she was. How lucky I was to have such a smart, stunning Aphrodite in my life. On and on they went in this fashion. Including in the end, in my own hand, under the heading RESERVED FOR DIVINE LASALLE, a lengthy epistle, love letter, from this very party. 'You have changed my life. I can't live without you. Your snapshot has been mangled by my kisses. You'd think a dog had got at it. Love. Love, Love, kisses manifold. I think of you and my heart thunders like horses running a derby. Yours forever and ever. Oh, my sunshine and life, my very breath!' Like that. On and on. In heart-breaking extraordinarily beautiful script. Cozy, elegant, refined. Wonderful grammar. Excellent paragraphing. Nothing misspelled. Not a dangling participle to be found. But no photograph, no student named Lasalle anywhere in the book."

"A town girl?" suggested the security guard, that pleasant fellow Chip, custodian of the civic pulse. "I usually, usually, customarily, preferred a town girl's outpost as my larder against the lonely weekend."

"Larder?" asked Karl.

The woman at the information desk spoke up. She was not happy. "I don't see the gravity here. We all have secret gaps in our lives. Some of us have bottomless sinkholes, black pits extending past the horned remoteness of China. Your laziness on this subject is a waste of our precious limited bodily resources. Better you employed those resources going carbon, confronting climate change, expurgating the Bible and the Koran…"

"The Kama Sutra?' offered Chip.

"…Attempt something important," continued the desk woman, rifling a hand through her raspberry hair. "Something rarified, principled, judicious, and ennobling. Why should I care about a vain man's stupid Lasalle, however celebrated he be?" She laughed to show she was kidding. Partly laughed. Her mirth wasn't of abiding issue. "I tell you sometimes I feel like ripping out my hair. Society has plummeted. Not only patients. The public is worse. This mores biz they tell me you write about, I could tell you a thing about that. Pants down to their knees, I can see their cracks! They stride right in demanding cigarettes! They vomit in our doorways, drink from the sanitizer bottles meant solely for hands. Well, goodness gracious, where do I stop? Your gap, Dr. Karl, painful though it be, is less grievous than many. I'm tempted to call it hackneyed rubbish. If real people can disappear, as they do every day, especially young boys and girls, why be surprised that someone who likely existed only in your mind should pull a vanishing act? That she's now a tiny figment stuck up there in your head should make you happy. I'd love to have a guy figment trapped in my brain. I'd work the little bastard night and day."

"A good memory isn't all it's cracked up to be," said Chip. "I'd be happy to have lived another's childhood. Uh-oh. Here comes the Cheese-Whiz brigade."

"Those fat girls are beyond hope," said the information specialist, kicking the desk chair until it went flying. They watched the chair strike a far wall, spring back as though in surprise, then careen in dizzying circles before it flopped over like something dead.

"I've always hated that chair," the woman said. "Almost as much as I dislike those fatties."

"They display admirable verve," Karl said. "Panache. Fortitude."

"What gruel! It is all pretense. Their sight sickens me. They bounce along like over-inflated balloons. They pose on street corners in obscene buttock skirts, showing red panties, pantaloons, waving syringes I know for a fact to be fake. They juggle their bazooms like lascivious whores. Yesterday, the ringleader told me she'd seen Jesus on a Starbucks couch cutting his toenails. Blasphemous idiot! She said sandals only came into existence because of the long toenails people had back then. She claimed the Romans held that long toenails were equated with success, which corresponds with the false nails and lashes women don today. How ludicrous. Those girls are so perverse, cavort so gaily, you'd think they think tomorrow they will be throwing confetti at newlyweds. Stop shaking your heads. I'm aware I sometimes make no sense."

"Illusion can be dandy," Karl said.

"I don't wish to personally engage with these issues," said Chip. He paused, sighing. "However, I suppose our friend here is right in thinking it's all a ruse. Clever, though. Antics obscure, perhaps replace, the pain. Nothing wrong with a good masquerade. They were arrested, you know. Police thought they were drunk. Drugged. A public hazard. Turned out they were clean. No booze, no drugs, nothing. They don't come near fatty foods. Actually, they've shed a bucket-load of pounds. Isn't that so, professor?"

Karl, trying to compose himself—a banana Popsicle might help—thought he might finally be beginning to understand Arendt's "banal" shtick.

Karl's sleep was not without interruption. In the dream a great winged bird announced he had a visitor waiting by his bed. "But I am in my bed," Karl said. The visitor turned out to be his father spun anew from ashes, and unrecognizable. His father, dead, had more to say than when alive. "They don't let us have beds where I am," he confessed in a stately, becalmed voice not his own. "They heave us all into enormous piles, in some kind of flood plain. You spend the whole of your death attempting to scramble free. Just when you think you've made it, along comes the flood to sweep you back again. It's like that Sisyphus story, the Camus version, I believe, that terrified you as a kid, imparting a notion of the futility of all human endeavour. Or it's more like your mother, daily, routinely, sweeping away the clutter, let's call it debris, we earnestly deposit every waking and sleeping second of our lives. Flesh flakes and dust demons, scaly detritus. Such as that. It accumulates even in a vacuum. It's a big headache for your astronauts."

"I have no astronauts," Karl said, at the same time reminding himself he was still asleep.

"Your mother sang as she swept, her way of bestowing joy onto the grim spectacle, and often, let's say, transgendering—if you'll forgive the word—our affairs into a recognizable paradise. Given your plateau achieved as a noted historian, I expect you recall the melody and lyrics of every song. 'Little Girl Blue,' what a spectacularly emotional song! Joe Johnson. Janis Joplin, Chet Baker, she could do them all. And clean that shack! My God! This was before your time but I laboured relentlessly, through forlorn years, building that shack."

Shack?

"A log cabin. Yours was a small side room containing an oak barrel utilized as a bathtub. That barrel had running water, hot in winter, cold in summer. We all bathed together, water being precious."

Karl was alarmed; his eyes, previously locked tight, now snapped open. "I don't remember any of that. Why are you here?"

"Here? The eternal question, Where is here? Those chubbies who so fascinate you are onto something with that future business. Never mind that Faulkner verity, the past isn't, etc. Why? How would I know? Some rank bastard scattered my ashes throughout the realm. Ashes, I ask you! Can that possibly make any sense? No? Well, the alternatives are gruesome, in any event. I'm going now. Lots of depots to hit and never enough time."

Karl felt he wasn't replete. "Lost my pep," dribbled from his lips in a deliberate mumble. "Talking to yourself does not always signify a fraught psyche," he heard someone say. A lone pajama-clad body passing along the darkened hall.

Something was missing in his perception of a sustainable reality. His response in earlier times, fame a wearisome shadow, was to find himself by losing himself in ancient *mores*. In "ethica," "ethology," "the Mores." In folklore, to put it another way. Dear old Prof. Winter, his Yale mentor, had properly warned that "if one is liable to be shocked by *any* folkways, he ought not to study folkways at all." The professor would likely shrug at the current folkways: a gun for every citizen, the war on women, mass annihilation, mass hysteria, celebrity worship, rising waters, becrazed evangelicals, a liberal conscience assailed—the mores as avaricious vultures ever circling. In Deep-in-the-Heart-Of this week they executed by lethal injection this year's one thousandth person. An elite legislative posse was studying why so few were women and children.

"Homer was blind, Beethoven deaf, Maupassant syphilitic, Monet a shrieker. Jesus a wilderness freak!" This the ramrod obese one shouted at Karl. "Virginia Poe, like Lady Gaga, is my ideal. What do you make of them apples, Dr. Dipshit Hotshot Historian?" She was

conveying a crippled arm, it perhaps an injury intentionally delivered by experts.

"I slipped on a Slurpee, you poop," she said. "Say!
My Daddy, a waste management aficionado, claims that
women err in believing men prefer the big-titty girl. I
mean real bazookas. He says most men want the plum
size. The Tea Cup Nellie, he calls them. How's a girl
to know? What's the historical view? Mores, that's of
Latin derivation. I've checked you out, Dr. Pulitzer-
nominated Shit. Is there a willie relationship in this titty
crap?"

"What is your real name?" Karl asked.

She paled. She looked truly horrified. "Janine el
Diablo," she finally said. "I'll truly fix your engine if
you ever get personal with me again. Poof. You're a
poof. Dollars to cupcakes, your big bazooka gal Lasalle
behooved the identical."

"You talk funny," Karl dared saying.

"It's blimp talk," she said, taking a swing at him with
the good arm. "I'm scooting. Deep-dish chocolate pie
awaits."

Did those obese cherubs sleep as nastily as he did?

Much later in the week Karl was summoned to the public phone. He heard his daughter's voice offer a jubilant
hello.

"I am in detox," Zulu said. "I have been here all
week. You will not believe how depraved we all are.
Voices in the head, body lice, bedbugs, bloody lips,
mangled ears and noses, that kind of thing. An aged
creature drugged to the gills told me today Matthew,
Mark, Luke, and John were like failed characters in a

Pinter play. If only they did not talk so much. That is interesting, do you not think? She might more astutely have conjectured Joyce or Beckett as Biblical scribes, in my view. Well, they were, some of us might aver. The shrinking bee population is her other obsession. She is forever shrieking, *Where will we get our honey?* I am afflicted by a poisonous radiance, but perceived in her light I am a blinding sunbeam. Daddy? Are you there? I fell off the trolley. I made a big, big splash, falling. I was truly horrendous. Like someone sleeping in her own puddle. I cruised through or gave away all my money, then came within an inch of selling myself. So now I am doing penance. I am once again undergoing the renewing process. I soon hope to achieve the vegetative state. Meanwhile, I am a little white mouse in a cage awaiting the developments accorded little white mice of addictive personality. I am dressed today in the little white playsuit addicted little white mice frequently prefer. 'What a darling playsuit!' people may say. 'But where is your sandbox, where is your little blue scoop and nice blue pail?' If we are polite and submissive, if we are good and earn the privilege, we are allowed one cigarette twice a week in what is called the Bessie Courtyard. I remember Dr. Bessie and his Bessie wife sometimes came to dinner when we lived on Wilberforce Street and you were Chair. Dr. Bessie might very well be delighted to learn your daughter is fascinatingly encamped in the citadel bearing his name. He was always a gentle, generous soul, is that not so? He liked clipping my chin. I once heard his Bessie wife whispering to a seatmate, 'What awful dresses! Some nice woman should take these dreary girls in hand.' Oh, rot, Daddy! Are you there? Three faux-gold benches depicting charging lions uplift the Bessie Courtyard, each saying in faded script Dr. Pepper 10, 2, and 4. Would not we all die? When I get my release I fully intend to sneak into your environs that unerring cognac you crave. I guarantee you an unblemished seal. Your Zulu is desperate for a bath, a manicure and pedicure and a hair stylist who practises her trade demonically. They are clairvoyant, those stylists, they see through to heaven, like those village smithies you liked dotting your literary landscape. 'Blond streaks to lighten your face, give credence to those sexy hips!' they like to say. You cannot possibly know what such coddling means to a daughter low in spirit as a freight car derailed. Not now, I mean, now I'm high and dry, sailing over the treetops of a roofless world. Do you remember the Man in my Life? The Nowhere Man? Ask him where he has been and he says Nowhere. It must be a wonderful place, that Nowhere. All my beaus went there. By the way, why I am calling, how is that amnesia of yours coming along? Is it in overdrive? Is it a four-gear or five-gear model, pedal to the floor? Will you buy me a new automobile if I remain good? My vintage DeSoto died of a heart attack. Spots on the lungs, cardiovascular disassociation, hardened arteries, malady of that ilk. That DeSoto you gave me on my sixteenth was older than the thirteenth century pope, whosit, you wrote your first book about. Celestine V, that is the name. The hermit pope who perished from a nail driven through his head. Am I refreshing your brain? Did the nail arrive while old Celestine was alive or was it implanted during one of his endless reburials? Such was your quandary. I recall my excitement upon discovering a full signature of pages where you assumed the point of view of the nail. Gertrude Stein could not have done better. Those silver coffins stolen over and over, then his remains usurped in the bargain. I memorized that book, you will recall, reciting it to pianola accompaniment and the clink of after-dinner drinks. I believe you were hospitalized when not long ago Celestine's remains were discovered beneath Abruzzo earthquake rubble. The nail still intact. Oh, Lord, those popes! I wonder if you recall the lovely poem you wrote for me when I was six, about a tribe in Paraguay, the Kadiveo and their cousins the Guykurus, whose women spent nearly their entire fertile lives on horseback so as to hinder the conception of children. It does not work, you told me; the riding, not the poem. Gee, I loved to the moon that poem. An AB AB rhyme scheme, fluid in the middle. Free verse, that captive bird released, orphaned to the wild, you explained. But Daddy? Are you there? Are you hanging in? The sanguine why behind this call has pertinence to that woman you call Ishmael—Lasalle, I mean. Is—*forgive me!*—is she my true mother? Is she? Would she have loved me?"

Often now when Karl reflected on this troubled daughter, one of three uncanny spirits haunting the universe, he visualized a solitary carrier pigeon, intent and disciplined, feathers tattered, combatting high peaks and baffling winds, thinking, in concert with every flash of star, "Ah, the mystery."

All three were tightly packed as mangoes, and twice as slippery.

Long, long ago, when this trinity still were children and it was this one's birthday, they had sat down to a candlelit dinner in a sunken garden somewhere in the south of France. At their insistence, sardines in olive oil, saltines, and canned pork and beans the fare. *Gifts for you, my lovely girls!* Each still wore, on thin silver chains, the tiny pendants around their necks. A fifth party had been present, surely. Lasalle?

"I look forward greedily to the simple life," said the birthday girl, "though I waft a fragrant perfume."

The sun waned. Throughout the day it waned and waned. It knew not what else to do. Karl thought of it as a yearning sun, wanting to go where suns never had ventured before. It wanted to bed the moon but the moon only turned the cold shoulder. Karl's eyelids became sticky, looking at that amazing sun. He requested permission to limp down to that establishment where one could secure alcoholic nourishment. In rather strident terms the request was denied. That privilege requires five stars, he was told. You have barely scratched the board.

The board, in any case, was constantly being defaced. It was a sphinx of obscenity defining a mores peculiar to the time and place.

Karl spent many hours observing the vista-deprived window. Each day something new was to be seen sliding down the glass—grapefruit remains, oatmeal, yogurt. Animal entrails. Someone had attempted painting on the window a green landscape in which sat a dwarfed cabin, smoke billowing from the chimney, but the glass rejected this initiative. An edict was circulated, giving rise to heart-rending depression among staff and patient alike: the obese girls had been separated, shipped off to undisclosed wings.

Hunger strikes were predicted. Waterboarding threatened.

TRADING WITH MEXICO

AFTER THE SECOND young man was stabbed, a delegation of officials from the Municipal Office arrived at the señora's door to inform her that such acts would no longer be tolerated. The señora greeted them with utmost civility, and they all sat out among the bougainvillaea and the potted begonias in her courtyard under a blazing sun. The señora plied the officials with tequila cocktails and delicious morsels from her kitchen, and soon enough the brains of this august delegation made the journey to more elevated planes. Scant mention was made of the stabbed boys. Laughter pervaded the hillside and everyone—from those occupying hovels by the graveyard at the crest of the hill to those in their fishing boats far out on the lake—knew the intended warning had come to nothing.

When the officials stumbled away late in the afternoon, they delivered profuse apologies for disturbing the señora on such a beautiful day over such a trifling issue. The mayor assured her that the incidents had now been put to rest; he confirmed his hope that she would not in future be troubled by village hotheads of diminished intelligence—known agents of El Diablo—who had so little to do with their time that they could always be counted upon to make mischief for decent people.

The previous night, a young man named José Garcia Benunito had been stabbed twice in the arm and once in the shoulder while attempting to crawl through one of the señora's windows. He fled in tears of humiliation down the Avenida, the señora's knife still lodged in his shoulder and his wounds leaving a trail of blood so thick that dogs lapped at it through the night without diminishing its flow in the least. José was found at sunrise shivering under the flowering dogwood in the Plaza Principal, the hair on his head gone an impossible white, his eyes sunk deep in his head, and so near death that the priest was summoned.

Later in the day, when it seemed the young man would not after all die, dry oregano, sugar and peppered cilantro were dusted over his face to appease his wrathful ghost; henceforth, he was transported by rumbling truck the thirty twisting kilometres to the hospital of the Virgin, in San Cristóbal. There, an amazing quantity of blood was pumped into him and for three days he slept a lifeless sleep.

Upon awakening, José Garcia Benunito refused to give any explanation for how he had come by his wounds or to breathe even the whisper of a complaint; with each new entreaty of those officials ranged about his bedside his eyes rolled higher into his head and he appeared to succumb to a sleep so inaccessible some thought him comatose.

The young man's silence was an issue for the saints in heaven and not a grave concern for those officials assembled at his bedside. Everyone knew his wounds were the work of Señora Caldera. The knife taken from his shoulder was one that many in their number, including the mayor, recognized from the numerous hours they had passed in the señora's kitchen; some among them, also to include the mayor, recalled this weapon from the olden days in his and the señora's youth, when she had nightly roamed the streets in search of her restless husband. As for the present, the knife's bone handle still carried traces of dough from her fingers, and inlaid silver script in the bone handle spelled out her illustrious lineage.

The doctor assigned to José Garcia Benunito's care was an aristocratic gentleman lean as a reed and pale as a cadaver. At every opportunity he stole away to speak with the victim's parents who, understandably, were distraught one minute and enraged the next. They wanted the señora hanged and their son made well. But issues of this sort were not the good doctor's concern. What concerned him was that his hospital had already pumped oceans of blood into the victim; now they had to send away to Oaxaca for renewed shipments of the precious fluid.

All of which, as he explained to the unhappy parents, was very expensive.

At this, José Garcia Benunito's mother, a woman of known vigour, ripped open her bodice and spat at the doctor's white shoes; she yanked sweaty bills from her bosom and hurled the bundle onto the floor. Not to be outdone, the father withdrew his wallet, ripped its contents into bits, and flung the whole wad into the doctor's unrepentant face.

"Will he live?" they asked.

"He lives now," the doctor said. "More of our Virgin we may not ask."

People living on the village Avenida were furious at the knife-wielding señora. They were furious with José Garcia

Benunito for letting himself be stabbed and for bleeding all over the countryside; they were enraged at the entire Benunito family for failing to keep the boy at home that fatal night; vociferous rancour was directed at those administrators who had dealt with the señora's earlier crimes so lightly. His blood had splashed all over the Plaza Principal. And where else could one's business lead one, if not to the Plaza Principal? Where else in this poor village could one go to beg, wheedle, cavil and cajole, and still find it mandatory to pay the outrageous price for what was needed? For the stomach, for the health, for the heart, for home and hearth and the piglets in the field? One was obliged to wade through a monsoon of blood even to get to the tortilla factory, or to sit down to beans and *cerveza* in the marketplace, which itself, more than one citizen said, was half-submerged by José's terrible river of blood. Young girls and boys could no longer take their evening promenade, the old women nibble their pastries, the old men lose themselves in checkers or chess on the plaza benches. All these amusements were a thing of the past. Social life had come to an abrupt halt. God's pity, it is *El Diablo*, it is Vengeful Fate, it is unforgiveable!—So went the story. Which story of course gave rise to rein-terpretation of stories of the olden days of the señora's youth when she had drained the blood of every woman crossing her resourceful husband's path, and his backside as well, not to mention, please, the day she stormed the very brothels of Ocuro, viciously attacking a profusion of beauties as they dutifully performed, and only her cousin the governor's intervention to save her own luscious neck.

On the fourth day after José Garcia Benunito's stabbing the same cadre of officials again arrived at the señora's door. She had stabbed another boy. This time they were in no mood to savour her cocktails or to banter about with irrelevancy. Señor Donati, the village mayor, refused even to take off his hat inside the señora's house or to sit beneath her bougainvillaea in her glorious courtyard, among the trickling fountains, the flit of humming birds, the wondrous statues of the naked nymphs her vanquished husband had long ago imported from mythic lands, much to the chagrin and bewilderment of the village's own unparalleled artisans. Señor Donati waved the weapon in front of the woman's face and told her in no uncertain terms that these stabbings must cease, or soon there would not be a single young man of marriageable age left in the village. She must go down on her knees to the victims' families and scatter abject apologies at every door.

No one, he said, could sit on the plaza benches without their sandals soaking in this vileness. Every good *doña* in the village had her petticoat rimmed with this abominable blood, children splashed day and night in the many pools and eddies, tracking its evil footprints into every office, shop, and home—as did dogs, cats, goats, chickens, donkeys! In consequence of her treacherous acts, one could not buy food or sell it, or reach the *funeraria*, or the Video, or approach the police station or post office or the telephone kiosk, the bus station, or so much as imagine reaching the Church of Our Lady, which was now encircled by a veritable moat of the heinous blood.

"The situation is intolerable," he told the señora, fixing upon her his sternest gaze. "That such acts of gross abandonment could be perpetrated against the harmless, innocent, pure, and true youth of this village by anyone in a family as notable, as revered, as idolized as your own—!" He was speechless, he said. He had to sit down and wipe his brow, and wave a subordinate to hurry with a fan before the heat of the day, the strain on his heart, the señora's homicidal mania, prostrated him. "A month's solitary confinement in a confession box would be insufficient," he said. "God would twist in agony at your tale."

Señora Caldera did not receive these assaults on the honour of her house with equanimity. "Such a fuss-budgie you are," the señora told him. "A cackling hen. A small stain of blood on a pebble and you and idiots of this village spew like a volcano." The fault was not hers, she said. Fault lay with the obscene youth of the village who for months now had been besieging her doorway in displays of mad lust for her daughter. The fault for these little mishaps with her knife resided with parents who could not control their sons' insane passions, and with yourselves, she said with an elaborate weave of her limbs, your lordship the mayor included, for the lax morality permitted in this village. "I have crawled on my belly before God and such is how we see it."

The delegation quit her *casa* in a huff, and for a long time stood stomping in fury on the vacant Avenida, the mayor slashing his silver-spiked cane at one and another. The very idea! How dare she! "Here," he said, "we may boastfully claim the pyramids of Teotihuacan, the peaks of Orizaba, the red serape of the great warrior Toluco. Untold wonders to rivet the eye and terrors to strike the heart, but nowhere else in all of Mexico do we have a woman so prideful of her shame!"

But here came rushing from her house three young boys in terrible flight. And here, in chase of them, the señora in a swirl of skirts and shrieks, her bosom heaving. She had discovered, she said, in the forbidden room where she hid away her valuables against the rainy day, these boys spying on her daughter. She was this minute going to consult the finest lawyer who could be found and bring suit against the village's elected delegates, as well as against those families who had allowed their lust-crazed sons to invade her privacy. She would bring suit against the entire village, she told them, since it doubtlessly was looseness of character and lax attitudes and a pervasive immorality spread by those who attended The Video where naked *gringitas* hung about in doorways and windows for everyone to see, the teats of these Delilahs like hanging fruit from the original garden, the teeth of vampirish *El Diablos* clinging to their necks, and this a thing that went on sunrise through sunset, inflaming the youth of this village to claw themselves upon the backs of any woman walking the street, old or young, ugly or pretty. "Shame, shame!" she cried. "The sickness, the horror, *Dios Mios!*— when in a village properly governed, in a civilized society, for instance in the time of her blessed father, these same rodent boys would be at home reading prayer books, reciting the rosary, engaging themselves in honest toil."

The fatigued mayor gazed upon the señora's enraged face with utter consternation. Was His Honour the Mayor not himself married to the señora's sister? Was he not, so to speak, of the same regal family? He took it very personally that the señora seemed now to be castigating her own sister and half the village in this wide net of blame she was weaving. And her father, that rogue and bandit! To mention in public the name of this wretch of a father who had fled to the Indies with the whole of the state's treasury!

It did not suit the mayor's purposes, however, to speak to the señora on this personal level or to remind her that each Friday evening through the past two decades they and their extended families—aunts and uncles, uncles and cousins—had dined together and been enriched by each other's company.

He was perturbed and in no mood to listen to more of her nonsense, or able to accept the smallest blame for offenses that clearly were the señora's own doing. If she wanted to waste her family's resources on lawyers and worthless lawsuits, and engage the court where his own brother presided, then such folly was beyond his comprehension. His throat constricting, his brow dropping sweat, his heart a blaring trumpet, he and his entourage sought escape.

Yet at this point all activity initiated by their various presences ceased. The sky brightened. Languid whirlwinds bearing the fragrance of cinnamon spun about their shoes and caressed their nostrils and every blossom along the señora's walls deepened in hue. The delegation fell into immediate silence, expressions of beatific indolence overtaking their faces. They brushed imagined lint from their shoulders, sucked in their slack stomachs, ran black combs through thinning hair.

The señora's incomparable daughter had emerged through the wide *casa* doors into the courtyard, accompanied, so it seemed to the men, by a chorus of song from the heavens more splendid than any heard from the choir at the Church of Our Lady. This paragon stood a moment under the tallest arch, beneath a thick canopy of bougainvillaea whose blossoms unfurled, dropping their radiance upon the girl's hair and cheeks and shoulders; the mango tree's fruit ripened before their eyes, the palm and banana trees stood straighter; the very air bristled with envy. She was the most beautiful woman anyone on earth had ever seen. She had been so since birth, and every year her visage had bettered. And, now, she was nineteen.

Nineteen, and of such radiance their knees weakened.

And yet...Was she not, merely, a woman? Yes. So let's stand straighter, each said to himself. Stop this fidgeting. Only a woman.

And yet, when she spoke...

She spoke: her voice airy and playful and such a perfection of notes the men feared they would faint on the spot. She smiled prettily at each of them, all in that moment before she lifted her skirts and swept down the steps toward them, the rings of whirling dust at the men's heels abruptly lifting, reforming around the advancing señorita's slender ankles.

"Mama, why are you squabbling?" the girl asked, adding in hurried undertone remember your promise to rest in the afternoon, dear mamma, please. To the men assembled her eyes narrowed ever so infinitesimally, and the cadence of perturbation marking her speech occurred in such petite quantity they thought certainly they dreamed it: Why do you flatter me, she seemed to say, why do you humble yourselves so and make so much the big fuss, when I am but a simple girl of uncomplicated design, not unlike your own daughters?

The men leapt as one to escort the exquisite señorita to whatever divine region she might choose as her destination. The señora, too, rushed over, fussing for some seconds to secure the yellow *rebozo* more becomingly about the girl's shoulders.

The men stared inconsolably at her yellow shoes.

For her part, the señorita paid no further attention to this group's posturing; unassumingly, she pranced along to that space beneath the window where the blood of so many boys had been spilled.

"Such a lot of it," she said, clearly astonished.

The men waited by, smiling and blushing, eager to see what the girl might next say or do. Her very presence elevated their minds to such a state of rapture that they could not restrain themselves from bobbing about on their heels, emitting childish giggles.

"!" the señorita said, staring into the fomenting blood. Or was it of the wall of red blossoms she was speaking?

The men danced at each other's side, asking: What did she say? Did the beautiful señorita speak?

Exuding soft sighs, the señorita parted a little from their company, drifting over to a stand of frangipani in rich bloom, the softly-hued petals all but transparent in the brilliant sunlight. Here she stooped prettily down, scooping a bit of sandy earth into each palm.

"I don't know why," she said to the mayor, "you should want to be so rude to my poor mother."

But the mayor heard no rancour in her criticism and grinned wider.

The señorita retraced her footsteps, stood by the purling blood, and slowly let trickle a portion of sand over a tiny russet stain.

"You are all so excitable," the señorita said.

The little group seemed not to know what to do with itself. The men wrung their hands and cleared their throats, looking with chagrined expressions at their chalky shoe tops, for the señorita's extended rebuke of them was not to their credit. It confused them that the divine creature was so little concerned over the stabbings. She does not know was the mayor's privileged thought. The mad mother has kept this news from her.

They watched her bend a little and kiss both cheeks of Doña Cochisa, wielder of knives. "Rest, dear mama," the girl said, helping her mother to lower herself upon the lip of a huge clay vessel set out to catch the rain. Indeed the mother appeared overcome by the events of recent days, her hair falling over her face, her eyes floating about without lustre or anchor, looking sixty if a day, when everyone knew she was scarcely past forty.

"I am certain you exaggerate our difficulties," the señorita told the assembly. "Such alarmists, dear me!" But she paused at sight of their wounded faces, quickly lighting her own with consoling smiles.

Everyone in the group now issued exclamations of apology, although each—and most of all, the mayor— was unsure of how, specifically, his performance today had earned the girl's censure. They did not in any measure doubt, however, that the señorita's comments were warranted, and all were convinced they would be the better for receiving them and in future sleep more soundly.

The girl brushed sand from her fingers.

"Now let's have no more unhappy talk. Today we live."

The aplomb and wisdom of the señorita quite shattered the men. While she had been under their noses since the day of her birth and they had long acknowledged her perfection, it altogether astonished them that now they had also to credit her with the brains of Solomon.

The señorita allowed the mayor to take her hand and kiss it, the mayor bowing repeatedly, while wishing he had a hat that swirled more magnificently. With each bow she rewarded him with sighs of mock exasperation, adding her own dips and curtsies. Soon the whole of the delegation was doing the same, and would likely have gone on in this manner, their congregation a circus of kowtows and swirling hats in the rising dust, as if the courtesy conventions of foreign dignitaries had taken possession of their bodies—had not the señorita finally said: Enough! I am dizzy! What shall I do with you? You are so like children!"

The men laughed and poked elbows into each other's ribs, so extravagantly resourceful, so complete in their nature did they now feel; so relieved that the pestilence had been put to earth; so fully certain that the amazing señorita had enshrined within her enchanting figure the power to forgive them the whole of their churlish nature.

"I believe mother now intends to invite you into the *casa* for more of her relaxing cocktails," the señorita said.

Señora Caldera obviously had no such ambition; she was not listening. A stream flowed near the house; she crouched there, running her fingers through the clear water. She seemed intent on capturing as many of the silver fishes as could be carried in her skirt. Already, it could be assumed, although with each attempt to snare them these fish eluded her, she saw these tiny fish dipped in a batter of masa and eggs baked in a bed of jalapeño pepper sauce and rushed to the table. No other village sauce—or mole, or chili rellenos, or any other dish they could mention—was the match of this madwoman's, that much they would give her.

"Mama?"

The señora looked up, startled. For a moment her body swayed dangerously over the water; she appeared, to everyone's eyes, not to know where she was. Her eyes swam. Spittle clung to her lower lip, looking exactly like a green folded worm. The daughter quickly wiped away this blemish.

Mayor Donati, for one, was troubled. The stabbing of the village's young men he had regarded as a matter of transitory significance—the stink would blow over—unrelated to the señora's ancient proclivity toward the disordered mind. If he dared state it in those terms. The acts she had routinely perpetrated in those days—such as chasing her laughing husband through the streets while waving sticks, knives, sometimes her departed father's rusted pistol—had been thought in those days to be dictated by the folly of youth, by the alien mixing of unnatural bloodlines, by betrayal and the infamy of rank passions of the heart when *El Diablo* on the one hand and *Mal de Ojo*, the Evil Eye, on the other rule that quarter. With this in mind, when the señora's husband was found dead in the street, few in the village had considered retribution for the señora's transgression either desirable or necessary. Compare her one sin with that randy devil's many, people said. Fate composes certain events. Fate writes the script and its designates, imprimaturs and legatees are powerless to swim against its course. Have pity on the woman. His body now rots in the tomb, but we are safe. The stars have their alignments, the universe its configurations, over which Fate and God preside, one and the same autocratic being, this Fate sometimes requiring your signature on the dotted line. As it is written, so shall it be. Why then trivialize the woman's deed with the cheap pursuit of justice? Why go to the trouble? Justice is but a dream and our lives are the proof. If fate has decreed it, then let fate sing out its full measure. If she is guilty, and who may doubt it, that divinity which resides in the heavens in its own good time will find its revenge.

It startled Señor Donati, therefore, to see for the first time the degree to which his friend the señora had succumbed to the dotage of old age, the vinegar of unreason; her skin was sallow, lined as a raked field; these old clothes draping her body had been better put about the tiles for dogs to sleep upon. A stranger would take her to be the beautiful señorita's grandmother. It made his hands shake to realize fate's hand could catapult one so swiftly; it worried him that the next time he looked in a mirror the same enslavement to time's ordeals would be visible in his own features.

"Mama?"

"Whatever am I thinking?" Doña Cochisa said at last, rising, astoundingly enough, with full agility. Restored. It was some trick of the light, his excellency the mayor decided. She was herself again; still the tigress.

"These gentlemen require fortification," the daughter said.

As the group threaded through the courtyard's lush garden, the señorita took the mayor's arm, allowing the others to drift on ahead. She seemed struck suddenly by a heightened mood, fitful one minute and in clouds the next; a deep blush coloured her face. With your permission, señor. You will permit me the favour of detaining you a moment? Of course, señorita. The pleasure is mine. With no little flightiness of manner she asked the mayor whether by chance or intuition he possessed the latest news concerning the fate of José Garcia Benunito. The mayor flinched at the long nails gouging his arms.

"He lives?" the girl asked. "He is not suffering? You have seen him?"

"Do you know this young man?"

"Distantly. As one knows a constellation."

The mayor could not believe his ears. She was lying. "Answer, please."

The mayor confessed that the boy's behaviour was most peculiar. "He appears to be afflicted with a perverse malady whereby whenever one questions him his mind diverts itself into inaccessible coma."

The señorita was not the least bit distressed or surprised. "But that's José!" she laughed. "I have not extracted a single sensible remark from him since we played together as children!" For all of the insult this description conveyed, she appeared delighted. She flung herself helplessly about, giggling and blushing, hiding her face in her hands when the astonished mayor sought to examine her more closely.

The mayor, no fool, with numerous daughters of his own, glimpsed in this juvenile behaviour the girl's true feelings. *Amor.* Everywhere one looked there was love. His own daughters were afflicted by the malady, as with mosquito bites: they pined, they screamed, they sulked.

The two halted and sat side-by-side on a tile bench decorated—long ago when the *doña's casa* had been a happier place—with the famous flying birds from the ceramica in Delores Hidalgo. He himself, at his own *casa*, possessed tiles much like these, painted by children scarcely old enough to walk, but inspired when it came to depicting birds, flowers, the skulls of the dead.

"You are on friendly terms, then, with José Garcia Benunito?"

The girl's fingers explored her sleeves, her eyes darting about in search of possible eavesdroppers, now encouraging the mayor please to drop his voice, to speak in whispers, to breathe word of their little talk to no one, least of all her mother.

"Oh, yes! I have been on friendly terms with them all, but mother has stabbed every single one regardless."

"But this José Garcia Benunito, who has come to our village a poor brainless orphan from the wilds of Chiapas, he is your favourite?"

"I see his face even when reciting my rosary. Perhaps especially then."

"But he was coming through your window!"

"Was he? How remarkable. Not my window, surely!"

Once the mayor was past his shock at the irreverent nature of this confession, he patted her knee and kissed her brow paternally.

She clutched his suit coat, twisting about so that her lips could utter more secrets into his ear.

"We have been secretly betrothed since the time of the tornado," she said.

The mayor had no memory of a tornado. Perhaps over the mountain, in Santa Ocuro where the gods and the earth's inhabitants were at constant war, but not here in this forgotten place.

She pressed her lips closer.

"I have not been a virgin since the tornado."

The mayor drew back, quite unsettled, indeed alarmed, by this revelation. He was not a priest; she should not be telling him these things. All the same, he was interested.

"This tornado, my child, when did it occur?"

"The year I was twelve."

"Dios mios!"

"José was twelve also. A mere boy, but still I loved him. The sky that day was filled with living beasts, with tree and tree limb, and the very roof tiles of this *casa*. It was hilarious."

The mayor understood now. She was joking. He patted her hands, kissed her brow: such an enchantress. So much the dreamer.

The tinkle of glasses, volleys of laughter, floated their way. They heard running footsteps and cries of jubilation. A clerk from Municipal Water appeared beneath an arch strung with lilac, gesturing wildly, his rear end wagging like an excited salamander. "The señora has promised no further murder," he said. "In return, she has extracted from me, in your name, one free truckload of water during the dry season."

Toward sunset the entire village was invaded by thousands of white birds. They descended upon Avenida de la mil Lunas, where their red beaks pecked the crimson stones clean of every stain. With the coming of night, their roosting embraced every inch of the señora's roof, trees, and walls, turning the night sky above the *casa* as bright as the Video windows, their dove-like sounds furring the air.

That evening a letter was brought to the señora's *casa*.

"Who writes us, mama?"

The embossed envelope was scented with a perfume Doña Cochisa, her eyes wet with rage, recognized of old. The flap bore the Benunito crest. Ages ago this same

crest had adorned every pillowcase and towel, every ser-
viette and handkerchief and tabletop and footstool in the
house. The crystal from Murano, the silver from Taxco,
even the mosquito netting over the marriage bed, even
the peacock underpants her vain husband wore, had been
so imprinted. Her dead husband had been such a boast-
ful man. The Benunito name, according to him, held a
place above all others. If God could seed the clouds to
make rain then he could spread his seed upon the earth,
and surely receive God's praise. Such dribble it was that
poured from his mouth. Such laughter when she sought
to gouge out his eyes with needles. She had burned every
object bearing the hated emblems, and would soon affect
the same upon this unpardonable letter.

"Who, mama?"

"That slut, Luchella."

"Why do you call her this bad name, mama?"

"Shush," the doña said. "Bring more candles."

The Benunito family, the letter said, wished to
announce the return of their son José to the land of
hope and charity. Soon he would again be among the
living. There was so much the humble boy would tell
of life in the underworld. There, a boy's humility, courage, and good breeding counted for nothing. Cocks the
size of elephants ruled the fire pits, dogs walked on hind
legs, donkeys brayed day and night. Mice made their
homes in each nostril. Snakes writhed on every street
corner. The poor boy's skin was raw as a slaughtered
pig's, still carrying the heat of his journey. One slipped
the spoon between his lips and the spoon melted, the
bowl danced, the letter said.

Señora Caldera read this portion of the missive with
rapt attention. She had an interest in the underworld.

Her dead husband likely would be there, strutting among the cocks and demanding his supper. She would like one day to ask the boy had he seen the Señor and did he know what were her dead husband's sleeping arrangements?

"What is it, mama?"

The señora shushed her daughter silent. Such words, she believed, were not for the innocent ears of children. She had the dear girl light more candles, and read on. A long paragraph devoted to the infamy of the boy's assassin incensed her. She had to wipe her glasses and settle a hand on her racing heart. The knife which had struck poor José was unclean, the note alleged; the contaminated blade had unleashed an infestation of maggots deep inside the wounds. The San Cristóbal doctor had favoured amputation. But a febrifuge distilled from ground bark from the almond tree, scented with papaya drippings, applied hourly, was keeping the boy cool, lucid, and handsome, although unfortunately he still lay comatose.

What rubbish, thought the señora. Everyone knew the bark of the almond tree was good for nothing. Some little prussic acid might be extracted, serviceable as a poison for the husband's porridge, but otherwise useless. The Benunitos had always been stupid.

"Who is a witch, mama?"

"Who? That slut, Luchella."

"Oh, mama!"

The señora could abide almost any subject, save that of the slut Luchella and anyone bearing the name Benunito. As young girls she and Luchella, not yet the slut, had been inseparable. At the age of twelve they had cut each other's hair and together presented their tresses to the cine manager in exchange for a month's free passes to the Delores del Rio revival. Together they had commandeered stallions grazing in a field and raced these beasts down the Avenida at full gallop, sending everyone scurrying. They had plaited each other's hair once it grew back, and forced castor oil down the throats of disobedient children in their charge. They had camped in banana fields, whispering secrets under the moon, smoked purloined cigarettes, and, coming home, had spied on neighbours undressing for the evening. Evenings, later on when they were of an age to do so without bothersome chaperones, they had strolled the Plaza Principal arm in arm, digging their elbows into each other's ribs, giggling with anxiety. Every passing boy held the potential, one day soon, of turning up naked beside them in bed. The Benunito brothers, alike as peas, caught their eyes.

Cochisa and Luchella had sewn their wedding dresses together, attentive as wrinkled grandmothers, told wicked stories about the insatiable appetite sacred to any decent marriage. Do not expect to walk, child, for the first week. Have gauze and medicines at the by. Drink buckets of kidney soup. A lubricant of lard and motor oil, applied to your crevices, will save the day. Do not expect Our Lady of the Saints to temper the wind to the shorn lamb. To thrive, see that you have your rightful time above him. Secure yourself with a firm grip of his ears. "Lay on MacDuff," as the *ingles* scribbler recommended. If he spits melon seed over your belly, before or while insinuating his piece inside you, know that you will have cross-eyed children. If you think to sleep in the arms of Hypnos after your soldiering, then know he will keep you up long and late for speechmaking in praise of his performance. Know that the expressions "pig in a pistle," "pig in a poke," "in a pig's eye," "eat a pig's ear," "pig out," "little piggy went to market," and the like all originate from behavioural practices carried on in the marital bed. If his piece lodges stiff, stubborn, and interminably inside you during the act, do not transport yourself as a pig dropped into scalding pot, but reach for your rosary beads and pray through till morning. By morning his piece will be drained and softened and easily removed by good tongs from the kitchen.

Their birthdays, even their wedding day, occurred on the same date—the one accidental, the other by design. When they married, in a joint ceremony at the Church of Our Lady, they married the same identical Benunito twins whose slim hips and black locks and slippery hands had waylaid them countless times over the years.

"Mama?"

The señora, still perusing the letter, was giving voice to a host of involuntary squawks, as though pricked by pins. The Benunito family and the unconscious boy, the letter said, would be paying a call at the señora's house tomorrow evening at seven. The coming nuptials had to be arranged. Now that Señora Caldera's knife had ruined poor José for any other woman in the village, the señora's daughter must take him for her own. Moreover—

For the next several minutes Señora Caldera peeled paint from her walls with her screams.

"Mama? Be gentle, mama!"

Moreover, there was reason to believe the youngsters already had "jumped the fence."

The señora raced from room to room, flinging open every window, as though poisonous vapours were seeping up through the tiles. "The slut!" she kept say-ing. "The contemptible hussy. It is time to murder every Benunito while they sleep!"

"Calm yourself, mama."

Then she had to slam her windows shut, because passersby in the street, seeing her there, were shouting up insane celebration, wanting to know at what time tomorrow was the party. What a joy, they said, that the village's two great families were at long last reuniting.

To clear her mind of these outrages and the letter's vile contents the señora rushed into her kitchen. She set about scouring every surface from floor to ceiling. She soaked and scrubbed every utensil, each pot and pan, and in the courtyard beat her carpets without mercy. Her daughter was set to work with a brush and pails of soapy water, cleansing the tile floors, the windows, the walls throughout the house. The señora prepared enormous cauldrons of *sopa*, of *arroz*, of *frijoles*, and patted out tortillas until the stacks reached the ceiling. *Lechuga* had to be picked and washed, *pepino*, *papas*, *tomate*, *zanahorias*; the *cebolla* peeled, *coliflor* and *espar-ragos* chopped, oceans of *salsa picante* prepared. She mouthed these words aloud, screaming. They wanted a party? She would give them a party. She sawed through the gristle of a pig and hammered flat two whole sides of veal. Puddings, custards, flan cooled on shelves while endless sheets of *pan dulce* were set to a brisk bake in her ovens. *Limon* and *lima*, *plátano* and *piña* were collected. *Langosta* and *pescado* had to be plucked from the waters, and *pollo*, *pato*, *jamón*, *chuleta*, *chorizo* secured from the market.

Señora Caldera hoped she would not have to stab the luckless boy again. If she had to do it, however, she hoped it would happen before the very eyes of his adopted mother, the slut, to whom she had not passed a civil word in nineteen years. Time warped the truth, certainly. The cart got before the cow, most assuredly. The mind was but a labyrinth of shadows, absolutely. No question the active imagination hatched the good egg and the rotten egg. Fallacy and fancy transmogrified into incontrovertible fact, naturally. Thus, on guard against those propensities, she had advanced into marriage with caution. The first time Benunito was seen smiling at another woman, she had not immediately thought she would drown herself. Nor on the second and third occasions had she dashed into the kitchen to obtain the cleaver. In the interim, she was making herself privy to a school of unimpeachable fact. Proof of these facts was not a necessity. Who needed proof when it was there every day in front of her eyes: the calumny, the hypocrisy, the betrayal. He woke up singing. Could she not from this gaiety deduce his movement and actions the previous evening? He was not a player in the cribbage tournament, as specified. He was not "working the falcon," whatever mangled glove he dangled before her eyes. He was not overseeing the new orchard planting, as testified. No, he was in Santa Ocuro with the whores, drinking pulque when not sucking red toenails.

He poked in the garden, he mended and polished tools, he repaired the roof, he constructed elaborate balconies, designed huge courtyard seats inflamed with one thousand bird tiles from Delores Hidalgo, he put in mossy pools with bubbling fountains and lilies of every hue. By donkey and his backside, he hauled in fruit-bearing trees taller than the belfry of Our Lady; he planted roses in a field large as a soccer stadium, shouting up to her from the plow he directed that if one rose could not win her heart then a thousand might calm her nerves; he led by its ears the donkey pulling the cart piled high with the plates from Puebla, the birdcages from Tzintzuntzán, the carpets from Turkey, the masks from Chiapas, the strange boxes built like cities from artists renowned in the capital. He did all this, no question, but when he was not thus engaged he was playing prince to the frenzied whores of Ocuro. He slept every night beside her under the monogramed netting and from his own deft fingers fed her slices of mango dripped with lime on a bed of greens arranged by the gods. He went to sleep in embrace of her and kissed her body in his sleep and uttered her name only. At four he was up again poking in the garden, planting trees, polishing and mending, retiling the roof, erecting the stone gates, porticos, balconies, raising the courtyard walls; digging wells, cisterns, adding hidden pipes that transported water to every room; adding new rooms, enlarging others; uprooting the earth for sunken tubs where she might bathe in full extension while regarding the heavens; adding wide windows and glass slides in the roof that showed the sky above drooping bougainvillaea; amassing a sail of bougainvillaea over the new walls, adding lilac, heather, honeysuckle, ivy; in the meanwhile filling her boudoir with a march of gowns, dresses, rebozos, perfumes, jewellery, handbags from the exclusive shops of the Zona Rosa in Mexico; importing sculptured deities, Vázquez paintings from the sixteenth century, Orozco from the twentieth, Tarascan divinities, glassware, vases shipped by his agents in Paris, in Rome, in Athens; collecting artifacts from Peru, authentic iron horsemen from Africa, cupboards from the Indies, fabrics from the Orient, shrines from Madagascar; and each morning, noon, and night ever there to feed the dripping mango into her mouth from his very own well-scrubbed hands. There to kiss her swollen belly, to recite storybook yarns of fairy and wizard, of bears that wore hats and spoke like humans, to the child kicking in her womb.

All this was subterfuge. It was illusion. All this was by way of soon making his escape to the whores awaiting him in Santa Ocuro.

One arrived at these conclusions by the application of logic, by stealth of intellect, by sound and solid reasoning.

He laughs, feeding her the mango with his own fingers and kissing her wet lips. If he laughs, it is because he is happy his time with her is nearing an end, and soon he can be reunited with the impatient, rapacious whores across the mountain.

One can read this in his eyes, can catch it in his voice as he hovers over her belly reciting the story of *El Principito*, The Little Prince, to his unborn child. How mysterious are your mother's tears, my little prince! Why does she weep, little prince?

One is not deceived by the dulcet tones, the cheerful countenance, the exuberant laughter. One hears in the soft rendition, the cocky banter; one sees the smug expression; one feels in his sweat when he touches her the powerful heat of one who is living a lie. When he strokes her, he wants her eyes sealed, which is why she keeps her eyes always open. He strokes her in the dark night, he utters her name, professes his adoration, declares his unending love, and all the while her eyes are upon him. His mouth is at her breast; her eyes are upon him. She will let him get away with nothing. He will not deceive her. She has evidence enough. It is there in his quickening pulse when he speaks the child's name, when he caresses her, when with his own fingers he slides the dripping mango between her teeth. Evidence is there in how he breathes, in how his breath can be felt on her flesh when she enters empty rooms he earlier frequented. Why then bother to sniff his collars, to root in his pockets, to track his every arrival and departure? Soon, yes, he will be with the whores in Santa Ocuro who will stride about naked in his boots, swing from chandeliers, pant with him until bedsheets drip immeasurable liquid. Santa Ocuro whores are the best in the world, of this she has no doubt, for everyone has said so since she was a swaddled child.

None of this is the fault of her husband. No, she had never thought that, even as she had chased him through the streets with knives at the ready.

The fault rests now, as it always did, with that slut Luchella.

Luchella Benunito had worked her wiles at their wedding. She had switched grooms. She had taken for herself the good brother, and pawned off on her dim best friend the lesser one.

"Mama? Mama, you should go to sleep now. Are you not tired, Mama? You are talking to yourself, mama. You will bring on your old sickness. Let me help you to bed."

"Please be quiet. I am thinking. I can think only when my hands are busy."

The señora, in her kitchen, is peeling another kilo of onions. Her eyes stream with tears, but there will be no rest for her until she has peeled a tub full, all to stuff into the mouth of that slut Luchella. To feed the army of Benunitos who have invited themselves for the morrow. She will work through the night, and when she is done she will look to see whether eternity will invite her to sit at its table.

"We must prepare for our visitors. The Caldera family has always prided itself on its hospitalilty."

"Yes, mama."

"Iron the tablecloths. Polish the silver."

"Yes, mama."

"I was never sick. The trouble was with my doctors, who prescribed impractical cures."

"Yes, mama."

"It was a mistake."

"What was a mistake, my adored mother?"

"It was your father's doing."

"What was, mama?"

"My time in the asylum."

"!"

"But I escaped."

"!"

"I was cunning. I bribed the doctors."

"You must have dreamt this, mama."

"Then I took the train across the mountain. The suitcase of knives was almost more than I could carry."

"A dream, my sweetest mother."

"I left that house a shambles. Blood flowed like a river. But your father was not present. He had been seen riding a bicycle through the market. So I went to the market. It is impossible to ride a bicycle through the Ocuro market."

"Shall I call the doctor? I believe you are sick, mama."

217

"What we must do is polish the candlesticks."

"They are polished, mama."

"And peel the onions."

"They are peeled, mama."

"Shut the doors. I feel cold wind about my neck and ankles."

"It's hot, mama."

"Do as you're told. You are not yet an independent woman."

"Yes, mama."

"There was no hurricane."

"Tornado, mama."

"Twelve-year-old girls do not ride white beds across the sky in a tornado."

"We did it, mama."

"You would have fallen off."

"We held on to each other, mama. It was this that saved us."

"When he was six years old this José shot a Chiapas man."

"Mama, mama, he was tied to a tree."

"He was hiding behind the tree. Six-year-olds like hiding behind trees."

"Tied, mama. His village massacred."

"We do not massacre people in this village."

"In Chiapas, mama. In the village called Acteal, in the municipality known as Chenalhó, in the Chiapas highlands. The state and federal governments were complicit in this attack, mama. They murdered babies."

"Who did?"

"The Red Mask."

"Leave me now."

"!"

"Marriage to a Benunito is out of the question. I was myself married to a Benunito."

"I know it, mama."

"I could not stand the name and went back to being a Caldera."

"Yes, mama."

"You have been to the house of the slut Luchella."

"You have forbidden this, mama."

"You have sat at her table."

"No, mama."

"Did you shut the windows? The doors? A cold wind is blowing around my ankles."

"I shut them, mama."

"Shoo the birds from the roof. Their cooing reminds me of…"

"Don't torment yourself, mama."

"Go away now. I prefer solitude when peeling … Where are my onions? I was cunning. My fingers were crossed when I promised an end to murder. Who did I say this to?"

"The nice man from the water department."

"Nonsense. What have I to do with water?"

Word spread through the village of the Benunito-Caldera social engagement; by daybreak a tide of the uninvited was already scurrying about in search of suitable attire. They by no means intended to miss the event.

The families of the other young men who had been attacked felt they had equal right to be present. They were resentful that the señora had not sent them formal invitations, embossed in the French manner. José Garcia Benunito was a feckless boy, and unconscious: what right did he have to the divine señorita's hand? He was not of this village. He remained a Chiapas Zapatista in his dead bones. That Benunito pair, Łuchella and Tomas the Henpecked, should have left him tied to the tree where they found him. The lovely señorita would be awash in gold once her old mother—how to say it?—*"Estirado la pata,* you dummy!"—kicked the bucket. Those Caldera people, since a time before Jesus wore shoes, had plundered every pocket. Let a peso or two dribble our way.

They summoned their wounded sons indoors and went to considerable trouble arranging their limbs in casts and slings; they taped wadding to their cheeks, made them practise their walk to achieve that demeanour appropriate for helpless cripples. In a coma, was he? Their own sons could better that. One crutch or two? Which offered the more dignified appearance? How best to sway the girl's heart, short of finding a Máscara Roja and shooting him dead?

"Roll your eyes into your head," they told these sons. "Moan."

"Stuff this root into your trousers. Pad your buttocks."

Horrific sores were grafted onto these sons' faces and bodies. Eye sockets were deepened with charcoal from the firepits, pebbles pitched into shoes, limbs twisted, grit rubbed into wounds. Cupboards were searched, vegetation scoured, and pots of dreary substances—the slime of toads, the innards of slugs, the shells of beetles—set to boil. Potions must be strung about their son's necks, along with amulets, rusting medallions, scarabs, talismans, crucifixes with real hair cut from dogs.

"Don't slouch. Stand up. Affix to your breast these skull bones. Call it the Second Coming. Think of it as a revised Day of the Dead. Zombies walk, as in the Video. Ours, after all, is a modern village."

Anyone looking at these boys would be impaled with sorrow; any decent girl, witnessing such suffering, would want immediately to succour them in bed.

"Unlike that Benunito rascal who is not a true Benunito but is Indian as we are."

"More so, as he is Chiapas born."

"Five or six years old, gun in hand, already a subsub-comandante Zapatista of the Liberacion Nacional."

"Found tied to a tree."

"Fortunately for him."

"What do you mean?"

"Otherwise he would have been slaughtered along with the others."

"I see. So the little ruffian is safely hog-tied to the tree."

"As that loudmouth Luchella and hen-pecked Tomas, on vacation, happily motor through the Chiapas mountains."

"Finding themselves in the tiny settlement, Acteal."

"Finding themselves in a massacre."

"Forty huts. Earthern floors. No electricity. No running water. No TV."

"1998."

"Fool. December '97."

"Tied to a tree. The famous Zapatista mask over his face. Armed to the teeth."

"A toy only."

"Did the Máscara Roja tie him to the tree?"

"No. They would have shot him. It was never learned who secured him to the tree. His parents were away, chased by soldiers through the highlands."

"Where they … how do you say it?"

"*Patear*, to kick. *Estirar la pata*, if informal. Kicked the bucket."

"And here arrives along the muddy village road the innocent Benunitos just as the Red Mask attacks good pacifists at their prayer meeting, likely under direct orders of our fine Presidente, the renowned Zedillo, now ensconced in what is called a chair, at Yale."

"Indicated. Not proven."

"Proved: A quarter of the village, dead. Soldiers in to hide the bodies, wash away the blood. Four pregnant women shot in the belly. Three Hernandez children shot dead, ages two, three, five. Seven in the Luna family; oldest sixty-seven, youngest eight months. Shot in the head, in the belly."

"As the Benunitos cavalierly motor the potted village lane, innocent as jaybirds on a limb."

"Three days until Christmas. Happy as can be. Likely asking each other what are all those strange explosions. Is it some local saint's day? Are they celebrating the X-Mas early? How strange it is up here."

"'The height makes us dizzy.'"

"Then to hear screams. To note a fallen body."

"There in the blink of a confused eye to contemplate what appears to be this small Zapatista child tied to a tree."

"Now known as José Benunito, all grown up and—"

"Don't say it. The annals of the living are yet to be—"

"Don't say it. Let us dress for the…"

At the Benunito house, it had been hoped that the jolts of the ride from the hospital in San Cristóbal would be sufficient to trigger the perverse boy's reunion with consciousness. This had not happened. He has ever shown himself to be a smart lad, why now is he being so difficult? I don't know, said Tomas, perhaps he is reliving that terrible day in Chiapas. I hope not, said Luchella, since that is a terrible day I relive myself every day. And will continue to, replied the husband, so long as our exalted government continues to insist that little boy tied to the tree shot a Máscara Roja during their siege of the village. Some of those criminal Rojas, remarked the wife, now serving time in prison—a slap on the wrist, interrupted Tomas. Every year they renew the insane charge, continued Luchella, her eyes burning, and into the courts scurry a legion of scandalous lawyers. Yes, said Tomas, it is ridiculous, and our own legion has taken our every peso to combat the insanity, but what can we do except— Yes, except carry on, concluded Luchella, although I for one could certainly breathe easier if this snapdragon loverboy would open his eyes. I am told loverboys require oodles of sleep, said Tomas. How otherwise could they be loverboys when arrives the hurricane? A tornado, dear one, said Luchella with a smile. But yes, you would have to be told, being yourself such a slouch on the couch, such a sad sack in the sack, a limp dick sinking into quicksand, to quote the Video. A clown beneath your gown, summarized the husband. A quickie for your chickie? said Luchella, always gifted the last word.

The snapdragon was laid out now in sweaty pyjamas on the good mattress brought into the kitchen. Barely breathing. The cadaverous doctor, Luchella Benunito claimed, had given him insufficient blood. A tanker truck should have brought in more from San Cristóbal. Her family had always been profuse drippers. Her mother, when Luchella was a child, had countless times sat her down, forgotten, in a far corner with a bucket beneath her nose.

Candles flickered in glass vials beneath the Virgin, which in this house they secretly called Virginia.

The boy lived. More of Virginia you could not ask.

"They have loved each other since childhood," Luchella told her husband. "Remember the tornado? It is destined they should wed. Ignore the señora's bitterness. She is insane, insipid, a cow. I have known it since the day she cut off all her hair for a ticket to the memorable classic *The Man Who Preferred His Donkey*. She was wild about that film. She cannot forgive us that your brother died before you, that her husband went to Santa Ocuro to wrestle with whores."

Tomas tightened his lips. His twin brother's crimes had never been proved. What one brother felt the other felt also. He had never himself had an interest in the whores of Santa Ocuro. Therefore, his brother was innocent. People should cease casting these stones.

"I cast what I wish," Luchella said. "Hoist our son onto the table. I sink or swim, as fate leads me. Cochisa was ever the sinker. She wanted to die a virgin, like nuns in a rainforest. The first time your brother touched her knee, she struck a rock against his head. Always she kept the same rock under her bed."

"Both of you rode brooms. You still do."

"Ha-ha. Very funny. Did I not say hoist him?"

"Luchella the Magnificent, you were called."

"By street urchins and randy boys such as yourself. Not in my own house."

"Whereas she was Cochisa the chinchilla, because of her mean little teeth."

"Ha-ha. Yet your brother must in the beginning have loved her."

"He never ceased loving her. Her antics amused him. They demonstrated, he said, her strong personality."

"Your brother Tomasino was attracted by her aura of doom. She was fated to die upon a rocky hillside, picked apart by vultures, but he would save her for the rainforest."

"She was worse after Vienna."

"Who would not be?"

"It is a blessing that the beautiful daughter escaped the curse. Intelligent, and of lofty nature in the bargain."

"Well. Aside from that tornado business."

"It's a metaphor, Tomas. You must cease taking everything so literally."

"Are you a metaphor?"

"Most certainly."

"Ha. That's why my hands go through your body when I straddle you in the dark."

"Try me in good light. Now stop being foolish and hoist our little stallion, please."

Tomas hoisted José Garcia Benunito on his shoulders like a sack of feed. He dumped the boy's dead weight onto the kitchen table, even as Luchella was scurrying to clear that table of jugs, gourds, and glass jars in which countless roots were seeking new life in water. Black ants streamed train-like across the floor. Luchella sprayed them with kitchen detergent and they scattered. The ants would carry away the house, if allowed.

"Lubricate his lips with mint," Luchella said. "Rinse his mouth with *cannelle*. Rub eyebright over his lids."

"Why?"

"To give the appearance of seeing. To endow him with the fourth sight."

"What nonsense."

"Careful what you say. We must walk on eggs."

"Why? "

"It is our nature."

The poor boy had not opened his eyes in thirty-six hours. He had not spoken. His tongue was clotted, his flesh purple. The cadaverous doctor had said the boy might well remain in this comatose state through eternity.

Luchella gave José's limp form a fine sponge bath in icy water, berating him the while. Explaining what she expected of him this evening at the señora's party. "It is in your honour," she told him. "Be natural. Make light of your wounds. Compliment the señora on her every move. Eat everything. Avoid looking into her eyes. She is wicked as a cat. Trust nothing she says. Her heart is as the garlic bulb, the ginger root: eternally deformed. She is bound to see in you something that offends her. She will absurdly think you resemble too much her dead husband. Grow a moustache."

She scented his body with a wash of cloves. She sponged *vainilla pura*, from Papantla in Jalisco, about his genitalia. She wondered at the sense of applying colour to his blackened toenails.

"Turn him."

Tomas flipped the body, giving an affectionate smack to the boy's rump.

Without pause, Luchella continued her massage: kneading, pounding, pressing. She twisted an ear, demanding that he listen to her, that he attune himself to the annals of fruitful love. "The comatose state is no excuse for a boy's disobedience," she said. "Do as your rogue father did me. Get the beautiful señorita alone and stick your tongue into her mouth. Nibble her ears and press your manhood against her at every embrace, although, of course, accidentally. Take her hand and while gesticulating at the stars have her hand mistakenly brush you there. Make her aware of the bargain she is getting, while at the same time stammering elegant apology. Your courtesies will impress her, as, at the same time they melt her resistance. This is an approach much worthwhile and a strategy practiced worldwide, in the same way that she ensures her breasts are always in the picture and the curve of her hip shown to best advantage by the well placed hand or the leg exposed by an invented wind. Nature will turn green with envy, as now you stroll with your beloved in the señora's garden. Press grapes between her lips, gathered by your own hand from the señora's vines. Equate the sweetness of her lips with the flavour of the red cherry, the plum, the peach, and her scent with the scent of a single rose in the señora's rose garden—planted, I should say, down to its every last thorn by the sainted brother of your father. But I digress. Ring your sweetheart within an island of lavish compliment. Let your every breath convince her that no one on earth is more desirable, beautiful, intelligent, wise, considerate. Her moral equal. Quote into her ears our Pablo Neruda: 'Darling, I hunger for your hot heart like a puma in the barren wilderness.' When kissing her neck wriggle your lips in a dialect of the Mayan Tzotzil, which will make her knees knock together and her toes tingle. Refer to native deities residing beneath the mountains, who kick up their heels, causing thunder. Execute the Chiapas dance of the Pig's Head, which brings water to a boil. Politely explain the intricacies of maize agriculture. If she gets snooty, call her a mean ladino while wrestling her to earth. Be funny without being stupid; women like that. Extol the virtues of the sunrise and the sunset and of your immediate family. Promise her an eternity of fulfilment each and every evening. Succinctly, then: be a Benunito. Be the young lover-stallion your father is."

José Garcia Benunito did not respond to these urgings. His mother, an ear to his chest, could hear nothing.

"Light more candles," she told the father. "Pray more earnestly to our Virginia."

"Our Virginia," Tomas said, "could benefit from a firm smack on her buttocks."

"She has none. But don't let that stop you."

Breathing deeply, Tomas had his eyes fixed on his wife, the chatterbox. On the hand poised at her hip, on the sweat ringing her neck and dripping slowly down her cleavage. Her descriptions of the wooing process had excited him.

"Move aside then," Luchella said. "Worthless man. If you do not ask, you do not receive. If you not demand, our Virginia does not notice."

She installed a mirror under the boy's nostrils. The resulting vapour was timid. But he had always been a light breather. Even if her poor son never reopened his eyes and if the looking glass had to be beneath his nostrils for one to know he lived, Luchella had every intention of seeing him wed to the beloved señorita. True love must assail every barricade. One must pursue it as the hunting dog pursues the quail's scent, as the…hot heart tracks the…tracks the puma. But she had already misquoted Neruda, no need to do so again. Not for nothing had José and his glorious chosen one endured the tornado. If the wedding did not come to pass she would never feel secure in God's heaven.

She heard the truck engine ignite in the yard and flew to the window. The machine was shuddering, gasping, emitting blue explosions front and rear; the wire-held doors fluttered like broken wings. It was no shame being poor; what a pity, though, that every cent of the Benunito riches had gone to her husband's brother, older by twenty-six minutes, and, thence, to the witch Cachisa Caldera.

"Where are you going, Benunito?" she called.

Her husband sat bunched under the wheel, grinning like a pet pig.

"To Santa Ocuro."

"Why?"

"To wrestle with sluts."

"Ha, ha," she said. "Take tons of money, otherwise even the most plump fatso will not have you."

Tomas, on his way to Santa Ocuro, ran the mountain roads at full speed, careful to keep his feet from going through gaping holes beneath the pedals as he harangued the multitude of Virginias quivering like hula girls on red velvet beneath the windshield. It had occurred to him that Señora Caldera's party must have music. Without music, there would be no dancing. Without dancing, Luchella would not have the best of times. He meant to return with the famous quintet, Five Blind Whores, playing that minute on the car radio; if all went well he would have just enough time to trim his mustache. To wipe a cloth under his arms and put on a fresh shirt.

Beep-beep!

He loved driving.

The beautiful señorita roamed disconsolately from room to room in her mother's house. Walls and floors shone; flowers crowned every teacup and goblet. Lamps were lit. Candles in a hundred candleabra, also. The clock from ancient Persia ticked in time with its sister clock from Babylonia. The hoopoe birds, long consigned to darkness, were back in place, newly polished, on the black onyx table. A golden bejewelled shoe, said to have adorned the foot of Bonaparte's Joséphine, was again occupying a pedestal. The Portrait Gallery, a trove of Caldera mayors, governors, presidents, and plain thieves who mostly had fled to foreign nations obligingly having no extradition treaty with this maligned land of sea and sun—the Hall of Shame, as it was known locally—had been dusted. In a dozen mirrors virgins small as thimbles or tall as herself examined her movements with bereft eyes. They were crying tonight for José Garcia Benunito and for her lost papa, reigning in Hades. So her mama said. The señora, last night, refusing bed to slice more onions, had seen him there amid the flames, cracking the whip while exhorting his minions, all of them formerly whores in Santa Ocuro, to more furious labour. "He isn't suffering," she said. "He rules the deepest pits and repents nothing. He feeds on hot coals and has slaves who fulfill every command. He is having himself a merry time. Our Church is in error. In that flaming cauldron incessant lust presides. Round-the-clock activity yet never orgasmo, only the memory."

"Oh, mama, how you talk!"

The Virgins were crying for her mama. To antagonize Luchella Benunito—to flood her with guilt, although it wouldn't—her mother had placed on display every photograph of her dead husband that could be found. Altars to his memory were arranged in every room. This was gruelling to the señorita because in all of them he looked exactly like Luchella's kindly Tomas. The Benunito families bore nothing but identical children. Sisters and brothers were the spitting image of each other, though younger or older. This characteristic apparently existed of old. Looking at a Benunito was like looking at stars in the heavens: every Benunito was a copy of every other Benunito, regardless of how scattered the tribe. Nor were the Benunitos the kind to stay at home; they were everywhere, busy making more Benunitos. In the state of Chihuahua, it was said, an entire town of forty thousand, growing rapidly, named Benunitojuatenea, and said further to be a paradise on earth, was populated by nothing but Benunitos. They drove automobiles named Benunito down Avenidas named Benunito, picnicked in Benunito Park, worked in companies, shops, and factories bearing such names as Benunito Ceramica, Benunito Zapateria, Benunito Petroleum.

According to the girl's research in the *biblioteca*, and her readings of her father's books which had escaped mother's torch, Poland, until the Nazis disposed of so many, had long been a refuge for Benunitos. The early Roman city Benevento, in southern Italy, existed as another corruption, its founder one Francesca Valpochelli Benunito, a woman of extraordinary ability who earlier had discovered that by combining pozzuolana, lime, stones and tuff with water she could create the useful material now known as concrete. The Benin River and Benin City on that river in Africa were named after a thirteenth-century explorer bearing the name Benunito. The fifteenth-century Italian noble family Bentivoglio came falsely by that appellation when

Pope Julius II erred in his spelling. Similarly, the Bay of Bengal by rights should today be known as the Bay of Benunito. An idiom widely employed by youth in her own village, and often heard from actors' mouths in the Video—'*neat-o!*'—was an obvious derivation of the hallowed name. It was a Benunito who sat beside Presidente Vicente Guerrero when in 1829 he signed the famous document ending slavery in the nation decades before the marauding *norteamericanos* so much as thought about it.

The first recorded presence of the Benunito family in Mexico and the Americas dated from the 16th century when a *bandito* revolutionary known as Benito Benunito rose from his peonage roots to storm the hated *obrajes*, textile factories imposed upon the population by the Spaniards, where slave labour was employed and entire families worked from dawn 'til dawn 'til another dawn without food or water.

Her own family, while younger, was equally illustrious. The Calderans had over and over amassed fortunes in lands and holdings, but over and over these had been squandered by natural resolve: they had been lost in wars and revolts, lost by papal edict, lost through land reform movements, through treaty and the perdition of time, with finally nothing left—until Cochisa married her father and became, briefly, a Benunito.

The *conquistadores* were first to trample the Caldera name, then the *gachupín* did it, then the creoles, then Santa Anna's troops, then the *ingles* President Polk through the infamous Treaty of Guadalupe Hidalgo whereby two-fifths of her country were ceded to *los Estados Unidos*, and one-hundred percent of the ten-thousand acre Caldera cattle land along the Rio

Grande. Her great-grandmother, so family lore had it, for years had been a spy-courtesan in the capital, her clientele consisting solely of the thousands of gringo soldiers at that time occupying the city, among them— to the family's great distress—the commander savage General Quitman, who had stormed Chapultepec and won California for President Polk in 1847.

Heaven's mercy: so much history for a little girl of three or four to absorb! But her Benunito father had insisted. "Off to the *biblioteca* with us!" he would shout of a morning, in rain and thunder no less, and here would clop the donkey Elmo leading the cart. "Education first!" father would shout, while busily returning the stupid donkey to its traces, busily turning the donkey in one direction and another because Elmo, like himself, wanted to go in every direction at once. "You can neither read nor write," he would say, cart wheels clattering round and round, their little father and daughter world in orbit, "but let that be not a detriment to your learning. The marvels of the age await us and one day you will hear blind girls sing, the heavens relent, and know my reputed traffic with the distinguished whores of Santa Ocuro is hogswill nourished by lunacy! The overwrought mind is a fertile field fertilized daily by curious logic, but even so, even so, my sweet petunia, I command you ever to love and respect your tortured mother as she suffers every sin devised, practised by, and inflicted upon her by our saints occupying heaven."

"And love, no less," he would say, "your adoring father, together with this stubborn donkey, for it was between the shuttered ears of one of this ass's ancestors that originated the universe's first good story. I refer of course to the *Satyricon* of Petronius, about A.D 50, and *The Golden Ass* of Apuleius, A.D. 150, more or less. Bone up, I say, on your history." Papa taught her much: why hens lay eggs. Why when unhappy they will not, why when sacral harlotry brought money into the temples harlotry was considered good, and bad when it did not; why rice is thought by some, for instance, the Javanese, to possess a soul while the potato does not; what was intended when the blood of Abel shrieked unto God from rocky ground; when not in a rut, the mores of a place is ever the turning wheel; what is commonplace today will tomorrow be an abomination; sacred dogmas are ground underfoot, and none too swiftly, if you ask me. All is ephemeral, including ourselves; let that be your guide.

He was a grand talker, her papa. Even as her mother, brandishing knives, chased him through swollen creeks, he was shouting philosophy, or verse, or enthusiasm, or history back at her.

In more recent times, the *Cristeros* intervened in her family's history when a *Cristero* fanatic, disliking a kinsman's *mestizo* face and shouting *Viva Cristo Rey!*—Long live Christ the King—put a bullet into his heart.

The local museum, with meagre holdings of any value, had on its walls the first photograph of the village, taken by the Indian boy her great-grandmother brought home from Mexico as alleged husband after the war. The army had been sent to the region to defend the state against Benunito-led reformers intent on secularizing church property, reducing the atrocities perpetrated by the army, and ending oligarchic rule.

The boy-husband this ancestor returned with could not read or write and had no fondness for the wearing of shoes or, for that matter, much apparel of any kind. When he was an old man, he still liked lazing about in a hammock, completely naked. His ancestors, he said, had laboured beneath the earth for a million years, then had climbed from beneath the earth on a frayed rope dropped to them by the gods Yes and No. The rope broke, and thousands of his people tumbled back inside the Deep, where he supposed they still resided, and where, in fact, a hundred other races likewise to this day persevered. Those who did not fall continued in the journey, which in his people's lore became known as the Journey of Ten Thousand Years. The Journey of Ten Thousand Years was called that, he said, because for most of his people it was not yet over. Even today, his people were miles beneath the earth, still climbing, still holding on, still grappling with rock and shale and suffering the deadly pestilence of the great gods Yes and No. Yes and No continued from time to time to dangle the frayed rope, even sometimes agreed to agree and amid lavish promise dangled what turned out to be an invisible rope, but his people had become wary, or wise, or cynical, and refused now to touch the rope or even to acknowledge its presence. She could remember, as a child of six or seven, one day sleeping with this naked gnarled old wizard in the hammock. A great storm ruptured the blue summer sky and lightning bolts waltzed over their heads like gypsy hordes excited by thought of a better life. She had woke the old man up, having seen with her peculiar infant powers that such a bolt was in aim for that very tree to which their hammock was tied. But the old man had lost full agility and one foot was trapped by the hammock when the lightning bolt streaked by their eyes to split the tree in half. The tree and its hammock, together with the very grasses within which they stood, burst into instant flames.

José Garcia Benunito, on some errand when the storm broke, had taken refuge at their gate; it was he, newly arrived from Chiapas and remarkable only for being known as The Boy Who Was Tied to a Tree, and himself naked, for some reason now eluding her, who hurried forward to remove the old man's foot from the inflamed webbing. It was the first time she had laid eyes on José Garcia Benunito—perhaps the very hour each had fallen irrevocably in love with the other and this despite her utter bewilderment at the language he spoke or the drawn look on his face. Thereafter, the old man's foot was permanently, totally, black. He could dip that foot in boiling water or walk it on hot coals; one could prick it with pins and he would feel nothing. Her great-grandmother in those days, honouring her time as a courtesan in the capital, favoured elegant attire in the western manner, these garments being sewn by hand from patterns ordered from the great fashion houses in Europe. Her hats were feathered affairs stacked high as a chimney, worn with laced boots which climbed button by button seductively up to her thighs; although she ate incessantly she remained trim as a stick, and chose, therefore, flowing silks which adhered tightly to her form, the skirts dragging the floor, airy scarves in flight from her neck when she and her naked old husband with his black foot joined others flocking nightly to the paseo in the Plaza Principal. The old man's nudity was scarcely noted by those taking part in the ritual, because his black foot was seen as proof of God's miracles, and he was, in any case, by this time greatly revered in the village for having dug himself up by force of integrity from the very bowels of the earth. Even the Padre from the Church of Our Lady of the Saints consented in this, casting a blind eye as the venerable old man and his elegant wife—both soon to enter the second century of their long endurance—promenaded about the square, their hands locked together, his erect penis, as she put it, taking the wind. Often they were joined in their promenade by the brave *chicosito* José Garcia Benunito and by herself, the two of them some eight or nine during this period: *chicosito* and *chicasita* skipping along in advance of the doddering pair, their hands clasped also, as already she and José Garcia Benunito comprehended in a foggy, undefined way that Fate intended them one for the other—which understanding the Day of the Tornado would later make official.

The photograph taken by the boy photographer with the naked feet showed six identical Benunito brothers and sisters in rebel's attire, brandishing machetes, spears, and brooms, bearing down on an assembly of well-armed soldiers of the republic. All six Benunitos—to the beautiful señorita's mind—possessed faces the exact duplicate of each other. Naturally, under time's speedy march, the photograph had been altered many times over by local artisans, colourists, and imposters hoping to be gifted such renowned heights, with the result that what one now saw in the museum's photograph, was an anonymous blood- splattered boy with a grinning face staked to a tree, toy pistol aimed at the backsides of one hundred soldiers fleeing up Avenida de la mil Lunas in fear of their lives.

Without this photograph depicting heroic if fictitious events in her own little village, to the señorita's mind, the world would never have known of the famous battle initiating the civil war known in the history books of her country as the War of Reform. Few villagers had ever heard of this war and fewer yet witnessed any reform.

But soon afterward, most agreed, soldiers again returned, this time in a force of five hundred. The five hundred rounded up the six revolutionary Benunitos and hung them from trees in the Plaza Principal, as a lesson in futility. Before fitting nooses around the victims' necks the soldiers built massive fires all along the Avenida, and set black pots to boil in the plaza. The soldiers drove citizens from their *casas*, making them witness to and participant in the grand occasion. One by one the renegades were dragged through the Avenida; the soldiers set fire to their clothing, compelling the people to hurl stones and flaming sticks upon the bodies or be shot where they stood. When the smoking bodies reached the plaza they were propped up against the facing wall of the Church of Our Lady, and the general of the army of the republic, after drum fare, engaged himself in a long speech, pronouncing upon the virtues of a stable, beneficent, and orderly government, and of that fate which awaited traitors. He then pulled a sabre from the first of the boiling pots, and in turn drove the blade into the eyes of each prisoner, tossing these orbs into the bubbling water. The señorita's own great-grandfather, now older than the century, hobbled on his black foot through the plaza and up to the general, spitting into his face. Upward of twenty soldiers descended upon him, in seconds hacking his body to pieces. The black foot was held aloft by the general, and another speech made, and still another, on into evening, and at last the foot, together with the balance of his corpse, was hurled into one of the six pots. A chair was arranged nearby, that the general might stir the pot with a long stick. He was well into drink by this hour, and sang, verse after verse, *The Victor's Lament*. Night fell and hard rains came. Gravestones tumbled over and slid about in the muck in the cemetery on the hill and rivers of mud poured down every path. As daylight showed, the soldiers were no more; the old man's corpse, black leg upright as a lance, was seen sitting with utter dignity in the general's chair. One might well ask how this could be. Señor Donati's father, at that time likewise serving as mayor, provided the one reasonable explanation. During the night of unparalleled rain, he said, a monsoon wind, determined to be the work of the unpredictable gods Yes and No, swirled about the plaza, of such force it whipped the uniforms from the soldiers' bodies and their rifles from their hands and the hair from their heads; the wind toppled the boiling water in the vast vats about the soldiers' feet and flung the hot coals of the fires into their eyes; the six blind and dead Benunitos strung up again in the trees were made to toss and dance there like painted participants at a costume ball. And the monsoon winds sent the general flying and lifted the old man's bones into the chair and ...

"!" was the señorita's response when first she heard this story.

What was I born into? she asked herself. Will marriage to The Boy Tied to a Tree save me? The last question was easy. José was not now tied to a tree. He was roped to her.

But it was not the weight of these events which tonight drained the beautiful señorita of her composure and brought grief to her every move. It was her mother.

The señora at times suffered a frightening lucidity, which she called spells, *mareos*, or *espasmos del llanto*, breath-holding spells often afflicting children, during which she could see into the past as a witch may see into a bubbling pot. These periods so agonized the daughter that her blood froze and to warm it she ran away to hide among the bristling skirts of the nuns at the Church of Our Lady. Her mother's seizures normally endured for three or four diabolical hours. At the end of these she would be herself again, soft as pudding and as loving as the Madonna. But the attacks in recent months were becoming more frequent and their effect more virulent. Her eyes saw through to hellholes unavailable to those not so afflicted; she perused quagmires and reeking bogs, every inch of these landscapes fixed with vivid detail. She walked with the dead, she said, inquiring of them the whereabouts of her husband, and bearing little gifts of poisoned fruit which she requested they take to him. The dead ate her fruit, laughing. He has fruit aplenty, they said. They put their bony hands upon her shoulders and spoke with ferocity of matters so grave she shook with wonder and dread; these sojourns made her see that her own crimes weighed as nothing against the scale of havoc these dead people said they had wrought, whispering each grim specific into her ears, while encouraging her to continue diligently her fine work on earth as this might bring her a modest respect in these firepits where the dead cavorted. The puny gods Yes and No were mere freaks, they said, when compared to…when compared to…well, they dared not breathe his name for their bones, already spindly, sore at elbow and knee, would surely be rearranged. Even your Video would despair of featuring us. Disciples at *The*

Last Supper of the Killer Tomatoes would turn their backs on us. Heaven and hell flies the flags of both worlds, these chattering spirits told her. "In brief minutes, one may ride the air currents separating the two habitats, though what is the use since one place is so much like the other. Both are replicas of your very earth, they said. The same couch potatoes, the same night stalkers. The poor now strive and achieve nothing, the middle class whose ancestry through the centuries is composed entirely of dust-busters toiling under merciless sun in sundry fields is now shrinking, all as the rich were getting richer through rewards for the purchase of land so long as they did not garrotte each other and paid sufficient homage to church and king. Oh, living or dead, all is in collapse and worsening daily. What can one say! There it is! Is it not disgusting? Yet the sun continues rising daily, offering a smidgen of hope even for hopeless zombies like ourselves, since in death lies resurrection, oh merciful Jesus, let us rejoice!

The spirits with whom the señora communed during these forays into lucidity had one consuming interest only; they wanted to know what were the latest releases from the Video, and when she told them of the endless car crashes, of exploding buildings and trampled bodies, of naked women with bleeding bosoms, with the long teeth of Dracula, and of monster aliens that could erupt from their mouths and bellies and vaginas at any given moment, the spirits nodded with satisfaction, opining that the worlds the Video projected were not significantly divergent from their travels on earth when they were counted among the living, nor were they so radically the opposite of those ordinary events transpiring in their current environment.

241

This was why she was stabbing everyone, because of her lucidity with regard to the earth's daily table of horrors. Her glorious daughter was perfectly capable of fending off the lustful fanatics coming through her window. It was with a clear head and a clean conscience, she said, that she was carving up these boys at every opportunity. When she did so, her husband in the netherworld twisted away from the whores labouring in his bed of ashes, moaning with pleasure.

The señorita understood perfectly well that her mother's conversations with the ghouls of the underworld had a more rational and basic explanation, one closer to home. As more and more boys sought the daughter's affection and José Garcia Benunito's shadow loomed ever larger, the señora's mind was returning with star-bright clarity to those days of her own courtship, betrothal, and alleged betrayal. This afternoon, in a discourse that still rang in the daughter's head, the señora had laid out her view of those days as clearly as if she were drawing a road map. "Luchella, the slut. Begin with that incontrovertible fact. The slut from the start wallowed about in muck with each of the two brothers. Yes, my husband and her own. No sooner than our vows were consecrated was your father rushing off to Santa Ocuro to trim the toenails of those red-headed spear-titted whores. God bless me, although I tried, I could neither climb the walls with him as they did or yodel with their same hypocrisy. He is supposed to be landscaping a garden, modernizing the house, seeing to his precious shipments from Europe. In fact, I see someone always there, a dark shadow, working like a dog through the day, no time for siesta, sweltering under the hot sun and in the evenings feeding me mangos from his fingers, but I know this mango artist is an imposter. He exists only in my mind, as was proved a score of times when I went to touch him. The truth! Don't weep, don't stare at me as if you think me an imbecile. Don't speak to me of your fabled *biblioteca*, of that dumb midget pony you called Elmo, I know very well he often employed your company as disguise for his mud-strumpeting with the painted trollops of Ocuro. For all I know you cannot yet read or so much as sign your name, so say nothing to me of that mad-hatter Petronius, A.D 50, or gaudy Apuleius, A.D. 150, whose rat-eared pages I have a thousand times hurled through umpteen windows. You are not the precious innocent everyone takes you to be …"

"!"

"… but a designing imp …"

"!"

"… fated to break-up how many happy homes?"

"Oh, mama, I beg you, please!"

"Part whore youself. I would not be surprised."

"Mama, don't make me cry! I love you! I promise to be good!"

"Tears! How wretched! One day you will learn the true worth of tears. What do you know of life, of marriage, a girl of nineteen, lean as a rake and not that pretty and likely soon to find yourself dispatched to a couch in Vienna? Tears. Your father watered the lawn with mine. Weeks your father would be absent and for all I knew he had fallen down a well. So he had, I discovered, and the Santa Ocuro sluts in the well with him and the well a bottomless cask of mescal and filth and his britches permanently arranged around his ankles. Small wonder I shed his name after his death. I was never a Benunito.

Never! And Luchella the Slut beating down my door every day to tell me what a saint her own husband was. No, wait, I have jumped the horse, we were not yet married at that time. But what a turncoat! Did I not tell you? Slut Luchella sold her hair to the oily cine manager for a single ticket to *The Brothers' Donkey*. The truth! It was playing at the old movie house on the plaza, later burnt down. Yes, by my hand, so immersed was I in my Faulkner translation. 'Barn Burning,' I believe that work was called. I was such a devout reader in those days. Susceptible to influence! A bit of kerosene, it was easy! Five centavos the film cost. Or a head of hair! We had to see it! The oily cine manager sucking our fingers and cuddling our knees as he sat between us eating honeyed popcorn. Us thirteen. Twelve. Ignorant as molasses. Don't look at me that way. The truth! I swear it. And hour by hour a weave of doctors through the house, weighing down my bedside, discoursing on one thing and another, making pronouncements: your daughter is ill, you must quickly dispatch her to Geneva where they advance the Master's work on the libido maelstrom, on dream and illusion, penis envy, cosmic disorder, anima, and animus!"

"Why have I never heard of this? Did you go, mama?"

"Quack, Quack."

"Did you?"

"Of course I went. That sadist sister of His Jubilation the Mayor, Philimina Donati, took me. In Geneva—or was it Vienna?—they were crazier than I was. But they cured me."

"¡"

"Those Freudian gymnasts made me whole."

"¡"

"I developed blisters on my backside from their infernal couch."

"Oh, mama!"

"I was only pretending insanity, you see. I had perused their books. If I confessed each time I opened a window, there filling the space with his wolf's head stood my father hoping to eat me alive, then they knew incestuous compounds explained my neurosis. I switched my own behind in support of this thesis."

"Who looked after me?"

"Idiot. You did not then exist. You were in the heavens, awaiting fruition."

During her mother's bouts with lucidity the insane truths she spoke compelled the daughter to clap her hands over her ears. To say a thousand times, "Mama, please!" *Por favor, mama.* Cochisa tracked her through every room. If she ran into the streets, her mother came running also, screaming the mind's ugly truths.

"Some other things you should know. One day I am in the garden planting oregano, basil, sweet peppers, mustard greens, and the earth moves. It moves, it rumbles. Trees topple. The very earth at my feet splits like a sliced apple. Something hits me and I fall unconscious. I awake to the night, the stars, and who do I see peering into my face but the man I take to be your father. At last he is back from Santa Ocuro. I cry out to him, I wrap my arms around his neck. I pull him on top of me. So heavy was he, my God. My God, it was like moving an elephant. I prayed to the Virgin, I said Dear Mary, please get this man on top of me. I did. I even appealed to Jesus. Get him on top of me. Damn him to hell but get him on top of me. Have him gnaw my neck;

chew my tongue. Have him knit me as one would knit a shawl. I ask you, how many shawls had I knitted in my time? I was the shawl queen of my state. In Geneva or was it Vienna, how many? But wait! There. He's made it. He is on top of me. Inside me. A bucking bronco. Through the night, galloping. Galloping. Inside me. Bones crack in my throat, my pelvis is a warship crashing waves of an angry sea. God believe me, I thought he was your father. He smelled nice, he smelled clean, he looked like your father. I believed he had renounced his wild ways, that God had changed him to be more like his brother. I tear off his clothes, I tear off mine, I rain down kisses upon him. So he likes sluts, I think, well, I will show him sluts. He fights me, he tries fleeing, but all my worries, the earth split before my very eyes, my certainty that the world is ending, has unleashed in me the wild animal. So young, I was. So ignorant. So much the tiger uncaged. It happens to a woman. Beyond wet kisses, beyond young reprobates' clammy hands stealing squeezes at your breasts, what do you know? Of the carnal appetite, I mean, when one is possessed with desire even if the world is ending in a minute and who wears this wolf head scaling your walls, clawing through your window. As the rooster crows, here the wolf comes. This time I am ready. I will turn the tables on that rabid wolf. Indeed. Oh yes, indeed. I am on top of him, he is on top of me, we are on top of each other and the universe is spinning, when I detect by some little flick of his tongue, by some little mole that grows by a nipple, by some little curiosity in his breathing, by some little spacing between the aroused toes, that this is not my husband. It is his kind and good brother. It is the man Luchella has stolen from me. You would think shame would have slackened my desire, that I would have come to my senses, don't you? Far from it. Yow! Yowch! I was even more feverish to have him. I wanted my rightful lover. I wanted revenge against Luchella the Slut and against your father who hires imposters to take his place. I became the true whore. Through the night and day hours, I outdid the nimble athletics of the supersluts of Santa Ocuro. Listen closely. Open your ears. That is why you cannot marry José Garcia Benunito. He is my own son. I cry that I have stabbed him. But the truth is you and he have the same father. God condemns such a marriage. Go babble your desires to the nuns. You may not have him."

Red-faced with shame, with rage at what fate has decreed for her household, Señora Caldera scurries away. The girl hears clattering footsteps, wails of despair so lamentable she drops limp as a rag to the floor. She cowers against the cold tiles, a child suckling on a thumb. A moment later comes the hollow slam of a distant door. Echoes. Vibrating walls. Then silence descends, sharp as a sword. The señora has locked herself away. She is underground in her secret vault. It is where she goes, when afflicted with these periods of mania and every secret must be revealed.

So the beautiful señorita now prowls the rooms, her heart aching. Life is misery. She is doomed. She is already dead. Fate's footsteps pitter-patter before her, a shrouded sister. Nature is her foremost enemy. The ground split that distant day and her mother lay with José's father. A lie, a dream, José was not yet born, not yet has been tied to the tree in the high sierras of Chiapas, there to witness the annihilation of his village, the killing of every playmate, of fathers and mothers.

Stray goats. Dogs. Cows. But the dark seed is planted. The criminal egg is hatched.

Her mother's tale is terrible and terrible, too, is the sickness that curdles her mind and terrible also is the truth her poor mother must never know. The day of the tornado. She is twelve, with José Garcia Benunito at the schoolhouse. He is telling her of the terrible day he was tied to the tree and the terrible path of govern-ment-paid assassins to the meeting house. There it is. Spare no one. By evening soldiers will be here to wash the walls. His parents, frantic to get into the mountains where Zapatista men and women are combatting *feder-ales*, have roped him to the tree. For his safety. Because he has let it be known he must fight alongside them. No, you must remain here, my son. Six is too young to perish for our cause. Elites have been granted our lands, now they demand our souls. Stay. Later, your grandfather will release you. But the grandfather now is dead. He has been shot in the belly. Máscara Roja has stormed the village. All these ignorant soft-hearted Zapatista indigos must be shot in the belly. See that pregnant woman? Shoot her please in the belly. So the Institutional Revolutionary Party, ruling these one-hun-dred years, command. Shoot those little boys while we are at it. Teach these upstart peasants a lesson. Never mind that we are ourselves peasants. Not one must be left alive. And here comes crawling a battered automo-bile over the muddy road. Dear me, what is that shoot-ing? Why is everyone running? My goodness, why is that little boy tied to the tree?

The skies go berserk; winds devour the earth. The winds lift them up. They rocket through the heavens, alongside tumbling calves, cows, goats, dogs. Chairs and tables and their very teacher fly by. Palm trees, banana trees, pail and bucket, fields of sugar cane, someone's black wig riding a broom. Someone's shoes, a hubcap, a pig's trough, a squawking rooster. They sail through black air into white air, into black air again. Rooftops and everything beneath those rooftops a tumult of spinning, whistling shapes. A four-poster bed with flapping lace canopy whips by, its path so smooth you would think it rolled on wheels. They whip and tumble head-over-heel in the racing wind; they are swept higher, spun; they hit a pocket of still air and plunge downward, shrieking in terror. They land softly on the floating bed, in a whirl of flapping canopy. Later, the sky calms, winds cease, all goes quiet and still. They are planted down on the bed in a green field. She is pinned to the golden bed. José Garcia Benunito is beside her gripping her hand. Not one stitch of clothing remains on their bodies. Their hair has been switched back, lying stiff as a board. Grit covers their skin head to toe. Their very eyelashes feel singed. A sudden gust and chicken feathers are everywhere fluttering; they and the bed in an instant are covered with feathers, as is the green grass, every bush and broken tree, the landscape as far as they can see.

They move, touch, explore. They love. They are a thousand miles from any place known to them.

"Philimina, please. What of this journey taken with my mother to Vienna?"

"Hush. Such things are not to be mentioned."

"Was she truly ill?"

"The woman is a rock. Whereas every moment you sing to yourself of your beauty and have not a brain in your head."

"!"

"The spirit had been frightened from her body. It was found again in this place you mentioned."

"!"

Under the mosquito netting, in her own room, the beautiful señorita is without strength even to remove her shoes. Lizards the colour of limes, catching her mood, cling motionless to the walls. Not a breeze stirs. If I close my eyes, she thinks, I will sleep forever. I will sleep and my mother's friends from the netherworlds will not find me. She will not find me. Only José Garcia Benunito will possess the power.

From the garden she hears the strange birds. All last night they had purled; not once during the whole of today has a wing lifted. Now they are at it again. It is a sign. They are summoning her.

Her dear mother rants and raves. Philimina, never before an unkind word to issue from her mouth, has shut the door in her face. Her beloved sleeps the sleep of the dead. The entire village is awash in ghouls.

2

During the night it rains. Little is unusual in this, as it is the rainy season. In daylight, under a cloudless sky, the sun a blinding gold, rain bursts occur and in what seems like seconds rivers that were but a trickle are washing away road and bridge, trees hammer down, a tumbling red-earth mud sweeps away all in its path while the vast lake, placid a moment before, visibly stirs, rises, inundates. Such is normal, expected, tolerated. Over the centuries recovery procedures are or not (mostly not) established, measures are or not (mostly not) put in place to minimize the inconvenience, to limit the danger to life and limb. This is nature and nature must have its way, or God must, so—excuse me!—are we not helpless? Are we not? So proclaims the mayor. In this manner are we reminded of our insignificance. The night cometh, Señor Death's hands are at our throats, when was this not ever so? In the meantime *Bueños Dias* to you, and to you, and to all of you, Yes, *bien, bien, estoy bien*, I am well and so I hope are you. Your hut washed away, *lo siento*, how sad, know that you are welcome to throw up pole and plastic in my yard. During the night the rain was perpetual and when we awakened—once more to golden sunlight, is this not true?—much that was familiar had been rearranged. Ah, but not to worry, no need to scratch your head, *mañana* all will be as it was before. The devil was caught by the tail and swung over the wall. Philimina tells me she heard him weeping while she was shaving her legs.

Along the Avenida de la mil Lunas naked boys and girls hardly old enough to walk are out with makeshift poles trying to catch the silver fish in the new river that rushes over the cobblestones; in the church moat and all about the Plaza Principal, where the black bones of our aged benefactor presides behind a barbed-wire fence, this scene is being repeated many times over. Everyone is unhappy. Although the fish are bountiful, not once—with pole or net or a thousand other stratagems—has anyone succeeded in actually snaring one.

A dusty green Lincoln town car of ancient vintage has been slowly ascending the Avenida's steep slope. It arrives in the Plaza Principal and a young *norteamericano* couple sit in it for several minutes before alighting. They have peeled a mango and with their fingers are dangling slippery discs above each other's mouths. The *chicleto* boys who have descended upon them, the *lenadores* man passing on his donkey, the squadron of children who would see to the safety of the dusty green automobile, together with the merely curious, can hear their laughter, can see the mango juice dripping down their chins. A small boy pulls from his pocket a dirty rag; he passes this rag through the driver's window and stands grinning. The visitor gives the boy a coin. The visitor wipes the woman's chin and hands, he cleans his own. He returns the cloth to the boy. *Gracias, amigo.*

De nada, amigo.

If the good travellers like this village's mangos, then surely they must like also the *piña*, the *tomate*, the grapefruit. Only a few *centavos*, señor.

Señor Donati, exiting through the carved doors of his municipal office, has noted the arrival of these strangers in the dusty car. He studies them with some disquietude, with some little stir of excitement, for they are the first tourists to arrive in this village in a long while. A blight has struck the village. Secret directives, the mayor suspects, have been issued from the capital. *Federales*, you would think, stand at the crossroads, turning everyone away. The tourists come to Oaxaca, they blanket Santa Ocuro and swarm surrounding regions, their numbers obliterate the rainy slopes of Uruapan, their footsteps carpet each inch of Parícutin volcano, but these same travellers avoid his impoverished village at all cost. It is said that unnatural activities transpire in this place. Here, it is said they dine on worm soup, wallow about in pulque, live for blue agave. In winter they heat their homes with electric eels pulled from murky depths. It is falsely said in other places that here the people worship bones, that the prize display in their tawdry plaza is a black foot mounted upon a wobbly chair. They weave no fine cloth, make no fine jewellery, no chess sets to astound the eye; no distinguished ceramics, no tinsmith, no architecture, no restaurant that isn't a filthy leaning shed. No pride, no history, no culture. Yes, most certainly there is the single autobus daylight into darkness threading the lanes, the cost whatever single *centavo* may be found in your pocket, yet still the preferred mode of transport is the donkey. See there that poor *indigena*, *niño* and *niña* strapped to backside and hip, and there the plump *mestizo* with pots on her head. Not long ago both would have had to leave this village before darkness fell. But I ask you, señor, was it not the same in your fabulous Venice not so long ago? Oh you historians with your amateur theatrics, will it kill you if just once in ten thousand years you trouble yourselves to get your facts straight? Everyone knows that here in this picaresque village, unrivalled in the arts and crafts, without parallel for beauty of landscape or señorita, unsubdued neither by nature nor despotic rule, we boast not one but three autobuses all in good mechanical condition and driven by cheerful drivers who will allow you to alight the moment you pucker your lips to whistle. While—to continue for a moment our discussion of this transport issue, the delivery of yourself and goods—we have limitless individually-owned collectivos plying a magnificence of routes, so that a person need not walk a single step unless he or she so wishes. I would draw your attention as well to our beauteous Colonial structures, few in number, granted, roofs thatched with worn palm leaves, granted, windows cracked, certainly, but of spellbinding grandeur, even so—even crumbling, as we confess they are. And I must adamantly beg that you execute vast ill-judgment in speaking so derisively of our "black foot mounted on wobbly chair," if such were your words. Surely you would not pass such a silly, not to say inane remark, if you knew the agony endured by the owner of this foot, a Maya descendent so revered it was said he invented the sun, or would have had he not spat in a general's face. This immortal it was, and his lady, who with bare hands constructed what is now known as the Church of Our Lady. The padre will tell you this claim is mythological rubbish; however, as we know the padre is in footstep with the Cardinal-Priest of Dorotea's own myth-making factory. None of which we need at present to stress too strenuously, since unlike ourselves all named are in pilgrimage to unrelieved happiness in kind heaven. Do I claim this humble church among the seven world wonders, no I do not. But from the unkempt plaza where you park your car look east through the open door of our church. Sweep aside the lazy dogs, the begging children, the vigilant goats, the squawking hens, as you cross the uneven cobbles. Jump the puddles, please. If your arrival is today, alas, you must walk ankle-deep in water. Enter at last the church door. Directly to your front, you will see, lit from within, a glass coffin. The coffin's roof, that is to say, is of glass panes inlaid in lead frames, while the resting place of the body is of highly polished black lacquer. The dimensions of this coffin, it will strike you, are curious: why is this coffin so unnecessarily long? Is this length of the coffin not extreme?

You are right, señor and señora. How observant you are. Listen, therefore, to the story of The Saint Who Grows in his Coffin. Once of our yesterdays, when our forefathers and foremothers were *niño* and *niña*, *chico* and *chica*, *probresito* and *probresita*, this coffin that you see held the severed bones of a nondescript, barefoot *Indigena*, son of Tarascan peasants and himself a peasant until he won the love of The Woman Who Bedded With Generals. It was this peasant *Indigena* whose act of bravery summoned the wrath of the gods Yes and No to slay our oppressors. Over the years his bones, of their own volition, reassembled. Each year he grows. Each year the lid must be lifted and his measurements taken again. The barber must be brought in to cut his hair, the beautician to clip his nails. Each year his suit must be refitted. Inch by inch, the legs of our Tarascan hero lengthen. Some believe they will go on lengthening until he can stride the earth and smite all oppressors. Three times in living memory have the carpenters lengthened his cabinet. Already you can see how his head touches upon one end and his heels upon the other. In another year yet again the glass coffin will have to be extended. This will of course necessitate enlargement of the nave; in time, the padre fears his altar shall be pushed back into the apse and he shall have to address the worshipful from a box hung from the ceiling. Well, since our church lacks a roof we may as well observe it also lacks a ceiling. In that regard, viewers have often found occasion to remark on the structure's affinity with the magnificent cathedral in, I believe, Barcelona, unfinished through three hundred years. Be that as it may. Yes, as it may. My point is that the steady elongation of our martyr's body under the glass is a miracle, but it is a miracle requiring abundant labour, which is why you see there the box to hold your offering. Unforseen difficulties, I tell you, do arise. As an example: soon a decision must be made about our hero's pillow. Our hero has told the padre in the padre's sleep that he dislikes the foam in the present pillow. He finds it lumpy. He cannot sleep. And it is true that sometimes when the padre arrives at morning vespers he finds our hero has turned over during the night. He finds him sleeping on his stomach, and the glass cracked from his thrashing. Our hero now desires a pillow of finest down, like those his wife and her generals slept on when his wife was a famous courtesan in the capital. It would be nice, too, to have a small table suitable to hold a reading lamp and, if not too much to ask, a glass of water. Perhaps from time to time, a shot of mescal. El Presidente brandy is another favourite.

Sometimes the padre jokes. He tells us our martyred *Indigena* has told him he wishes the beautiful señorita Caldera would sleep with him the occasional night, as refreshment for his memory. Do you know of our beautiful señorita Caldera? If you saw her you would fall to your knees in adoration. She is the most beautiful woman in creation, and perhaps the sweetest. Everyone says so. And smart, in the bargain. She can recite in full *The Little Prince*, learned while in her mother's womb. She will tell you all you may not wish to know about the famous early scribblers Petronious and Apuleius. I give you a tasty morsel directly from the liberating text: *Sayeth the ass: "If you, little shitter, place a shantle of grass unto my tongue, I shall relate for history's benefit the most glorious story ever. Thank you. There existed once on earth a woman on earth whose beauty surpassed the beauty of every goddess immortal in the heavens, and every minor goddess*

*claiming title thereto, and her name was Psyche. Psyche. Can
you not hear? I include in this all beauties in every orbit,
under every sun. And under each sun stood likewise our hun-
gering love-devotee, mercurial Cupid, who was as one with
the populace. "A beauty!" cried he. "Such perfection! My heart
leaps. Dios Mios!"*

The padre told his supplicants: Such talks are pre-ex-
istent tales in the camouflage of make-believe. Ask
yourself: What was the word before there was a word?

Avoid the lovely señorita's difficult mother, however:
she drinks nightly from the river Lethe. It is said that emi-
nent Viennese doctors installed an assortment of trap
doors inside her brain, only to discover these trap doors
did not open or close properly. They then drilled tiny
holes into this apparatus and filled these with the finest
lubricant, a remarkable oil designed to remove rust from
the trap door hinges, making these doors at least serviceable. Apparently the procedure was somewhat slipshod.
I myself can neither rebut nor uphold these assertions.
My best advice to you is to avoid crossing the path of
this woman. On the other hand, our señorita is the nine
daughters of Zeus rolled into one. When she walks,
whirlwinds accompany her ankles. Birds twitter, cats
purr, plants produce lavish blossoms. Tears that fall from
her eyes fall as fine cut-glass crystal. I myself have in my
kitchen a chandelier fashioned from these tears, which I
could sell to the *Museo Nacional* for a truckload of money.
All the young men in this village share our martyr's
dream. They would sleep with the señorita also. They
would have her hand in marriage. But a tornado struck
our village some time ago. So people say. A thousand eyes
saw this apparition sailing the heavens in a golden bed,
entwined in the arms of our local celebrity, Benunito. A

good boy famous for being tied to a tree in Chiapas, that tree now a noted Zapatista monument. Why? Because the dreaded government in the capital claims he shot a paramilitary criminal of the Máscara Roja. With his toy pistol, no less. They have sought endlessly to have the child tried and imprisoned. President Bush of the prideful *Unitos*, and Mr. Cheney, *subcomandante* of the arrogant *Unitos*, and Mr. Rumsfeld, Attorney General also of that progressive entity, over the years endeavoured to send the child to Cuba's evil Guantanamo prison, sitting on land won to them by dishonourable treaty. I mention this merely in passing. It is not necessary that you delight my ears with your informed contrary opinion.

The señorita's heart since that day has been reserved for this fortunate boy, who unfortunately lies today in a coma. Perhaps he will forever be in this coma and the beautiful señorita's tears will then be sufficient for us to build an entire city of nothing but the finest cut-glass crystal. If so, for a few pesos, I shall at that time conduct you on a tour of its every wonder. The Blind Whores of Ocuro? Do I understand you to be inquiring of this chart-topping group superior to all in the performing arts? The Los Primos Prize, the Latino Grammy, frequent La Bolero winners. So many accolades! You have seen our leaflets? The Blind Whores will set your heart racing; they are priceless Madonnas, wizards of stage and—excuse, please, I was about to say "of stage and bed," but what do I know of such matters? Indeed, they are coming. I suspect they are astride scooters this very minute, churning over lofty mountains to our paradise.

All true, his Excellency the mayor thinks, holding still and importantly on the municipal steps. Though the speaker has gone a bit overboard in praise of those blind whores. No, he can't say much for the young generation's music. To his old ears, today it is all either unmusical rap or galloping drums, piercing chords, and dumb indecipherable lyrics. Yet, it's true those blind girls are maniacal on their scooters. They motor the curvy mountain roads faster than Zeus. Naked, according to Tomas, except for bejewelled faces and thigh-high black and red boots.

Ah. Well. No problemo.

He remains in contemplation of the travellers who have arrived in the green car, sighing to himself. His imagined tour guide has neglected to tell his imagined *turistas* of the recent plague of village stabbings or of the latest marvel, the coursing stream stocked with fish that swim and feed as living fishes do, but whose every fibre from skin to intestines appears to be composed entirely of genuine silver.

What a shame it is that lamebrain big shots in the capital view his village as an unenlightened place where nothing of consequence ever transpires.

The mayor's heart is filled with pride that at last this deplorable situation has altered. Tourists have come; he must make this pair feel welcome. He likes the look of the man. He is sober. He looks approachable, capable; his white feet are shod in the local sandals. Finest leather from the finest cows, with soles cut from the finest tires of the best automobiles. The *coaterina* about his shoulders is the genuine article. He has an alert face. His expression speaks an unguarded enthusiasm. He has viewed the black skeleton of the village benefactor perched on the chair behind the wire fence, and reacted positively. He is not the suspicious type, guarding his wallet. The green car he is willing to leave under protection of barefoot boys who have received the assignment. The green car is packed with baggage and mementoes of extensive travel through this country—ceramics, blankets, blouses, bird cages, carved chests, boxes, tin ware—but he does not trouble himself to lock the doors or so much as roll up the windows. He does not slice his eyes to see if his fine automobile retains hubcaps, gas cap, antenna. He is therefore generous, affable. Already he is dispersing money—plenty of it, what a godsend!—to the rabble of boys and girls who will wash his car. He is buying chicklets. He is scratching the heads of befuddled pariah dogs. *"Hola!"* he is continually saying. *"Buenos diaz! Como esta."* Good. He is even speaking—only five words, mind you—the language.

But what of his companion? How might the mayor remark on this other visitor? She is slender. Tall. Her hair is long, tangled, one might say. Looking unwashed, one must admit. A redhead, but such a red redhead! A redhead with yellow shoes on her feet!—which is why no one in the plaza can let his eyes depart from her excellence. This redhead is perhaps from a bottle? But why not? Let women everywhere employ the bottle, since it makes them so beautiful. Even pulchritudinous vixens on the Video posters, blood dripping from their nipples, serpents erupting from their ears, demons catapulting from the navel—even they have luxurious hair from the Nice'n Easy bottle.

This woman from the green car looks agreeable. That much he can say already. But the mayor—whatever little steps he takes to right or left, no matter how much he pivots or inclines his head—has yet to see her face.

So, then: you are the mayor. Go nearer.

"A man in Santa Ocuro told us we should see the fish," he hears her saying. "We followed his vehicle all the way here. He wants us to meet his son José. Do you know this José? José is in a coma. But much of this I find all so incredible, because back home a good friend is also named Benunito. Is it not amazing that the first person we should run into in Ocura should be another Benunito? We have read of this boy José in the international press. He has become something of a beacon, because so many want to see him imprisoned: your country, the Americans, ours as well. In Canada, we have a somewhat similar situation: the fifteen-year old Toronto boy who, I believe, under attack, hurled a grenade, killing an American. During Mr. Bush's regrettable war. Thence, illegally, to be incarcerated in evil Guantánamo through the wicked years. Are you understanding me? You will forgive, I hope, my fatal Spanish. May I continue? We understand there is to be a grand wedding between the comatose boy and a beautiful señorita Caldera. Such a celebration! But how will the boy say 'I do,' if he is in comatose? Does the groom say 'I do' in your spectacular country? Perhaps someone can nod his head for him."

Such a talker is this redhead. The mayor ventures nearer. He likes this woman's voice. She is addressing old Eguchi, who cleans the church but never himself. Who goes barefoot and dresses in rags and has not a brain in his head. A disgruntled, leaky old man who never speaks civilly to anyone. But here he is, grinning ear to ear. Already in love with the *inglesa gringita* with the red hair and yellow shoes. What is it with these yellow shoes? How many has he seen in recent days?

The mayor now stands not two feet from the woman's backside. He inhales her perfume and old Eguchi's rot. But isn't this strange? Whereas in the past one has shuddered to stand in old Eguchi's presence because of the stink, the stink now seems to be of little substance. Certainly, the visitor appears to have no objection. Old Eguchi's odour mixes with the *inglesa's* natural sweat, and air is made sweeter. It seems to the mayor that old Eguchi is standing straighter, that a few minutes' conversation with this redhead—not that Eguchi has said a single word, only nodded in that way he has—has changed him altogether for the better. Old, yes, but such a pleasant-looking man: how funny it is that until this moment the mayor has never noticed. Toothless still, haggard of face, dressed in clothing picked up from a ditch, but invigorated somehow. It brings tears to Señor Donati's eyes, to see the old man's transformation. What magic spell can this traveller from the green car possibly be weaving? Old Eguchi is clearly in a state of enchantment. And now the old flakehead is actually speaking. And how well-spoken he now is! He is telling the visitor about the Man of Bones, whose figure presides over this plaza. What he submits as fact is far wide of the truth, but may one have everything?

"At the wish of his wife," old Eguchi is saying, "after spitting in the general's face and his body chopped apart, our Man of Bones was burnt by raging fire through the long night, in that same chair up by the cemetery. But the chair would not burn, nor the bones crumble. The village awoke the next morning to discover the skeleton here seated on its chair in the plaza, mounted on the chair you see inside the fence. A chair impervious to flame! Ages ago this was. But somehow some of these bones, or another's bones, came to reside in a glass coffin inside the Church of Our Lady. Our Lady has taken an interest in this. She tends him. I have seen myself Our Lady descends from her niche and trots along to his recumbent figure, holding in her hand a goblet filled to the brim with God's mercy. Now each day the skeleton grows. Some will tell you people are digging up their own family bones and fitting them to his. I do not myself believe this, although, as you see, he now has three legs. He has multiple arms and eighty-six ribs one day, and none the next. I died of fright one morning, seeing him there with two heads. Arrive here in the wee hours and you will see the chair empty. You will hear the Man of Bones walking in the night. If he calls to you, which is his wont, lower your head and hurry on. It is said he is searching for his beloved."

"My goodness," the woman declares.

The mayor at last steps in. Visitors must be honoured; they must be encouraged to stay long and reap the rewarding experience. He must remember to show them The Video, which will dramatize the fact that this village is a progressive place, in tune with the march of the times.

"Welcome, stranger," he says, "to our village."

The woman turns. He would go on in the normal way: he is the mayor, after all, and excels in the social graces. He has a reputation for witty repartee. This no one can deny. But the woman's countenance shatters his composure. Her face! That face! He shivers. His heart beats faster. He can feel his flesh crimping. He looks upon her face with amazement. It is extraordinary. It is unbelievable. He does not know what to think. The deity must be up to some trick. Because this woman, aside from the colour of hair, the paleness of skin, the blue eyes, the dimpled cheeks, the full lips, the fine hips, the cheerful breasts, the—oh let's not go on—is the exact duplicate of the beautiful señorita Caldera. The very twin!

His gaze goes to her feet. Lazy whirlwinds are spinning around her ankles. Rose petals scent the air. All around the plaza can be seen shrub bushes renewing their fragrance. He has always been told he is imaginative. Perhaps that is the explanation.

Old Eguchi sees this, too. He pulls at the mayor's arm. "Another beauty," he says. "Are more stabbings to ensue or are we at last to know peace? What are we to do?"

Night is falling. Vespers are done. Already the belfry here in the plaza has tolled the day's end, and bells from lesser churches in nearby villages responded. The church insists the day ends at eight. At six, the *paseo*, at eight go home. Pat your tortillas. Prepare your mole. Cook your meat, if you have it. Eat. Go to your hammock or straw. Sleep. Normally, with allowance for The Video, people did so. What else was there to do? But tonight, hooray, there is the señora's party. The mayor must hurry home, wash and dress. He will wear the tuxedo. The official medals. The red chest-ribbon. Another inch of elastic added and surely the trousers will fit. But he cannot tear himself away. Miraculous business is transpiring.

The two visitors kneel side-by-side at the stream, scooping hands into the water. The woman squeals with pleasure, holding by the tail a wriggling fish. A second later the fish transforms itself into genuine silver.

He even sees the Taxco stamp. The man, too, is holding up a fish. Before their very eyes, the wriggling ceases, the fish becomes solid silver.

A trick. These two are magicians.

For some minutes now they have been pulling these amazing fish from the water. A crowd has assembled and more are running toward them down the street of a thousand moons. The old and the young, the lame and the healthy, all are rushing to witness the miracle. Hurry. Feet, let me go quickly. The mayor wipes sweat from his face. He is mesmerized; he cannot believe his eyes. All the same, this is an old story; he has seen its repetition a thousand times. The *norteamericanos* will fish until they have emptied the stream. They will return to their green automobile and drive away with every ounce of village wealth. They will vanish across the border, never to be seen again. They will steal the fish just as predecessors stole New Mexico, Texas, California. Yes? But wait. This appears not to be the case. To the mayor's amazed eyes, this young man and this young woman are pressing into eager hands each fish they pluck from the water. Old Eguchi, smiling, holds several. Old Eguchi will in future wear fine suits; each day he will have his face lathered by the barber. The chicklet boys are lit with zeal as they convey the little fish to the infirmed, the stricken. How amazing! But, ah! I see. They are following instructions. The visitors' hands go on dipping; their hands go on giving. The little fish are jumping into their hands, so desirous are these fish to attain their destiny. Soon all within the plaza will be as rich as the governor, as rich as the politicians in Mexico. Already Madras the jeweller has set up a table replete with scales and troy weights; already lines are forming. Weights are announced, values declared, transactions concluded. Now the happy visitors are wading into the stream, beneath a canopy of flying fish. People are past their earlier hush; awe has given way to celebration: long live the fish! To the mayor's wonderment greed appears absent. There is enough for everyone. The padre is scrabbling about on hand and knee, sweeping into his frock the errant fin, the shredded scale, the odd flake of skin. For the church, let us assume. No doubt he will buy a down pillow for the martyr with the black foot in the glass coffin. A fish lands at the mayor's feet, slithers momentarily, and no one reaches to grab it. A dog sidles in. The fish dangles from the dog's teeth and everyone laughs at the dog's perplexity as the form alters. The dog drops his treasure, licks it, paws it; then eats it anyway. The air is thick with the odour of fish. People are jumping into the stream. They enter for the pure pleasure of doing so; they would enlarge upon the merriment. This after all is the evening of the señora's great party. A holiday should have been announced, and would have been, were not all those who occupy council thrones in the municipal building a pack of weasels, no insult intended. Others are running home with bottles, cups, bowls filled with the wonderful water. In days to come the elixir will cure snakebite, erase cataracts, melt bunions; a drop of it in the soil and your corn will spring higher. Eggs will be as the size of boulders.

Birds nesting among the Man of Bones swoop and dive.

Tears are pouring down the mayor's face; he has never been happier. He wipes his eyes and sees the *gringita norteamericana* approaching. She is wet from head to toe, yet radiant. Her eyes are lit like the sun.

She means to press silver fish upon him. Señor Donati cannot refrain from capturing the visitor's hands, from kissing her brow, from clicking his heels.

The Blind Whores are warming up instruments. The Padre tut-tuts. He is reminded the new pope would approve: Russia has Pussy Riot. James Bond has Pussy Galore so no problema. *Plink, plank, plunk. Toot, toot.* People are eating, drinking, making merry. An hour ago, on tables along every available wall, a hundred gleaming platters were stacked high with exquisite foods. Now you see shredded bones, overturned goblets, congealing liquids, discarded dishes. Floor and earth are littered.

Sensible people have taken to the garden. Inside rooms are packed with howling relatives of the young men Señora Caldera has tried to murder. Claims are being made, rights established. The wounded men, hobbling about in deformed peculiarity, resemble survivors plucked from a battlefield.

José Garcia Benunito's comatose form has yet to find its place of honour. His bed is too wide for passage through any door. First they must disassemble the bed. To disassemble the bed they first must decide where to place his body. To lean him against a wall like a bag of laundry would be inappropriate. To dump him into a chair would frighten the children. His corpse-like figure has been dressed for the occasion most peculiarly. The garment does not fit. It seems meant for a child, and is indeed the very replica of what he wore as a youngster tied to the tree in Acteal. The fit matters not. The famous Chiapas mask of subcomandente Marcos who defied a nation and won international regard for his people adorns his face. More than one person complains about the many odours rising from his skin. It is said he should be in the cemetery under a stone slab. Luchella sweeps from room to room, declaiming on the virtues of a quiet man. She has been hunting the señora. Where is the crazy woman? Luchella wants to know why there are altars to her own husband throughout every room.

Señora and señorita have yet to make an appearance. There is speculation and indignant complaint about that. That the señora's motive in creating the Benunito altars requires deep thought everyone agrees. Have the Benunitos supplanted the Virgin? Has God been shunted away into the tool shed? They remember the departed scoundrel only too well. He kept the Santa Ocuro brothels afloat and tried his moves on every woman within range of his horse's endurance. Every day he galloped further. It is said he galloped all the way to the capital and made love to a hundred women in a single afternoon. The village has not seen his likeness since. A thousand children bear the image of his black mane, his brooding eyes, his teeth that turned to steel the day he died. When his horse went lame, he travelled on foot. Women by the score pined for his knock every night. Women at an untold number of wells said, "First you must wash my feet, then I may happily oblige." He is in line to become sainted, beatified; in that connection he has many rogue predecessors. The poor soul, bless him, wore himself out. He lived for love and if not for love then for love's distant cousin. Before his twenty-first birthday, his bride was washing his corpse. Before he was cold in the ground she had renounced his name.

A lie! others say, Tomas among them. So many lies! May your tongue incubate fleas if ever you speak again!

Such a man he was! A saint who stands side-by-side with Emiliano Zapata! Side-by-side with our hero who bears the nom de guerre subcomandante insurgente Marcos. Was it not the Benunito brothers who transformed this lacklustre village into a model showcase for the *Ejercito Zapatista de Liberacion Nacional*? Yes! Was it not they who created our autonomous school, our autonomous justice hall, our autonomous health clinic? Who made the radio broadcast something other than static? Did they not stand masked beside brave Marcos in the city beneath the clouds, in humiliation of the turncoat Presidente Zadillo who signs the San Andrés Accords in Lacandan jungle in the granting to us a semblance of equality, but who delivers nothing except more soldiers and paid assassins to annihilate or hold us in chains? As has every president since. Racist, conniving, triple-lipped bastards! Cannot once our small-minded amateur ledger keepers, historians, scribblers, trouble themselves to get the facts straight? To quote our friend the mayor. And you, Doña Caldera, what a lump you have been. What a delusion you have lived. Your husband's long absences, where was he? Not, I assure you, with the whores of Ocuro but in the jungle combatting soldiers, reconstructing villages, combatting racist landowners, seeking out paid informers, spies infiltrated by the government. As are, for that matter, the maligned whores of Ocura, who one week practise the profession and the next have taken up arms in the jungle-track of felons intent on another massacre. A ruse, a tactic for safety, this double identity. Scarlet Pimpernels. Zorros. This village has one such informer, I regret saying: the padre whose ear is at every door. He reports to the Cardinal-Priest in Dorotea, who motors by limousine to the governor, who goes on cat feet to the president, who hums one tune publically and another privately. One-tenth of the population oppressed, neglected. The world's poor—they and their kind, say, are spawned by Satan—drop skirt or jockey strap, soliciting. Drop them, and here the ignorant women come running: *Me next, sire! Do me, please sir!* So say the powers-that-be. *More babies, please sire, that we may feed at your trough!* Tell me that isn't the current thought among worldly leaders. Deny it. Then hustle in your thugs to Acteal to shoot us in the belly.

Kind sir and madam: do not imagine for a minute Tomas and the woman you call Slut Luchella were innocently vacationing through Chiapas highlands, happening by happenstance upon the massacre in Acteal and the boy tied to the tree.

Some relatives are saying the absent señorita—where can the creature be?—was the provocateur and the señora merely her instrument in the recent attacks. The señorita, they say, thinks herself too good for any mere mortal. The jeweller, whose eyes shine like rubies on a plate, muses that sight of the señorita's naked beauty must so excite a man that his every pore bleeds. To see this vision naked, they would allow the very soles of their feet and their ears to bleed. How unfortunate that she would not find this attractive. Several young women take this opportunity to stride magnificently one way and another. It exasperates them to hear the girl's virtues constantly illuminated. What does she have, after all? Her eyes are vague, hair skimpy, her lips akin to those of the goat, her fingernails chewed, breasts so diminutive they could fit a peanut's shell. Hips? She has none. Legs? Stove pipes. A stuck-up prissy ignoramus. A sheltered neurotic. Worse than her mother! That hair! Those nails! Those yellow shoes! Rusty heels! Bad breath! A big nose! As for her famous whirlwinds, they have never witnessed these. Who wants dust blowing at one's ankles? Why are men so perverse? Beautiful, indeed! She's a stay-at-home simpleton, a mouse, not in groove with the times. Who cares about ancient whiz-kids like Apuleius? Mention the Video to her and what does she say except, "I have no patience for make-be-lieve." Tornados? What tornado? What tripe people speak! And that José! Another nitwit! What boy of any intelligence would fling himself into a hammock ignited by lightning to rescue an old shit's black foot!

Parents agree. What my daughters want is a tradi-tional boy who puts his shoes on each morning at six, is at work by seven, labours without complaint until the six o'clock evening hour, flags the *collectivo* home and enters our door at seven, kisses me, pecks his wife and children, congratulates us on the chicken mole, and by nine has removed his boots and is restfully snoring. To judge by the faces made during this recitation, the description is far afield of these daughters' expectation. A generational problem, thinks the man from the water department, whose own daughter's demeanour is, as usual, beyond worldly criticism. Clementina, 16, works side-by-side with him in Water. As ice caps melt in universal warming, her one thought is water. Thus those caravans trucking aqua to Zapatista villages when the government poisons the wells. The water is charged to the mayor, who may or may not know, as he has always been a bit foggy upstairs. Or so believes Clementina, noting that the condition appears to assail everyone at a certain age: in this village all men past the age of forty. Clementina now wears a cast on her right leg; she drives a truck in the caravan and weeks ago was run off the road up near La Realidad. *Pendejo!* she said. *Cogete un burro!* Fuckhead. Go fuck a donkey. All in the district adored Clementina for her venomous mouth, even those *pendejos* who would see her tumbling to death in a valley.

No one can say enough about the miracle of the fish. One man argues that these same fish will tomorrow turn into black ash, and for his trouble receives old Eguchi's fist between the eyes.

José Garcia Benunito is hidden in a closet until his rightful place of honour may be established. One by one, people stashing away their cloaks, looking for a toilet, open the door and shriek. Pepe the undertaker, of whom one might have expected better, faints.

The Blind Whores' music echoes through house and yard. Thatched roofs a kilometre away, loosened by rain and wind, shiver, slip, and slide. All day people have been studying the sky. A haze obscures the mountains. Hard rain is falling up there. Already small creeks are forming. They trickle here and there in the estate, dampening shoes. Stepping onto what appears as dry green grass your foot sinks ankle deep.

The mayor's pigs have broken free of the pen. They stop short, crouching, oinking madly at sight of the Blind Whores. The musicians have numerous children racing one way and another. They carry secret envelopes on which is pencilled the recipients' names: *Our sisters send affection and hope to see you again soon.*

The jeweller is open for business; he has his weights on a table at the front gate.

The Ocuro banker sits opposite, accepting new accounts. A free tortilla press, today only.

Creditors bearing aged unpaid bills mingle and mix.

Those arriving early at the fiesta have noted a sweating horse tethered to a frangipani tree inside a side gate. Who belongs to this beautiful animal has been a question asked time and again. I have seen that horse before. It is certainly familiar. The horse is saddled. Its flanks quiver; snorts and hoof-stomping erupt at any approach. The hide glistens. The horse is sweaty. It has been ridden hard. It views with baleful eyes those passing.

Later on, a man of uncommon appearance will be seen feeding this horse an apple. His face is masked. A pirate's eye patch covers his right eye. A Che Guevara cap covers his head. He is well-armed, the chest strung with bandoliers. He is smoking a pipe. In the whole of this village no one smokes. Tobacco is a luxury they must deny themselves.

People are saying: I've seen that hombre before.

They are asking: Was that the wind-devil subcomandente I saw?

Philimena Donati leans heavily on her cane. She swears she heard him say: No victory for those who walk on their knees. She has sore feet. Rebel slogans disturb her. Most things do. These blind *putas* have not the genius Tomas Benunito claims for them. One plays the tuba. Philimena hates the tuba. They should cover themselves. If there must be music let it be good mariachi tunes. Che Guevara wore a Frenchman's hat. A beret, she believes this item is called. This man's head was hidden by a soiled labourer's cap. She saw no eye patch. It pisses her off that people can get so few facts straight. Their observation power astounds her. In the afterlife she hopes to God there will be none of that. If so, she will quit the place. There flits the stubby padre, rotund as a sitting buffalo. He eats like one. At least today the black cassock looks clean. The cocky roach has obscenely thin ankles. He's going sockless today. He thinks he looks sporting in those dirty sneakers. Oh, but I am in a foul mood. Oh God, who by sin art enraged and by penance ne'er satisfied, look down upon these fools astray from the devil's campground and by the power of thine arms crush them. Philimena laughed, thinking this. In Vienna, she had experienced the joys and ravages of romance. With lovers she had known the wonders of London, Paris, Rome. They had wrinkled the sheets of a hundred beds. Then, thank you, Jesú, it was over. Scoot back to Vienna, collect the imbecile, and go home.

The padre circulates. He wonders why he is always the last to know what is going on. The cassock was brushed this morning by lazy Yolanda, in damnable service to him. But did she remember the daily sprinkle with holy water? She has yet failed to destroy the giant termite hives in trees where his favourite napping hammock is hung. Turreted structures descend like upside-down cathedrals and seem coated with concrete—shit, saliva, mud. The little bastardos have tubes running every wall. Stalactites hang from every ceiling. The Las Abejas bitch bypasses these when cleaning.

The padre believes an Evil Eye stands as sentinel at his every turning.

What vicissitude his thin shoulders must bear. That wretch Philimena has her sight glued upon him. The woman is unbearable. He bows her way, he smiles. He looks to the bandstand, voicing his opinion that modern life is a curse. A storm of rebuke pours his way. How repugnant are drab negations on this special day of days. Mayor Donati is dispatched to have a word with him. But others are already having that word. Why must you always be such a sourpuss? God will allow no sourpusses in the heavens, which may explain why you remain among us. It is a brave chiclet boy saying this to God's beach-ball messenger. For this the boy will have his head thumped and toy figures representing the Invincible Four removed from his pockets. In a moment people will be saying this brave chiclet boy who walks bent at the waist fell into a magic stream and his bones were mended. The boy himself will have to tell them this is not so.

The pacifist Las Abejas group has decided to hold a prayer meeting on grass beneath a range of avocado trees. The earth proves too wet and they must move on. The grape field is wet also. They decide individual prayer wherever they may find themselves is the solution. They will pray for the souls of the mothers shot in the belly and for the young children killed, and for José Garcia Benunito whose soul perhaps is still roped to the tree. The Las Abejas were those murdered in Acteal.

It is observed by many that rain is descending the mountains at a worrisome pace. The dewy air instils a chill. Women seeking abandoned shawls open the wrong door and scream again. Their cries excite the birds and Señor Donati's pigs, which screech also.

The day's rumoured events are recounted regularly: An old man called Nuez de la Nuez, Nut of the Nut, falling into the stream, had his rheumatism cured. A white goat with the face of the Virgin licked the leg of sick

Rafael, and Rafael instantly threw away his crutches and danced the Dance of the Deer. The Blind Whores have drunk from the stream, which is why they are playing as never before. Another mouthful and they will see again.

The Blind Whores hear gurgling water beneath the makeshift stage on which they play. Rain in the distant hills has thickened. The musicians have no worry about that. Air in Santa Ocuro is always moist. They are wary. Those thugs called the Máscara Roja are again active. EZLN radio has issued warnings. Eighteen of these Tzotzil racists were imprisoned for the Acteal killings. Many have since been released. Their ranks have swollen. They go by other names now.

Numerous fiesta-goers are asleep in chairs, strung against walls, stretched out on the tiles. Under the garden bougainvillaea, lately infested with white birds that for two days did not lift one wing, dozens more sleep the sleep of exhaustion, some still clutching drink.

Where is the señora? Everyone asks this. Have you seen the señora? Where is the lovely señorita? Why are they inflicting the cruel pain of absence upon us?

José Garcia Benunito's bed has been commandeered by Señor Donati. Asleep, he chases runaway pigs as beloved relatives, knives stabbing, chase after him. The undertaker, Pepe, is in close watch of the padre. He has never liked churchmen, and this one particularly. The padre is always sniffing, sniffing. He has for no good reason boxed the ears of Pepe's son, this also. Pepe has noted the horse. Business takes him all over the region and he often has seen both horse and rider. It is subcomandante Marcos' horse. So the subcomandante is here on some mysterious errand. What errand? Marcos has remained out of sight in recent years. The government in Mexico had finally succeeded in discovering his true identity, and broadcast the name. A week ago in Realidad the great man made a surprise appearance. He was, he said, as of that day, no longer movement leader and spokesperson. Henceforth, he said, the new Zapatista voice would be that of subcomandante Gabriel. Long live subcomandante Gabriel!

Yes, long may he, but who is to be this Gabriel?

Señor Donati is first to hear this question from Pepe's lips. The mayor is dazed. Pepe's report hardens his brow; it is too much for him. He is only an insignificant official in an unnoteworthy place. Which donkey shall carry the wood, carry the water, which decorative lantern shall go where. Which family quarrel shall I settle today. How many will we bury this year. Such is the sum of his usual duty.

The sun is setting on Señora Caldera's wrecked grounds. For extended hours she has been locked away in an otherwise uninhabited chamber. Around her are open trunks over which is strewn the sporty attire her husband wore. His polished boots stand toe-to-toe nearby, as if she has set them out for the dead man to step into. A ring of carnations adorns her grey hair. She has dressed herself in a gown of soft white cotton. The seams are split at the waist, under her arms, and all along her heavy shoulders. The repose of death does not dignify her face. On the floor is an unfinished letter she was composing to her daughter. Dough from her hands has hardened on the pen still crookedly attached to her hand.

The señorita, upstairs on her bed, has not opened her eyes in many hours.

The door opens. Dress for the weather, she is told.

Rain has quit the mountains. It arrives here, slackens, and quickly ceases. An electrical storm rattles over the village. The sky blazes. Lightning fires in every direction. The entire village is cast into darkness.

Subcomandante Marcos addresses José Garcia Benunito.

Wake up. You now are Gabriel. Take the horse.

The green automobile of the *norteamericanos* motors leisurely from the village.

Where do we go? It is the señorita speaking.

Remains to be seen is the answer.

ACKNOWLEDGEMENTS

The author thanks the editors of the magazines and anthologies where the following short stories did (and will) appear: "The Historian," in *The Antioch Review* and *Best Canadian Stories 2015* (Oberon Press, John Metcalf, editor); "Sara Mago et al," in *Exile, The Literary Quarterly*, and *Best Canadian Stories 2016* (forthcoming), and the Exile/GloriaVanderbilt *Carter V Cooper Short Fiction Anthology Series, Book Five* (2015); "Slain by a Madman," in that same magazine and anthology series, Book Four (2014).

I also extend thanks to John Metcalf, whose editorial hand on *Swinging Through Dixie* frequently bailed out the clueless author.

ABOUT THE AUTHOR

Leon Rooke is a novelist, short story writer, playwright, poet, editor and critic. He was born in rural North Carolina, but has been a resident of Canada for many years. He has published over 30 books, and about 350 short stories have been published. Over the course of his career, Leon Rooke has been writer-in-residence at numerous North American universities, including the University of Victoria, Southwest Minnesota State University and the University of Toronto. Rooke is also the recipient of numerous awards and honours, including the Canada-Australia Literary Prize (1981), the Governor General's Award for English Language Fiction for *Shakespeare's Dog* (1985), the North Carolina Award for Literature (1990), and The Carter V Cooper prize (2012).